STOUT OF MY LEAGUE

LOVE ON TAP
BOOK 4

SYLVIE STEWART

ROLLING HEARTS PRESS

COPYRIGHT

ALSO BY SYLVIE STEWART

Most titles available in Kindle Unlimited

Ale's Fair in Love and War (*Love on Tap*, Book 1)

Smooth Hoperator (*Love on Tap*, Book 2)

Deja Brew All Over Again (*Love on Tap*, Book 3)

Asheville Collection (Standalone Stories from the *Love on Tap* World)

* * *

Poppy & the Beast

Hot Flashes and Hockey Slashes, Hot Flash Hookups, Book 1

Mood Swings and Hockey Flings, Hot Flash Hookups, Book 2

* * *

Between a Rock and a Royal, Kings of Carolina, #1

Blue Bloods and Backroads, Kings of Carolina, #2

Stealing Kisses With a King, Kings of Carolina, #3

* * *

The Fix (Carolina Connections, Book 1)

The Spark (Carolina Connections, Book 2)

The Lucky One (Carolina Connections, Book 3)

The Game (Carolina Connections, Book 4)

The Way You Are (Carolina Connections, Book 5)

The Runaround (Carolina Connections, Book 6)

** * **

The Nerd Next Door (Carolina Kisses, Book 1)

New Jerk in Town (Carolina Kisses, Book 2)

The Last Good Liar (Carolina Kisses, Book 3)

** * **

Full-On Clinger (FREE ebook for a limited time)

Then Again

Happy New You

About That

Nuts About You

Booby Trapped

To my mom, who drove me to countless baseball and softball practices and who has always had an ear to lend and hug to give

PART ONE

Author's Note: While *Stout of My League* can be enjoyed as a stand-alone, it contains spoilers for books one through three of the *Love on Tap* series. For this reason, you may enjoy reading them in order. For those reading the series in order, Part One's timeline begins *before* the epilogue of book three, *Deja Brew All Over Again*.

CHAPTER
ONE

I MIGHT NEED A MEDIC

LYNN

"It's not rocket science, sweetheart. It's a wiener!"

Don't lose your shit, Lynn. You need this job.

I've been working this summer gig for three weeks, and these words have become my mantra.

"Hello?! Are you even listening?" Ennis continues in that snively tone that makes it feel like bedbugs have taken up residence under my skin.

"Got it," I respond through clenched teeth as my tongs fish the fleshy wiener from the pit of steaming hot dog water. I shake it before depositing it into a bun. I've just added a new life goal to my list: become a vegetarian. It'll go right between earning my PhD in physical therapy and devising a foolproof plan for my new boss's death that won't land me in jail. A girl has got to have goals, right?

"Remy, I gotta run to mezzanine one. Keep an eye on the new girl," Ennis shouts over his shoulder before disappearing out the back door to the concession stand.

My coworker's only response is a subtle flip of the bird in

the door's direction. "Ignore Anus," Remy mutters with a scowl.

My tongs freeze in midair as I fight a grin. "Did you just call him Anus?"

"I have no idea what you're talking about," Remy responds as he shoots me a naughty wink and blows a swath of blond hair from his eyes.

It may only be my third shift working concessions at Ardent Park with Remy, but I already know he'll be my life-line this summer.

I fold the hot dog into its foil-insulated wrapper and move on to the next one. Ennis expects me to have at least a hundred ready to go when the gates open and all the Asheville Arrows fans descend for tonight's game.

It's still afternoon, and it's a regular weeknight game, so the concourse is dotted with other stadium employees hurrying to their assigned duties and stations. I'm amazed at how many people it takes to make a Major League stadium run. Almost as amazed as I am at the number of rowdy fans who start swarming like locusts a couple hours before game time. As far as I can tell, baseball fans love three things: hot dogs, home runs, and young players in tight uniforms. I don't get it, but I'm not into organized sports.

The physiology of the athletes? The way they use their bodies, joints, muscles, and connective tissues? Absolutely. The injuries that come from the performance of said sports? Bring it on. Give me a torn rotator cuff or a hamstring strain any day. But the sports themselves, I find boring as hell. I much prefer long runs with my favorite playlist in my ears in place of a team sport. I don't need balls to make me happy. I deal with those enough at home.

Okay, *ew*.

What I mean is there's enough testosterone flowing through my family tree that the last thing I want to voluntarily witness is a bunch of sweaty jocks chasing a ball and smacking each other's asses. No thanks. My four older brothers supply all the toxic masculinity I can take. Why else did I make sure to go away to college?

Speak of the devil…

"Your ass is ringing," Remy says just as my brother Cash's ringtone blares from my phone.

"Shit." I forgot to turn off the ringer. At least Ennis isn't here to mansplain phone etiquette in the workplace to me.

I snatch the device from my pocket and switch the Johnny Cash song to silent before sending Cash to voicemail. Each of my brothers has his own ringtone, paying homage to his namesake. "Ring of Fire" for Cash, "Keep on the Sunny Side" for Carter, "Thank God I'm a Country Boy" for Denny, and "King of the Road" for Miller. Though I'd murder any one of them in their sleep if they dared reference *my* namesake, Loretta Lynn. I mean, sure, she kicked ass more than a time or two, but what barely twenty-year-old woman wants to be named Loretta?

Remy parks his behind against the counter and crosses his arms over his chest. He's cute, with a devil-may-care attitude and messy hair that remind me of my brother Miller. Of the five of us Brooks kids, Miller is the closest in age to me at twenty-two.

"Boyfriend?" Remy asks, not bothering to hide his nosiness.

"Worse. Brother."

This makes him laugh. "That bad, huh?"

"He's offended I'm not working for him this summer." He's also undoubtedly fretting about my state of well-being given some of the recent family upheaval we've had, but I'm not getting into that. Cash loves mothering me, but Mama is plenty capable of that on her own—not that I need it.

"Oh, yeah? It can't be worse than here, can it?"

I consider that for a second. Serving beers at Blue Bigfoot would definitely pay better than running concessions at the ballpark, but being under my brothers' constant surveillance makes it so not worth it. Besides, my Sports Science and Kinesiology program director at App State told me if I put my time in here, I can use the access and proximity to score some face time with the Arrows athletics and rehab team—and maybe even get some shadowing in. She's all about the hustle, which makes me a big fan. Even the chance of witnessing these professionals at work is worth bathing in all the hot dog water in the entire stadium. Well, almost.

Remy scoops chips into plastic nacho containers while I continue wrapping hot dogs. Just as I turn to ask him where I can find more wrappers, though, my attention is caught by a woman's voice shouting, "Help! Please! Somebody!"

I spot her immediately, crouched on her knees beside the prone body of a slight man with graying hair. My brain shifts into emergency mode, and I vault myself over the counter as I bark at Remy, "Call 9-1-1!"

I reach the woman at the same time a tall, dark-haired passerby does. He hits his knees and slides his fingers along the man's neck, checking for a pulse, while the woman dissolves into tears and pulls at the man's shirt, crying, "Tom! Tom! Don't die!"

I force a calm, controlled tone. "9-1-1 is being called. What happened, ma'am?"

She doesn't take her eyes or hands from the man, but she's getting in the way of the guy trying to help, so I gently take her arm to physically direct her my way. He shoots me a grateful nod, his sharp jaw clenched in concentration. "Ma'am, is this your husband?" I ask.

"Y-yes!" she stammers before finally focusing on me with teary eyes. "Tom!"

"Okay." I grab both her hands as Dark-Haired Hottie—yes, we're in the middle of a crisis, but emergencies don't render a girl blind, now do they?—bends forward to feel for signs of breathing. "Tom is going to be okay. What's your name?" I ask.

"L-Lydia." She looks around my mama's age with streaks of gray in her brown locks and deep laugh lines around her eyes and mouth. Shit. I'll bet Tom put those there.

"First aid and an ambulance are on their way." Remy appears at my side with a cell phone pressed to his ear, and I nod before turning to Lydia again.

"You hear that, Lydia. The ambulance is on its way. Tom is going to be fine. Does he have a heart condition?" I ask, firming my hold on her hands when she tries groping for her husband again. I forgot the stadium would have first aid staff available. Where the hell are they?

"He's been doing so great with his diet. I don't understand," she wails.

Dark-Haired Hottie, kneeling at Tom's side, raises his head and gives it a subtle shake, making my heart plummet into my Chucks. I yank Remy down to his knees with one hand and transfer Lydia to his hold, giving him a wordless command to keep her out of the way. Then I slide over in front of Tom until my thigh comes flush with Hottie's.

My voice drops low. "Do you know CPR?"

His tense jaw remains locked as he replies with a curt,

"It's been years. I can't remember the ratio of breaths to compressions."

I give my head a sharp shake as I realize I'm on my own. "No breaths. That's old-school. Go find the medical staff," I command as I position myself above Tom and locate his sternum through his Arrows T-shirt.

Here goes nothing.

TWENTY MINUTES LATER, EMTs wheel Tom to the waiting ambulance while Lydia sobs grateful tears into my hair and hugs me harder than even my hug-smothering mama could.

"I don't know what I would have done if you hadn't been here," she gushes. Remy helps disentangle her limbs from my body, and I send him a grateful half smile.

"Anybody would have done the same. I just held him over until the pros got here."

"Come on, Lydia. Tom's waiting. You don't want to miss the ambulance ride, do you?" Remy guides her away, and I exhale a breath of relief that feels like it's been pent up inside my chest since Roman times.

"Damn, you're one cool customer," a deep voice says from behind me, and I turn to see my dark-haired rescue partner.

My responding laugh comes out shaky. "Not really." I suspend my hand between us so he can see how badly it's trembling. "Adrenaline."

"Nature's perfect drug. I'm a big fan." His smile is a little lopsided and a lot handsome—something I'm able to appreciate more fully as my brain descends from panic mode and settles back into my body. In fact… *damn*. All of him is even more handsome than I realized, from his pretty espresso eyes to that sharp jaw, broad shoulders, and a set of firm thighs protruding from beneath his athletic shorts and making my throat dry. I try to swallow, but it gets stuck. And now I feel a cough coming.

Ennis, of all people, saves me. "Hey, new girl! These pretzels aren't going to heat themselves!" he shouts from the concession stand. *New girl?* Seriously? *Everyone* here is a summer employee.

The stranger's eyes leave my face to narrow in my boss's direction, giving me a chance to thump myself in the chest and croak, "I gotta get back to work." Even if I'd rather hang out and stare adoringly into his brown eyes a bit longer.

Ugh. *Priorities, Lynn! If you get your ass fired, you won't get to schmooze with the athletics team and get a leg up on everyone else in the program!*

Sure, this guy is hot, but hot is only a distraction. One I don't need. Nope.

He nods, finally bringing his gaze back to me. "Yeah. Me too. I'll see you around, though."

And then he's gone, and I'm back to tonging gross wieners and preparing my pro-vegetarianism speech to deliver to my decidedly carnivorous family later tonight. It isn't until after the game and we're doing cleanup that I realize Dark-Haired Hottie's parting words can only mean one thing.

He works at the stadium too. Which means our paths might cross again.

Would that be *so* bad?

MEN ARE ANIMALS (AND NOT THE DOMESTICATED KIND)

JOEY

"I'll have another *Hop Squatch*," Paulie orders, and I hold back my groan. I was ready to go half an hour ago, but I'm Paulie's ride, so I can't exactly ditch him here at the bar to get drunk and make shitty choices without me.

"You got it," Jodi, the server, responds with a wink before tucking her order pad in her apron and sauntering away. I'm confident the extra swing to her back porch is only there for Paulie's sake. The bastard is ugly as hell, but somehow his status as a star second baseman makes women blind. Go figure.

"Another one bites the dust," he boasts, his eyes following Jodi's ass as she disappears into the crowd surrounding the bar.

Echoing my thoughts, my buddy Gunner says, "You do know if you were a garbage man, the only tail you'd get would be roadkill, right?"

Paulie scowls good-naturedly as he lowers his empty

pint glass to the table with a *clack*. "Bullshit. The ladies can't resist all this."

"Has he always been this delusional?" I ask. I've only been on the Arrows' team for one season, so I don't know the guys as well as our left fielder.

"Yes," four voices respond at once, and Paulie flips each one of his teammates off in sequence.

It's an unusual mid-season day off, so a few of us decided to kick back at one of our favorite watering holes, Blue Bigfoot Beer, here in the River Arts District of Asheville. The brothers who own the place are pretty cool, and who wouldn't want to throw back a few while a giant collection of Sasquatch memorabilia stares you down from all angles?

"Come on, Paulie," Gunner continues. "It's a universal truth, and you know it. Pro athletes get tail because women love the idea of dating a famous person—athletes are the holy grail for some reason. It's a status thing."

"Or a money thing," Riley, our third baseman, adds.

I spin my water glass on its white bar napkin and wade in. "Nah—I still got tons of women when I was dirt poor and sharing an apartment with two other guys in the minors." I'm not in a hurry to get back to that living arrangement anytime soon, but it's one of those dues a ballplayer has to pay if he wants a shot at *the show*. Lucky for me, it all paid off. Now I just have to work my ass off and hope it sticks. Nobody tells you being in the majors comes with the constant fear of getting knocked back down to the bush leagues.

A part of me almost misses the old days—not the black mold in the shower or the midnight dinners of cold pizza or fighting for couch space, but some of the normalcy for sure. When I got moved up to the Baltimore Black Dogs a couple years ago, I admit I enjoyed not only the paycheck but the attention too. Having people recognize you in public and ask for selfies or autographs is a definite ego boost, especially after working so hard to get there. But some of it is not all it's cracked up to be—like the women.

Cleat chasers in the minors are nothing compared to those in the majors. A farm-team cleat chaser is a local girl who likes baseball, hard bodies, and a good time. A big league cleat chaser is a woman who can play a better game than any ballplayer I've ever met. And she's always got a plan with a capital P. I'm not sure if the P stands for pussy, power, poser, or all three, but I don't need another lesson. I'm a quick learner, and getting traded to a new team taught me that women who go after ballplayers don't stick around when the chips don't fall exactly as they've planned.

"Truth," José, our center fielder, chimes in before turning to Gunner. "Women just love athletes. Though you'd better watch all your 'tail' talk around that girlfriend of yours."

Gunner grins as only a lovesick asshole can. "Elizabeth is the exception to every rule."

Everyone groans until Paulie decides he's not done being the center of attention yet.

"Look, I can't help it if my body draws all the ladies." He throws his arms out to give us an unobstructed view of his chest covered in a T-shirt that reads, "Be Good to Your Wood." He's the definition of a flexer, but I can't help but like the guy.

Despite being one of the quieter members of the team, I've had no trouble fitting in, thanks to the true sense of camaraderie among all the Arrows members, Paulie included. Maybe it's because we're a new franchise in the league, or perhaps it's just this particular group of guys, but

I feel at home on this team in a way I never did during my first stint in the majors with the Black Dogs. It's hard not to feel a sense of rejection when you're traded—to start questioning your skills and catching a bit of impostor syndrome —but these guys make the environment feel a lot like a family.

Jodi returns with the table's drink order and another wink for Paulie. "You guys all good?"

"I'd be better if you took me home tonight." Paulie goes all in, drawing another round of groans.

But Jodi only laughs with a flip of her bob. "Sorry, Paulie, but I've already got a date. Maybe next time." The woman is a genius. I'll bet a hundred bucks she's got a boyfriend and spotted an easy mark in Paulie for a killer tip.

The table erupts into laughter, and I clap a hand on my teammate's shoulder. "It takes a strong man to admit defeat."

"No way! She already had a date! That's not my fault!" He tries to save face while insults start flying, and we draw attention from nearby patrons with our antics.

A blonde from one table over slides off her chair and leans in over Paulie's shoulder, laying a manicured hand on his bicep. "I'd ditch my date for you, number nine. Just sayin'."

There's usually a decent degree of anonymity at Blue Bigfoot since it's not a sports bar. Still, there are always fans —and cleat chasers—who follow the players around and try to determine a pattern of behavior. I'm guessing this girl is one of them.

But Paulie's not a complete asshole, so when the blonde's date returns from the bathroom, he holds off her advances and chats with the guy for a couple minutes before the boyfriend wisely escorts his woman out the door.

My teammate's expression is way too smug when he drops back into his chair and reaches for his fresh beer. "God, it's good to be irresistible."

"Cash is a good-looking guy," José comments out of absolutely nowhere.

We all fall silent and turn to look first at José and then at the long bar on the other side of the room where one of the proprietors frowns down at the beer he's pouring.

"Something you want to share with the class, Riviera?" Riley asks, stifling a grin.

"You're a bunch of children," José responds with a scrunch of his dark brows. "I'm evolved enough to be capable of objectively evaluating another man's attractiveness without my balls shrinking inside my body."

Chastened, we all turn back to give Cash Brooks, Blue Bigfoot owner and bartender, another perusal. He's tall with dark hair and broad shoulders.

"Okay, I can see what you're saying," Gunner is the first to admit.

A couple more mumbles of agreement follow before Paulie demands, "Why are we checking out the bartender again?"

José's lips quirk. "'Cause I'd bet money if a woman met you and Cash on the same night without knowing anything about what either of you do for a living, *you* wouldn't be the irresistible one."

"That's just cruel." Paulie pouts.

"That, my friend, is the truth." José runs a hand over his shaved head and takes a healthy swallow of his amber-colored beer.

But Paulie's not giving up. "I think you're underestimating my charm."

Gunner coughs out a laugh. "Says the guy who took his last date through the Wendy's drive-thru because, and I quote, 'Their nuggets are on point.'"

I almost choke on my water while another round of laughter hits our group.

Paulie narrows his eyes at the bartender and then swings his gaze back to José. "Care to make a wager?"

"Dude, Cash has a girlfriend," José informs him. "Haven't you seen the hot blonde he eye fucks every time she's within a hundred yards?"

"God, I love a woman in glasses," Riley waxes.

I can't dispute that Cash's girlfriend, Hollis, is undoubtedly hot, but I'm more of a brunette fan. My mind flashes back to the gorgeous brunette from yesterday at the stadium with her long, wavy hair and huge caramel eyes. She handled that situation with the cardiac arrest like she was a seasoned EMT instead of a concession worker. It was kind of awe-inspiring.

"I'm not talking about Cash. I'm talking about one of you fucknuts. I'll bet a thousand bucks I can best all of you and get a date with any woman here—without mentioning my job."

"If I weren't married, I'd be tempted to take that bet just to get you to shut up," José says.

"Oh, I'm absolutely in." Riley rubs his hands together and starts scanning the room for a candidate.

"Same woman. You each have one try." José lays out the rules. "The rest of us get to choose who it is. I'm not letting you give yourself an advantage by picking some obvious cleat chaser who'll recognize you."

"Sold," Paulie agrees, while Riley nods.

"Her." Gunner's tone is decisive as he throws a subtle chin to the glass doors of the patio, where a leggy, dark-haired woman is silhouetted by the sun as she enters the bar.

"I'll even let you go first, Paulie," Riley says with a degree of self-assurance that's probably not unwarranted. He looks like a movie star, and he's funny as hell.

Paulie's chair scrapes back. "Watch and learn, gentlemen."

I shake my head and lift my glass for another sip when the doors close behind the poor woman of the hour and I'm finally able to make out her features. But my arm freezes when I recognize her.

It's the brunette from the stadium.

My pulse jumps in my neck as a feeling close to panic wraps around my entire body. What is happening to me?

I'm not a believer in signs—much to my mom's dismay—but running into the same girl twice in one week can't be a coincidence. Can it? It's got to mean… something.

But that's stupid. The panicked feeling is Paulie's fault. Sure, I like the guy, but it would be cruel to subject this poor woman to his shady advances, right? She's way too good for him. That must be it. But there's not much I can do now that Paulie is halfway to her, so I clench my jaw and instruct my heart to slow its wild galloping. If I learned anything from our first encounter, this girl is perfectly capable of handling a pushy ballplayer. Hell, she could probably handle a charging bull without breaking a sweat. The thought, however, does little to calm my heart rate.

Luckily, it takes less than ten seconds for Paulie to strike out in stupendous fashion while all the guys at our table do their best not to stare or guffaw. All except me, because I'm suddenly not finding anything amusing about this situation.

Before Paulie even returns, Riley is out of his seat and running his fingers through his movie-star locks to tame them. "Looks like I'm up to bat."

Before my brain can even send a signal to my legs, I'm on my feet, one arm extended to block Riley while I lurch forward and blurt, "I got this," and take off in the brunette's direction.

Here goes nothing.

LYNN

Ew.

That guy is the physical embodiment of an unsolicited dick pic.

I shake off my unpleasant encounter with the overly confident patron and scan the taproom for Jeremy Rossi. He texted yesterday asking me to meet him here, although I have no idea why. But since meeting up with him would probably piss my brothers off, I found myself incapable of declining.

Jeremy is my oldest brother Carter's friend and former colleague. If I had to guess, I'd say he's in his mid-thirties. He's also a shameless flirt, which is why my brothers don't want me within a hundred yards of him without them present to "protect" me. I swear, if this were a century ago, I'd be locked in the attic by those jokers in the name of protecting my virtue. They've clearly never read any psychology books, though, or they'd know brotherly behavior like that almost always blows up in your face by causing said little sister to rebel and sleep with the entire football team.

Not that I ever went quite that far. I prefer a more intellectual type—someone who can not only spell misogyny but knows what it means and despises it as much as I do.

I'll guarantee that Paulie guy couldn't spell it with a whole bag of Scrabble tiles and a dictionary. I'm guessing his query of "Girl, are you a beaver? Cuz, *dam,*" was supposed to be a pickup line? Yuck.

"Hey there," a voice says from behind me, and I turn with a frown, expecting to see Paulie again. But my frown flips upside down when I spot a familiar face.

"Hi!" I'm sure I'm smiling too hard, but what are the chances of running into Dark-Haired Hottie at my brothers' brewery? "What are you doing here?" Okay, that was a stupid question. Luckily, he doesn't call me out.

"Just grabbing a drink, same as you, I assume." His voice is a deep rumble, and I'm amazed I can make it out so clearly over the chaos around us. Blue Bigfoot is packed tonight.

I shrug, for some reason not wanting to tell him I'm meeting up with someone—even if it's not a date.

"Save any more lives since the last time I saw you?" he asks with another of those half grins I remember from our first meeting. Damn, he's cute. And I'm pretty sure his eyelashes are longer than mine. So unfair. Equally unfair is the way his T-shirt molds to his muscular chest in a way that's somehow the furthest thing from the flexing bros who walk around staring at themselves in every remotely reflective surface Asheville has to offer. He strikes me as someone who has no idea how hot he is, which makes him that much more tempting.

"Nope," I respond. "It's been exclusively hot dogs and nachos—which will probably result in some heart attacks later, but not on my watch." Oh, god, did I bat my eyelashes at him? Gross.

"I worked ballpark concessions when I was a teenager." He grimaces, and even that is hot. "Do they still use that orange nacho cheese that in no way contains actual cheese?"

I laugh and hope to God my brothers haven't noticed me yet. "Absolutely, although we're not allowed to call it cheese. It's 'nacho sauce' now. I'm guessing there was a lawsuit involved."

When he nods, the motion causes a section of messy hair to fall over his forehead. My fingers itch to brush it back. Sluts!

My internal argument with my phalanges (98% in Human Anatomy, thank you very much) means I barely hear his response. "Ah. Makes sense. So, uh, was it my imagination, or is your boss kind of an asshole?"

"Anus," I reply without thinking.

Dark-Haired Hottie opens his mouth, but nothing comes out.

Fuck!

"Hm." He bites back a smile, and I want to punch myself in the face. "Even though it's the same thing, why does that sound way worse?"

I cringe at myself but manage to smile. He's so freaking *nice*. "Sorry—I wasn't trying to deliver an anatomy lesson. His name is Ennis. But everyone calls him Anus—not to his face, of course."

"Wow. That's…"

"Yeah." I wrinkle my nose. Never in my life did I imagine engaging in flirtation over buttholes, yet here I am.

Time to move on. "You work at the stadium too, right? What do you do?"

He visibly hesitates, which I find odd, before he finally replies, "I work on the field."

"Landscaping." I nod. "That doesn't sound like too much fun in this heat." But it does explain the muscular thighs and the defined biceps straining his cotton T-shirt. Did he hesitate because he thought I'd think badly of his profession? I've got nothing but respect for anybody who busts their ass to make a paycheck, no matter what they do. Hell, I schlep hot dogs and heart attacks.

"My job has its perks." He shrugs and extends his hand. "I'm Joey, by the way."

"Lynn." I take it with a smile and don't fail to notice the calluses on his palms. Damn, those would feel extra nice on certain neglected body parts of mine. His hand is dry and warm, and I know I'm keeping hold a little longer than I should, but he's not pulling back either.

"It's nice to meet you, Lynn." Am I imagining it, or did his rumble just lower another notch? My clit confirms we are not imagining anything, especially when he continues, "So, uh, can I buy you a drink?" See? A girl doesn't want beaver talk. She apparently wants buttholes and drink offers instead.

"Lynnie," a vaguely familiar voice interrupts, and I fight a scowl as I see Jeremy approaching us. "Sorry I'm late." Damn.

Joey's frown is back, so I blurt out in a rush, "Hey, Jeremy. This is Joey. Joey, this is Jeremy. He's my brother's friend."

Jeremy's gaze shoots to me, and I can't miss the knowing quirk of his eyebrows. Idiot. But since the jig is up,

I continue, "Give us a sec, Jeremy," before shooing him away.

"Sorry. I didn't realize you were meeting somebody."

"Yeah." I mean, I'm not about to be a bitch to Jeremy just because my vagina has decided to offer herself on a plate to this hottie. "I think he needs some advice or something." It's honestly my best guess for why I've been summoned.

"So, raincheck on that drink?"

Yes, please. "Sure. You know where to find me." I offer him jazz hands for some reason.

Joey tilts his head and hits me with another lopsided grin that has me wishing I were wearing a skirt instead of shorts so I could simply drop my panties and hand them over right this minute. "Yeah, but I should probably get your number just in case you get fed up with the anus and quit."

My smile takes over. Getting distracted by a guy for a short while suddenly doesn't sound so foolish. It is summer break, after all.

"I DID NOT EXPECT this from you, Lynn," Jeremy says in a scolding tone a few minutes later when I approach the table where he's parked his behind. How did he snag a table in this crowd? When I shoot him a questioning gaze at his comment, he expounds, "So casually breaking my heart like that."

I can't fight the eye roll. "Yeah, right." He's such a flirt. Luckily, he's the harmless kind. It's not like Jeremy is unattractive; he's just not my type. And he's way too old for me. His idea of a nice date would be fancy wining, dining, and being seen by the right people, while mine would be lying on a blanket in the bed of a pickup in the middle of nowhere and stargazing while the Counting Crows play on the truck radio (yeah, I'm kinda old-school). You can take the girl out of the country and all that.

"What's so important I had to come over here on my day off?" I ask, settling into the chair across from him. Jeremy and I don't know each other all that well, but when he and Cart had a falling out, he texted me as a go-between while patching things up. That, and we both like to win at Words with Friends.

"What else did you have to do?" He frowns at me, and I notice his carefully styled brown hair doesn't dare to flop over his forehead like Joey's. Pity.

"Wouldn't you like to know?"

"Who is that guy anyway?" He's going to get wrinkles if he keeps frowning this hard.

"I'm leaving if you keep pulling this big-brother BS on me." When he throws both hands up in defense, I continue, "He's just some guy from work." I don't need him blabbing to my brothers.

"Isn't he a little too old to have a summer job?"

I attempt to spear him with invisible daggers, but he remains unharmed. "My boss is like forty. And, besides, Joey can't be older than maybe twenty-five. Now, why am I here?"

Jeremy sighs and leans back in his chair. "Okay. Sorry. I just wanted to check up on you."

I can feel my eyebrows attempting to merge into a hideous unibrow on my forehead. "Seriously?"

"Yeah." He shrugs before leaning into the table again and resting his forearms on top. "Look, I know you guys have had a lot of shit swirling around your family these last few months, and Carter's not exactly being an open book, so..."

He trails off, and I firm my lips before biting back. "You're not worried about *me*. You're trying to get me to spill the beans on all the Brooks family drama!" And there's no shortage of it, that's for sure. The bar almost got shut down, Miller got arrested, Mama's house got trashed and nearly burned down, Carter took down some crooked politicians, the bar had a break-in, and we all finally met the doctor who was responsible for our dad's death. That's a lot of drama for six months.

"No, I'm not!" Jeremy insists.

"You're worse than Adrina, you nosy old busybody! If you want to know about Cart, I've got a brilliant idea. *Ask Cart.*" My voice drips with sarcasm. "I've been telling you the same thing for weeks." I push my chair back, annoyed that I had to drag my ass down to the River Arts District to engage in playground games with grown men—until I remember I wouldn't have run into Joey tonight if it hadn't been for Jeremy. Still, he can suck it. "Busybody is now my goal word in our next Scrabble round. Nineteen points— even without any bonus squares!"

"Lynn." He lurches over the table and grabs my arm to keep me from fleeing. "I swear, it's not what you think!" When I pause, he takes the opportunity to continue in complete earnestness, "I care about you."

But before I can react—whether that might be to laugh, vomit, or sigh, I have no idea—a menacing growl interrupts the conversation from tableside. "What the fuck did you just say to my baby sister?"

Jesus, Mary, and Jolene, here we go again.

JOEY

LIV:

The silent treatment is a form of abuse, you know.

I glance down at the text from my cousin. Instead of entering the weight room, I pause outside the doors to bite the bullet and reply.

ME:

What are you talking about?

Her response is immediate, and I can picture her tiny thumbs swiping away at her phone screen. I lucked out and got all the height in the family, leaving Liv at five foot nothing with the proportions of a fourth grader. Her personality more than makes up for it, though.

LIV:

You haven't returned any of my texts, you asshat.

See what I mean?

ME:

In my defense, I didn't realize your twenty texts regarding the lack of variety in Starburst products at your local drugstore required a response.

LIV:

Duh. You could have at least sent proof of life.

ME:

I've been busy.

Something she knows because she's the biggest baseball fan I know, and she's been following my every move since I started playing on farm teams seven years ago.

LIV:

I don't respond well to being ignored. You know this about me.

I do. Which is why I'm not currently doing my light game-day lifting in the weight room with half of my teammates.

ME:

You have Brett all over you 24/7. Don't pretend you're lonely.

Her boyfriend, Brett, is a stand-up guy who always strikes me as a man who knows he's got a good thing and is in no way prepared to fuck it up. Good man. And he's equally as obsessed with baseball as Liv, so they're a match made in baseball heaven.

Speaking of Brett, a new notification appears at the top of my phone screen.

BRETT:

Is Liv giving you shit for not texting her back? Sorry, man. I left the room for thirty seconds.

ME:

No worries.

BRETT:

I'll get Bo to bug her for a walk—one sec.

Liv has a giant Great Dane who's basically a big baby—drool and all—and she treats him like he's her child. Which kind of makes sense since she's a large-animal vet and spends every day completely unintimidated by animals ten times her size who could crush her like a grape.

LIV:

Is Brett texting you about me?

ME:

No.

Gotta stick to the bro code. I rest my shoulder on the wall outside the weight room and give in to my cousin's demands.

ME:

What's up? How are you? Anything exciting going on? I miss you.

ME:

There. Is that better?

LIV:

Yes, thank you. [sunglasses face emoji]

I can't help my grin because I do miss her. Liv is more like a sister than a cousin. I grew up in Montreal with my immigrant Chinese mother and French Canadian father, while Liv was in North Carolina with my aunt and uncle, both Chinese immigrants who still live in Greensboro, where Liv is too. We visited back and forth all the time growing up and emailed and texted whenever we were apart. And she's always been my biggest fan, something I don't like taking for granted—especially since my parents still want me to become a lawyer or neurosurgeon instead of playing ball. I should have texted her back, if only to give her a hard time about her sweet tooth.

LIV:

I'm just texting to tell you we're coming to
Asheville to visit for your next home game.
Can we please score some good tix?
[praying hands emoji]

My smile grows. It'll be great to see her, especially after our back-to-back away series starting tomorrow.

ME:

You know I've got you. How many?

LIV:

Just two. Ted and Haley will be at some
comic book convention or something, and
Gavin and Emerson refuse to travel with us
anymore. Wimps.

I made the mistake of staying in a hotel room next to Liv
and Brett's last winter on a trip to New York, so I don't
blame their friends one bit. I put in earplugs and blasted a
white-noise app, and I could *still* hear those two fucking like
wild buffalo through the wall. Let's just say breakfast the
following morning was a tad awkward for Brett and me. Liv,
on the other hand, sat happily devouring her pancakes like
me having my cousin's orgasm noises branded into my
consciousness for the rest of time is not fucked up in the
least.

ME:

Got it. I'm late for pregame weights, so I'll
catch you later. Be nice to Brett.

LIV:

I'm always nice to Brett. In lots of ways.
[winky face emoji]

ME:

Please don't make me vomit before a
workout.

LIV:

[devil emoji]

I move to shove my phone back in my pocket but pause
at the last minute. I'm already late, so I may as well take
advantage. My thumb hovers over Lynn's contact for a
second. It's only been a little over twelve hours since I got

her number. I really should play it a lot cooler than this, but…

ME:

Hey. It's Joey.

The ellipses start bouncing, and my pulse joins them. *Jesus, this is getting ridiculous. You need to focus on baseball. She's just a girl, you moron.*

LYNN:

Hey!

A cute as hell girl.

ME:

How'd your therapy session with your brother's friend go last night?

LYNN:

Not so well. My brother interrupted and made an idiot of himself, as usual. No wonder his friends need therapy.

ME:

You're only masquerading as a concession worker, aren't you? You're really a doctor.

LYNN:

Ha! I wish. But I am working on a PhD in physical therapy.

ME:

Wow. Impressive. I never made it past my sophomore year in college.

If I'm not being honest about everything, at least I can be honest about that. Baseball has always been my dream, so I dropped out when I got a shot in the minors, and I've never looked back.

> LYNN:
>
> Well, I haven't made it yet, so hold your applause.
>
> LYNN:
>
> I looked for you after my brother acted a fool, but I guess you'd already left.

> ME:
>
> Yeah. Had to get up early for work.

Not a lie. Afternoon games mean we show up to the clubhouse early. But it feels weird to hide anything from this girl, especially after the harrowing way we met. Well, harrowing for the rest of us, but maybe not for Lynn, who handled it like she pumps dying people's chests every day.

The memory has me thinking about my mom and her signs again. I never come through the stadium via the gates, but I'd had a pregame appointment offsite that day and came out to my truck to find a flat. It had made me late—which pissed me off—and I'd had to Uber to Ardent Park and haul ass through gate security instead of via the players' parking lot and entrance. I just happened to be walking by when Tom hit the deck and Lynn came to the rescue.

I should just tell her the truth—that I wasn't completely honest when she asked what my job at the stadium was. I'm not even sure why I didn't correct her when she assumed I was on the grounds crew. Part of my head was still stuck on the bet that I'd hijacked, and the other part was just so into this girl that I didn't want to risk glimpsing some familiar wheels start turning in her mind upon mention of my real career. Finding out Lynn is one of the legions of scheming cleat chasers would be like standing at the plate with a full count and seeing a perfect fastball coming your way, only to strike out when it turns out to be a crafty circle changeup.

The fact that she didn't recognize Paulie should tell me she's probably not an Arrows devotee and is just working a summer job while she's in grad school. I wouldn't expect most fans to recognize me since I'm new to the team and not a local star like Gunner or Caleb, our starting pitcher. But people still surprise me on the regular when I'm out and about in Asheville.

LYNN:

Gotta get that field primed for this afternoon's game?

ME:

Something like that.

God, I'm an asshole.

ME:

You maybe want to get that drink after the game?

It's my last chance before I go on the road for the next six days, and I don't want to give her time to change her mind.

LYNN:

Sure. I get off an hour after it ends.

ME:

I'm not off until after you. You want to meet up somewhere, or can I pick you up?

LYNN:

I'll meet you. You name the place—just not Blue Bigfoot.

ME:

You didn't like it?

Maybe she's not a beer fan.

LYNN:

I prefer to spread my patronage around Asheville. So many small businesses, you know?

That's cool, so I suggest another craft brewery downtown, and we decide on a time. I'm clearly shit at hiding my good mood because the first thing Gunner says to me when I take up the leg press station next to him is, "Still riding the high from winning that bet last night? Better watch your back. Riley's out for your blood after checking that girl out properly."

I frown at him, my elation fizzling like a doused campfire. "Her name is Lynn." Not *that girl.*

When I returned to the table after getting Lynn's number last night, José was all over Paulie to fork over the thousand bucks he'd won. It hadn't been my intention to use Lynn in their bet at all—I just couldn't stand by while Riley hit on her when I wanted her for myself. So I really didn't have a choice. And since they'd all clearly seen us exchange numbers on our phones, I couldn't exactly lie and say she'd turned me down.

I do a double take when I catch Gunner's shit-eating grin. Damn, I'm an open book.

"Oh, this is gonna be fun. *Lynn* has got you tied up in knots already. Elizabeth is gonna be fired up about this one."

Fabulous. Just what I wanted—two nosy lovebirds all up in my business.

"Focus on your lats, will you? Your batting sucked on Friday," I lie, but it does the trick and gets my friend off my back—for the moment, that is. I'll have to make sure I don't slip up and tell anyone I'm taking Lynn out tonight. The last thing I need is a whole team of guys up in my business, especially when I have no idea what the hell I'm doing.

LYNN

"Where are you off to all dressed up?"

"I'm not speaking to you." I frown at Cash where he stands in the entryway to the den. He and Carter are both on my shit list for the stunt they pulled last night. In fact, I'm taking advantage of the Arrows' upcoming away games to get out of town and avoid those pea-brains altogether. The beach is calling, and I am fucking going. "What are you doing here anyway?" Cash practically lives at Hollis's place these days. They're like one big happy family of two humans and three ridiculously cute dogs.

"I thought you weren't speaking to me."

"I'm not. Bye." I turn to the front door, eager to get on my way.

"Wait! I'm sorry, okay."

"And what is it we're sorry for?" Mama steps into the hall from the kitchen, and I cross my arms in preparation to throw my brother under the bus.

"The usual. Nosing into my business and acting like a

complete Neanderthal. Humiliating me in public. You know the routine."

Mama's head whips my brother's way, her riot of brown curls swishing. "Cash Brooks, your sister is a grown woman who can take care of herself."

Cash scowls and perches his stupid hands on his stupid hips. "Jeremy was practically professing his love for her in my taproom. What was I supposed to do? Besides, Cart started it."

Mama looks down her nose at him like a proper boarding school nun, and I think I can actually see his balls shriveling in his jeans. Good.

He's not wrong about one thing, though. Carter did start it. That idiot actually grabbed Jeremy by the collar with his meat hands and threatened to end his life if he didn't explain himself to my brother's satisfaction.

Not being as big of a moron as my brother, Jeremy wisely backtracked and explained that our family has welcomed him so thoroughly that he feels like he's one of us—and has a responsibility to look out for all the Brooks crew. I've gotten the sense he didn't grow up in the best family, so he's welcome to ours as far as I'm concerned.

But honestly, what was he thinking in the first place telling me he "cares" about me? I mean, what is that? He doesn't even know me. It's clear I either need another Words with Friends opponent or he needs to get a girlfriend.

By the time Cash crashed the party, Carter had released Jeremy, but he hadn't finished cussing him out—or drawing the attention of half the taproom. I was beyond relieved to find out Joey had already taken off and hadn't witnessed the whole thing. Especially the part where Cash offered to hold Jeremy down while Carter publicly castrated him right there on the barroom table. Talk about wholesome family fun.

"Lynnie is about as interested in Jeremy as Mango is, and he doesn't even own testicles anymore," Mama declares while I cross my fingers that her words penetrate Cash's thick skull. As if needing to put in his two cents at the mention of his name, Mama's pet skunk wanders into the hall and stomps his feet on the wood floor. I grin, despite my lingering anger at Cash.

Mama continues her lecture. "Your dad wouldn't have disrespected your sister like this, so I don't know why you boys continue to do this when she's an adult just like you."

Cash inexplicably laughs at that, and when we both glare at him, he proclaims, "Dad one hundred percent would have been right there with us, carving knife sharpened to take Jeremy apart, and you know it!"

When Mama doesn't contradict him, I glance over to see a few traces of guilt in her expression. "Mama!" Would Dad really have been this protective over me when it came to guys? I'll never know since he died before I reached the stage where I saw boys as anything more than annoying farting machines. I always make a concerted effort not to focus on the time I missed out on with my dad, but it hits hard out of nowhere sometimes.

If it meant I got to have him back, I'd let him chase away the entire male species if that's what he wanted to do to show his love for me—as warped as that is. But it's hard to give my brothers the same grace.

"I'm gonna be late," I say, preferring to explore my feelings in the privacy of Priscilla, my ancient beater of a car.

"Have fun!" Mama shouts to my back as I close the front door behind me. I notice Cash doesn't echo her good wishes.

HOW IS it possible he's even better looking than I remembered? I try not to audibly sigh as Joey approaches the high top where I've been sitting for only a few minutes. The early bird gets the worm, after all. Although I hope it's far bigger than a worm in this case.

Mother magnolia, I need to shut up.

Joey's tousled black hair begs for my slutty fingers again as his strong, denim-covered legs bring him my way. His jeans are paired with a collared dri-fit shirt and cloth slip-on shoes tonight, making me happy I opted for a sundress. The warm smile that stretches his lips when he catches sight of me transforms his face from uber-hot to out-of-this-world-hot.

He looks like the product of a sexy biotechnology experiment where Simu Liu's genes were carefully combined with Chris Pine's in a stroke of genius worthy of a Nobel Prize. And all for me. At least for tonight. A night without any interfering brothers or crappy bosses or weird declarations of "caring."

"Lynn," he says in that deep rumble I'm already becoming addicted to. Without a fraction of hesitation, he goes in for a cheek kiss, not giving me any time to freak out at our proximity. He smells like copper, sandalwood, and fresh-cut grass, and I'm pretty sure I moan a little. Luckily, he's already pulled away, so he doesn't hear.

I could seriously eat this man up with a spoon. I just hope he doesn't turn out to be a caveman like my brothers—or that Paulie buffoon from last night. But he couldn't possibly, could he? God isn't that much of a bitch.

"You probably don't get to watch much of the game while you're working, do you?" he asks after seating himself and asking about my afternoon.

"No, but that's okay. I'm not a baseball fan."

"Really?" His eyebrows spike, and he almost looks like he wants to laugh.

"Nope. What is that look for?"

"Nothing. It's just kind of amusing that you work at a baseball stadium, but you don't like baseball."

"Oh, well, that I can explain. First, I needed a summer job anyway. Second, I really have a passion for nacho sauce." I clutch my heart while he grins at me. After I take a sip of the water the hostess poured, I reveal the truth. "Okay, that's a lie. The director of my program suggested that if I got a job around a sports team, I might be able to get a little one-on-one time with some of the athletics and rehab staff. You know, check out the program, maybe see the treatment spaces and learn about how things operate there."

"Ah, I guess that makes sense." He rests his forearms on the table, and my eyes are caught by the defined veins and muscles. Gotta love a man who works with his hands. "But couldn't you just apply for an internship or something?"

"Ha! Do you know how many students fight for sports team internships? I don't stand a chance, especially at this stage in my education. But I can hustle with the best of them, don't you worry." I plan to finish undergrad in three years instead of four. That way I can start the PhD program sooner.

"I'm sure you can, from what I've seen so far." The look of admiration in his eyes has my heart, brain, and womb all crooning gospel hymns while my clit sings harmony. I hope my thoughts aren't broadcasting themselves too loudly, but just in case, I break our eye contact to check out the taproom.

I've been to this brewery before, and while it's quaint and has a cool vibe, it pales in comparison to Blue Bigfoot. But I'm probably biased. I notice there's only one server in the whole place, but I'm in no hurry. I'm much more interested in the getting-to-know-Joey part of the evening than the drink part.

"Can I ask you a question?" I bring my eyes back to him, suddenly determined to find out all the important things.

"Shoot."

"Do you like Scrabble?"

That's clearly not what he was expecting to hear if his eyebrows are any indication. "The board game?"

"Yeah."

"Why do I feel like this is a loaded question?" He's amused. Good.

"Probably because it is." I add a smile to soften my response. I can still like a guy if he doesn't enjoy word games. I'm not a monster.

He's unfazed, making me like him all the more. "Okay, then, can I ask *you* a question?"

"Shoot." I echo his earlier response.

He leans across the table, giving me a close-up view of his coffee eyes and those obscene eyelashes. When he speaks, his voice drops an octave and picks up a little gravel. "Did you know oxyphenbutazone is the highest possible scoring word in Scrabble?"

I experience a tiny orgasm on the spot, and I know my face gives me away when my only response is, "Wow."

Joey throws his head back and laughs a deep, hearty chuckle I can feel in my clit. I'm tempted to take my eyes off him to scan the taproom and see if anybody else is witnessing the same miracle of hotness I am, but I'm determined not to miss out on a single second of it.

When he finally gets his wits about him again, he says, "So I take it you're a Scrabble fan."

It takes everything in me to adopt a fake bored expression and shrug. "I can take it or leave it."

His grin goes lopsided again. "We should connect on Words with Friends. I play it to wind down at night."

Be still my heart. He is the perfect man. I could be in real trouble here.

"Absolutely. My handle is *lynnqqueen*. 'Cause I'm the queen of q words."

His finger slides absently across the condensation on the outside of his water glass, and I swear it gives me goose bumps. "Mine's boring. It's just my initials and zip code —*jmm28801*."

I know I'm grinning stupidly at him, but I can't help it. Although picturing him bare-chested in bed as he drops words on the board will in no way help me sleep at night, I'm willing to make the sacrifice.

"Game on," I respond before switching tack. I need to know more about this perfect man. "So, do you work for Ardent Park year-round?" I have no idea what goes on at the stadium outside the summer months.

"No," he replies, but instead of expanding on that as I expect, he takes a sip of his water and changes the subject. "What kind of music do you like?"

Hmm. I decide to let him off the hook and answer his question. "I'm a genre-free music fan. As long as I can dance to it or sway to it, I'm in. Bonus points if it has killer lyrics. Double bonus if it's from the nineties. What about you?"

"I pretty much stick to rock. I grew up in Canada, so the alternative rock scene was stellar."

"Oh my gosh, I'm so jealous." I lean forward. "Where in Canada? Not that I've ever been." Our family isn't exactly loaded, meaning childhood vacations tended to involve camping somewhere within driving distance of Asheville.

"Montreal. I think everyone has a love-hate relationship with their hometown, though, right?"

I nod. "Agreed. Even though I only go to school an hour from here, it's still nice to get out of my hometown. I've heard Montreal is beautiful."

He leans forward again, and we're close enough that I can make out the subtle differences in the shades of brown in his irises. "It is. And the food is fantastic. I'm convinced you have to speak French to make a decent crepe."

I laugh at that and ask, *"Parlez-vous français?"* It's the extent of my French.

"Oui, mon premier mot était en français," he responds, making my jaw drop.

"I was kidding! You actually speak French?"

He shrugs like it's no big thing. "I grew up with it. I also speak Mandarin."

"You're a polyglot. Or a linguaphile? Both?" I wave a dismissive hand between us. "No wonder you like Scrabble!" I'm so in like with this guy. "I took Spanish in high school, but all I remember is how to tell you that Juan and Carlos went to the beach."

"Well, it's important to keep tabs on those two." He's adorable.

"I was always better at science and lit. But it would be cool to be fluent in another language."

"Sorry about that." The frazzled waitress appears at our

side, a pen tucked behind her ear and another in her hand. "What can I get you?"

Joey gestures for me to go first like the gentleman he clearly is, and I order a Cheerwine. Joey grins and orders himself a lager before the waitress bustles away.

"You know there's no actual wine in Cheerwine, right?" he asks with not a hint of condescension.

"Duh. But I wouldn't be a proper North Carolina native if I didn't order our state's signature soda. I'll worry about the diabetes later." It really is sort of disgusting, but I still love it.

This might be my best date ever, not that I date all that much. I was very good at getting into harmless trouble in high school, making out with lots of boys in backseats and generally having fun—something that drove Cash absolutely batty. But I've never technically had a boyfriend. My first time having sex was in my first semester at college with a visiting student from Spain named Joaquin. He was cute, super smart, and—most importantly—not an asshole. The way he said my name with his accent—*Leen*—made my knees a little weak. I'm afraid I might have broken his heart a little when I told him I only wanted to be friends, but that was better than pretending just so I didn't hurt his feelings. Besides, I'm too busy chasing my career dreams to have a boyfriend.

But sharing some fun dates with the perfect man? That, I can do.

JOEY

God, she's cute. And gorgeous, intelligent, funny—the whole package. She's almost too good to be true.

And speaking of the truth, it's time to confess before I dig my hole any deeper.

The waitress comes back and sets our drinks in front of us, and I wait until she leaves to spill the beans. But Lynn raises her red Shirley-Temple-style drink, smiling at me in a way that hits me in the chest like a line drive.

"To Montreal crepes and North Carolina Cheerwine," she says.

I clink my glass with hers. "And first dates." I need to make my intentions clear before I go on. There's a slight flush to her cheeks at my words, which I find adorable as hell.

We each sip our drinks, and my lager tastes perfectly smooth and bitter. "So, I have to tell you something."

"Oh god." Her face falls. "I knew this was too good to be true. My brothers didn't get a hold of you, did they?"

I can't help but laugh at her panicked expression. "Brothers? No. Why?" This, I've got to hear.

She shakes her head and drops her drink onto the paper napkin on the table. "You know in movies and books, there's always a family with four or five burly older brothers and one little sister who they treat like a fragile newborn bird?" When I nod, she raises her eyebrows and finishes, "Tweet."

I drop my chin to my chest and laugh again, which only makes her scowl at me. "It's not funny. I'm the youngest in my family, and all four of my brothers are complete cavemen. I've literally been carried from a date's car in a fireman's hold by one of them."

"I think it's kind of nice."

"That's because you've never met them. They're overbearing children in men's bodies."

She tucks a lock of dark hair behind her ear, and I follow the movement. Her delicate fingers glide from her hair and back down to the table, where she wraps them around her glass. What I wouldn't give to have those fingers brushing across my skin, wrapping around my cock, doing all manner of things that would bring that flush back to her cheeks.

But I'd be happy spending all night just looking at her too. From her thick, shiny curtain of hair to those wide caramel eyes rimmed with dark lashes to that slender neck. She has a birthmark on her collarbone that I want to kiss and a gorgeous set of breasts that look like the perfect handful. I'm going to be sporting a giant boner under this table if I don't rein in my thoughts.

"So, what is it that you wanted to tell me?"

Well, at least my boner problem is solved. She's going to be pissed, isn't she?

I take another sip of my beer and keep both hands

around the glass. May as well enjoy one last taste in case she throws it in my face. "It's just that… I wasn't completely upfront with you last night. When you asked me what I do at Ardent Park, I mean."

Her brow creases. "Oh? You don't work in landscaping?"

"No." I shake my head and take one more breath. "When I said I work on the field, I was being deliberately vague, and I should have corrected you when you assumed I was part of the grounds crew. I'm actually… well, I'm actually *on* the team."

"What team? The athletics and rehab team?!" She looks mortified, so I'm quick to explain.

"No. The *team* team. The Arrows. I'm a shortstop." I grip the glass almost hard enough to break it while I wait for her reaction. When it comes, it's not at all what I expect.

"A shortstop," she repeats back to me with a tilt of her head.

I try biting back my grin, but I fail miserably. Lynn is the *furthest* thing from a cleat chaser I think I've ever met. "Yeah, a shortstop. I play kind of between second and third base and stop hit balls from getting to the outfield."

Her responding nod isn't very convincing. "So, you're… a baseball player?"

"Yeah." There. I've confessed, and I'm not wearing my beer.

"Oh. Okay." She shrugs and takes another sip of her drink. Her pink lips are now stained red, and I want nothing more than to haul her across this table and get a taste.

"Okay." I nod instead and take her in, a feeling of complete contentment settling over me. I can't escape the sense that something big is happening here, but I refuse to analyze it in favor of simply enjoying the moment.

When we've watched each other in silence for a few beats, Lynn leans forward and lowers her voice conspiratorially. "This doesn't change my opinion on baseball, though, just so we're clear."

All I can do is laugh and thank fate for bringing this breath of fresh air into my life. No matter what happens from here.

"YOU'RE NOT LURING me out into the middle of nowhere to chop me into little pieces, are you?" Lynn asks from the passenger seat.

"You probably should have asked that question before you got into my truck."

I glance over with a grin and see her shrug one of her bare shoulders. I need to write a thank you note to the inventor of short dresses with tiny straps. "Oh well. At least I know my brothers won't rest until they track you down and avenge me."

"See, I told you they were being nice."

She barks out a laugh. "Seriously, though, where are we going?"

I didn't want to say goodnight after our drink at the brewery, so I asked if she wanted to go for a drive. She accepted on the condition that she got to control the radio, so right now we're listening to a nineties throwback station and driving down a deserted country road. I lean forward in my seat and tilt my head up to the dark sky. Perfect.

"You'll see," I answer as I turn onto a dirt drive flanked by two soybean fields. I come to a stop about twenty yards in and put the truck in park, leaving the engine running for the radio but shutting off the headlights. "Wait there," I tell her, hopping out and rounding the truck to open her door. When I extend my hand, she takes it, a reluctant smile on her cherry-stained lips. I never knew until tonight what I was missing out on by not giving Cheerwine a shot.

"What are you up to?" Lynn asks, glancing around into the darkness before dropping her head back and letting out a gasp. "Oh my god."

I watch her face for another couple seconds before tilting my own head back and gazing at the clear night sky sprayed with a million stars, each one visible from our vantage point. "Not too shabby a view, huh?"

"It's breathtaking," she whispers. "We get some decent stargazing at my house, but nothing like *this*. It's incredible."

Her eyes stay rooted to the sky while I glance back down at her profile and step closer. When I take her hand in mine, she finally shifts her gaze over to me and smiles at me so soft and sweet it has my stomach swooping like a crazy pop fly.

"You are downright dreamy, do you know that?" she asks, her smile turning mischievous.

"And you're gorgeous." I pull her hand so she sways into me, and I use my other hand to cup her jaw. She smells like coconut sunscreen and flowers, and when I dip my chin to go in for a kiss, she meets me halfway.

The first brush of our lips is electric. I take her bottom lip between mine, then get a taste of the top one, grazing it lightly with my teeth in the process. Her lips are silky perfection, as I knew they'd be, and I can already taste the cherry from her soda. I draw back a fraction of an inch and feel her warm breath on my lips as she exhales.

"I love this song," she whispers before leaning back in and gently sweeping the tip of her tongue across my bottom lip. I vaguely register the song in the back of my mind as Counting Crows's "Round Here," but I can't give it any proper attention when every cell in my body is focused on kissing this gorgeous woman. I grant her tongue immediate entrance but can't help taking over the kiss as I slide mine against hers for a proper taste.

Cherries. Sugar. Heat.

My cock swells, begging for equal attention, and when Lynn lets out a little moan, I adjust to deepen the kiss. She slides both hands up my stomach to my chest, leaving a trail of fire along my abs and pecs that shoots straight down to my dick. I groan and snake an arm around her, my hand skimming up her back. The pads of my fingers glide along the silk of her dress until they meet dewy, bare skin, and I pull her into my chest, trapping her hands between us and feeling the length of her body flush with mine.

Fuck, she's addictive.

This kiss is making me feel drunk, and I want to push her against my truck and hear what she sounds like when she comes. But the timing is all off. This can't go anywhere tonight. I'm leaving early in the morning for a week, and the last thing I want is for this to be some cheap one-night stand.

When I tear my mouth from hers, we're both breathing hard, sharing the same air while the song on the radio switches to a raucous number from Nirvana. Lynn rests her forehead against mine as we catch our breaths. With our proximity, I can't make out her features, but I sense her smiling when she says, "Damn."

I let out a low chuckle, responding, "You took the words right out of my mouth."

CHAPTER
SEVEN

MY FAVORITE CONDIMENT

LYNN

Is this really happening? I mean, I'm not an idiot, so I know it's happening, but how in the world did the universe just deliver me my dream date, Counting Crows and all!? Do I owe someone my firstborn now? Is my soul promised to Beelzebub without my knowledge?

I know it wasn't the smartest thing in the world to get in a stranger's car and let him drive me to the middle of nowhere, but I have this palpable gut feeling that Joey is one of the good guys. And after that kiss? Now I know he's not only good, he's talented. The way his tongue dissolved me into a puddle of gooey hormones was expert-level. And I did not miss the impressive press of his package against my stomach when he pulled me into him.

I'm gonna have to explore the entire gamut of baseball analogies when I reflect on this later.

"Lemme drive you back to your car," he suggests. And while I want to argue that we haven't explored the blanket-in-the-truck-bed portion of my dream date, I know it's the smart move to leave things where they are for tonight. I let him retake my hand and open the passenger door for me.

He really is dreamy as hell.

The normal me would be looking for flaws or waiting for the other shoe to drop (because it *always* does), but I've somehow ditched her for the night. Instead, I'm some foreign version of myself that believes in diving in headfirst and worrying about reality later. She rarely comes out to play anymore, but I'm feeling her hard tonight.

Hell, I didn't even balk when I found out Joey lied about his job. Well, lied is probably a bit harsh, but still. Usually, I'm out the door Road Runner style when a guy gives me any indication that he's a game player. Or a Neanderthal. Or a jock (too many cringe-worthy teenage memories of bro chest bumps and chugging contests). But it's easy to imagine why Joey might not want to advertise. I've heard some of the women talking in the stadium bathrooms—you'd think they were bartering over solid gold sides of beef instead of watching a bunch of men throw a ball.

In fact, Joey wanting to hang out without first trying to impress me with something a lot of women would find irresistible almost makes me like him more. He's sweet. And hot. He's basically my favorite condiment—hot honey. And he tastes just as good.

The baseball thing… yeah, that's not ideal. I'm not into fighting over a guy, and I don't like being the center of attention. But it's who he is, and I do like *him*. This is stupid anyway. We're not even dating, so I refuse to give it that much thought. We'll just see where this goes and have some fun along the way. Easy peasy.

But even as I tell myself that, it's impossible to ignore the way this already feels almost fated.

Gulp.

"So, tell me more about your family," Joey says as we reverse course back to Asheville.

I glance over at his profile. "My mama is a complete nut, but she's a lovable one. Besides that, it's just the degenerates. Oh, and our family skunk."

"Your family what?" He laughs.

"Skunk. His name is Mango, and he might be a bigger troublemaker than all the rest of us put together." Truth.

Joey's narrowed eyes flash my way. "I can't tell if you're messing with me or not."

I grin. "Not one bit. He had his sprayer removed as a baby, so he doesn't stink or anything. He's kind of like a mix between a cat and a dog, except I'm pretty sure he's smarter than both." When Joey just shakes his head, I repeat, "I told you my mama is a nut."

"I grew up with dogs, but the weirdest that ever got was when I wanted to name one Smegma." When I snort-laugh, he hurries to explain. "I heard it on the school bus and thought it meant something entirely different. I'll never forget the look on my dad's face when he had to explain it to me."

"Oh my god." I cringe. "That is beyond disgusting. But at least it's original. I can guarantee he would have been the only Smegma at obedience school."

"True." He nods like he's giving the idea some serious thought.

I roll my eyes. "What about you?"

"Only child here." He checks for traffic and turns onto a main road leading back to town. "Just me and my parents. Pretty boring." He glances over again. "You didn't mention your dad. Is he not in the picture?"

"He passed when I was thirteen."

"I'm sorry."

"Thanks." But I wave him off. Nothing kills a vibe like talking about a dead parent. "My mama thinks that's why my brothers treat me the way they do—they've got some misguided notion that they need to fill his shoes or something."

"I can see that. Besides, it's kind of a big brother's job to protect his sister, isn't it? I mean, I don't have a sister, but I've got a cousin I'm close to, and when I found out her ex was cheating on her, I broke his nose." He shrugs. "It's what we do."

Alarm bells start ringing in my head, but Joey clearly doesn't hear them because he continues, "Guys are protective. At least the good ones are."

"Ugh." I'm not about to hide my feelings on the matter.

But Joey is more amused than anything. "Are you telling me if some guy cheated on you or you found out he was a drug dealer or something, you wouldn't want somebody to interfere?"

"If you mean interfering by giving me information about said loser that I didn't already have, then yes. If you mean stringing said loser up by his nuts, absolutely not. I can take care of myself."

He wisely backs down. "Okay, fair enough. I take it your brothers are the stringing-up-by-the-nuts kind of guys."

"One hundred percent. It's ridiculous." I frown at him. How did we get on this topic anyway?

"I think I'm going to start agreeing with you. Because, at this point, I get the idea I'll need full pads and a cup if I ever meet them."

I facepalm at that and laugh, but he's not wrong. "Are you telling me you're a drug dealer and a serial cheater?"

He turns to me and puts up two fingers in salute. "Never. I swear on Smegma's grave."

All I can do is shake my head.

Twenty minutes later, we're back downtown, and Joey hasn't revealed any more signs that he may wear a loincloth and hunt saber tooth tigers in his spare time. We pull into the small parking lot of the brewery, and he maneuvers into an empty spot near Priscilla before getting out to open my door for me again.

"So, the team is going on the road tomorrow morning, but I'd love to see you again when I get back. You up for it?"

I take his hand and slide off the seat, my sandals crunching on the gravel. "Absolutely."

He doesn't let go, instead lacing our fingers together as he smiles down at me. My stomach swarms with ptero-dactyls. How I know they're pterodactyls, I can't say. They just are.

"In the meantime, I'll hit you up on Words with Friends, lynnqqueen."

There's that deep rumble again, and it has me fighting a shiver. So he punched some jerk in the face. Big deal. I'm sure he deserved it. All I can do is smile up at him. "I hope you're not a sore loser."

He barks out a laugh, and I get to watch the show again. I can't decide what's more beautiful, the sight of this man laughing or the stars in the sky out in the country.

When he brings his head back down, his eyes are still crinkled with amusement. "Next time, you pick the place. I didn't realize you don't like beer, so that was my bad."

I shake my head, still a little distracted by his hotness and the pterodactyls. "No, it's fine. I'm not actually old enough to drink, so it doesn't matter."

As my words hang in the air between us, I feel a shift, like a spell being broken. And for the second time in twenty-four hours, I want to punch myself in the face because Joey's grin falls faster at my words than a greasy stadium dog in a toddler's hands.

Me and my big mouth.

WHICH CAME FIRST—THE BABY OR THE MAN?

JOEY

I freeze, the hand holding Lynn's going cold as her words register.

Did she just say she's underage?

But wait, she told me she was studying for her PhD—and she saved a guy's life like a seasoned pro. I pegged her for twenty-four at the very youngest! What is going on here?

Was she playing me? It certainly wouldn't be the first time.

She must read my expression perfectly because she drops my hand and holds her head in both her hands. Her movement, unfortunately, shifts the neckline of her sundress, giving me a view right down the front. Fuck! I'm a complete pervert!

"Oh my god, I'm not a *minor*!" she barks out loud enough that a passing couple glances over to check us out. Shit! When she realizes we've drawn attention, she lowers her voice to almost a whisper and says, "I'm twenty."

"Lynn, I..." I trail off because I still don't know what to say. Yeah, that's better than, say, eighteen, but she's twenty years old, and I'm on the verge of twenty-nine. That's not okay. She was a teenager less than a year ago!

"It's really no big deal." Her voice has a slight edge of annoyance now, and I still can't figure out how we ended up here.

"You said you're studying for a PhD." I finally get out a full sentence, my defensiveness audible.

"I am." Her lips firm into a rigid line. I'm pissing her off, but this is serious to me. I need to watch my every step with the league—and with my own moral code of conduct.

I take a step back and prop my hands on my hips. "So you're a child genius or something? You skipped five grades?"

She mimics my stance. "No, I'm in the undergrad Sports Science and Kinesiology program that feeds into the PhD Physical Therapy program. There is no bachelor's or master's degree in physical therapy."

"Oh." Okay, so maybe I reacted a little harshly, but... "I'm twenty-eight, Lynn. And you're *twenty*."

"And?"

"And that's kind of a big deal."

She throws her hands up. "And last I checked, this was a first date. Nothing is supposed to be a big deal on a first date."

She has a point. But, damn, I really like this woman. I've never felt an immediate spark like this with anyone. It feels like our tenth date instead of our first. And she's twenty years old, hardly more than a girl. I'm at a complete loss.

"Well, well, well!" A booming voice catches our attention, and I look over to see Paulie closing in on us, José not far behind. Of all the luck.

"Crap," Lynn curses, her face losing color. She opens her

mouth to speak again but closes it as her eyes catch on Paulie's hand descending onto my shoulder. This is so not good.

"Our boy has good follow-through," Paulie bellows gleefully just as José catches up and grabs his arm.

"Come on, Paulie, leave the nice people alone." He doesn't try hiding the urgency in his tone. What the hell is Paulie thinking? As far as he knows, Lynn isn't even aware I'm a ballplayer, much less his friend.

"Do you… know each other?" Lynn asks, her dark eyebrows scrunching together.

"No!" José tries saving me, but Paulie is still oblivious. And loud.

"Know each other? We're on the same team. Don't you watch baseball, sweetheart?"

Lynn's chin snaps back so fast, I'd be unsurprised if she sustained a whiplash injury. *"Sweetheart?"*

"He's had a few drinks." José tries laughing it off as he jerks on Paulie's arm again, but the idiot stays rooted to the gravel of the parking lot.

"He's your *teammate*?" Lynn eyes me, looking like she just smelled a dog turd.

"Unfortunately," I mutter under my breath, but Paulie interjects once again.

"Okay, you don't like 'sweetheart,' I get it. But I didn't catch your name last night when you made me lose that bet."

Fuck! Another look Lynn's way shows eyes now filled with equal parts fire and ice.

"Bet? *What bet?*" she demands through clenched teeth, and I swear she grows three inches in height with her anger.

I shake Paulie off and move closer, in full panic mode now. "It's not what you think. I promise."

But Paulie is only too eager to answer her question as he, too, shifts closer, evading José's grip. "José here said I couldn't get you to go out with me without telling you I'm a pro ballplayer."

"Yup, and that's the end of the story. Time to go now! Nice to meet you!" José yanks hard on Paulie's arm, sending him stumbling sideways. He uses his temporary imbalance to steer him away from us and back to the sidewalk, but not before Paulie succeeds in fucking me over with a few last words thrown over his shoulder.

"You won fair and square, Martel! Enjoy the spoils!"

Lynn stares at me, eyes wide, cheeks flushed, and her silky lips dropped open. "I was a *bet*?"

"No! It wasn't like that." I reach out to, I don't know, take her hand or squeeze her shoulder—anything so she'll listen to me. But she sidesteps my hand and puts several feet of distance between us.

"So you're saying that Paulie guy was lying?"

"Yes. No. Okay, you were part of a bet, but I didn't make the bet!" I'm desperate for her to believe me and understand what's going on here. But what *is* going on here? She's too young for me. This is wrong. But at the same time, I've never had this level of instantaneous and fundamental connection with anyone in my life. It can't just end like this.

But that's apparently not my choice to make.

Lynn digs in her purse and pulls out a set of car keys. "Are you being serious right now? You get all bent out of shape because I'm younger than you thought I was, but you and your juvenile jock friends made a bet to see who could *fuck* me first?" She stalks to an old beat-up Mazda a couple spots away, and I follow.

"No! That wasn't the bet! And it wasn't even me!"

She whirls around at the driver's door, her dark hair wild around her face and her chest heaving. She looks like a goddess. A vengeful one, but gorgeous and vibrant all the same. "Does it really matter?! Everything is a joke or a contest or a comparison of dick size to guys like you. You strut around in your toxic testosterone club and treat women with no respect at all. Believe me, I get enough of this shit from my brothers, I don't need it on a date too." She yanks the door open and drops into the seat. "Have a nice life, Joey whoever the hell you are."

Her door shuts with a loud screech and a bang, and I step back so I don't get run over as she peels out of the parking lot—and out of my life.

And she's right. Fuck. She was one hundred percent right about what she said, and I am a complete and utter douchebag.

Fuck my life.

I SENSE movement in my peripheral vision and glance over to see Gunner Nix's lips move as he sinks down into the empty seat next to mine on the team plane. I guess the headphones covering my ears didn't sufficiently project my desire to be left alone. Confirming his intentions, Gunner yanks the headphones from my head and drops them in my lap.

"Do you want me to sic Skye and Elizabeth on Paulie?" he asks.

Goddammit. Does every-fucking-body know what happened?

Gunner answers my unspoken question, his voice low enough so nobody else seated around us can hear. "José told me what happened. I told him to keep it under wraps."

Thank God for that, at least.

"I'm fine," I lie. I just want to get to Chicago and kick some ass.

"On a scale of one to ten, how mad is Lynn?"

I narrow my eyes at my friend. "You ever seen *Godzilla vs. Kong*?"

Gunner's eyebrows almost connect with his close-cropped hair. "Which one is she in this scenario?"

"*Mecha*godzilla."

"Eesh." He winces and scratches his beard. "Was it the bet, or had you still not told her about your job?"

"The bet." I shake my head. "But I didn't do myself any favors by freaking out about her age right before Paulie showed up."

"Why? How old is she?"

"Twenty."

He rocks his head back and forth as if weighing the information. "What kind of twenty?"

"What do you mean?"

He shrugs. "Head in the clouds, drama queen twenty? Or solid head on her shoulders, more mature twenty?"

Damn. "Definitely the latter. Man, the reason I cockblocked Riley is that I'd already met her last week. She works concessions at Ardent Park. Remember when I was late and Coach read me the riot act?"

"Yeah." Everybody heard me tell Coach about my flat and an emergency in the stadium, but I didn't go into detail.

"Lynn gave CPR to this guy who had a heart attack right in front of us. She saved his life like she was just filling a drink order and then went right back to work like nothing happened. I felt like I needed a shot and a nap, and all I did was watch."

"Seriously? That's pure clutch, man." He runs a hand over his buzzed head. "So I think it's safe to say her age is just a number, yeah?"

Double damn. "Yeah. But I fucked it up."

He claps my shoulder. "Women get mad. Just ask Lizzie. She gets mad at me all the time, but she always forgives me in the end. Call Lynn and say you're sorry. Hell, I'll talk to her and tell her that stupid bet wasn't your idea."

I don't respond, mostly because I have no clue what to say. I dug my own grave.

Drew, our first baseman, pokes his head over one of the seats in front of us. "Yo, Nix. Can you send me that audiobook you were talking about?"

I take the opportunity to retreat into my head again, replacing my headphones and pressing play for the tenth time on Counting Crows's "Round Here," and promising myself it will be the last time I listen to this song.

Three minutes later, I hit play again.

LYNN

ONE WEEK LATER

"Hey, new girl! How many times have I told you the pretzels need more salt!?"

I draw in a breath and recite my mantra in my head before saying *screw it* and turning to my boss. "Ennis, it's already such a salt lick. I'm shocked we don't have random cattle dropping by for a sit-down meal." I'm really in no mood.

Sara, another of my coworkers, stifles a laugh by the soda machine and Ennis glares at her. "Enough with that attitude," he sniffs before stalking to the other side of the booth.

"Can you give me a hand, *Lynn*?" Sara emphasizes my name, talking louder than strictly necessary. Ennis pretends not to hear.

I join her with a grin of appreciation. It's the first home game in over a week, and I'm on pins and needles. It doesn't help that the announcer's voice is loud enough out here for me to hear every word. And despite my determination not to pay any attention, I know Joey has already had a few good plays tonight. Not that I care or anything.

The entire three hours leading up to game time, I was jumping out of my skin every time I spied a tall, dark-haired figure in my peripheral vision. But I've relaxed a bit since the team took the field, and I know I'm safe from any visiting ballplayers.

Not that I expect Joey to hunt me down. I was quite definitive the last time I saw him, so he's got to know where I stand. And it's not like I want to see him or talk to him again. He's a jerk. A meathead. A caveman. And that's the furthest thing from my ideal man. If I were looking, that is.

But my conviction in the matter didn't keep me from being abnormally subdued on my beach trip with my friends last week. Sadie, my dorm big sister—and favorite senior this past year who I'm going to miss like crazy next year—even sat me down for a chat to find out what had me so blue. When I told her the bare bones of the story, Sadie agreed the whole thing sounded shady. And I trust her one hundred percent, so I know I'm wise to steer clear of Joey and his toxic circle of jocks.

Too bad I still can't seem to shake the blues.

I suppose it could have something to do with the unanswered texts sitting on my phone.

But this is so not me. I don't let men get me into my feelings like this, so I need to find a way to shake it off and get on with my life.

"Where are the hot dogs?!" Ennis shouts, and for once, I'm happy to return my focus to greasy stadium food and my asshole boss.

"STILL NO SIGN OF LARRY?" I ask my brother Miller as I sidle up to the bar at Blue Bigfoot the next day before opening.

"Sadly, no. I'm afraid he might be gone for good," he replies, blowing his dirty-blond hair from his eyes as he wipes the bar down.

"Damn." Larry is Blue Bigfoot's mascot, a Sasquatch statue that belonged to our dad and was carved by an old friend of his before that friend became a famous sculptor and started earning a ton of money for his work. The statue has sat by the cash register since the day Blue Bigfoot opened, but it was stolen a few weeks back when the brewery had a break-in. "And the cops still have no leads?"

"Nope." This comes from Carter, my oldest brother, as he and his girlfriend, Sunny, approach from behind me, and he throws an arm around my shoulder. "You speaking to me yet?" he asks, not looking nearly as apologetic as he should.

"That depends. Are you sorry?"

He adopts an expression that tells me he's about to lie, and Sunny smacks his arm for me.

"Never mind." I roll my eyes. These numbskulls are going to need to reimburse me for the eye surgery I'll need to repair the damage from all the eye-rolling they cause me.

"Well, he scared Jeremy off, by the looks of it, so he'll have to eat humble pie with both of you at some point," Sunny shares before looking up at her boyfriend again. She's so much shorter than him, it's almost comical, but I love her for taking on my big bro, no matter how much he annoys me. "Is there any way you guys can commission a new Larry from Morton Frye?" She squints at me.

Miller laughs almost hard enough to send his forehead into the bar. "Did one of you win the lottery and not tell me?"

"That bad?" Sunny asks, and we all nod in response. I don't know the exact value of Larry, but I'm fairly certain it's way more money than any of us have seen outside of a game of Monopoly.

We all ponder that momentarily, wishing for things that can't be. But we Brookses are used to that, so it doesn't take long for us to brush the thought aside and get on with it.

"We're heading out to grab lunch. You guys want us to bring something back?" Cart offers. I notice we're not invited on this little lunch outing, which tells me I might not want to know what they're actually doing. Gross.

"No, thanks," Miller and I reply in tandem, clearly thinking the same thing.

As soon as the happy couple is out of earshot, Miller confirms my suspicion by saying, "I don't think I can eat a burrito that's witnessed those two going at it."

I snort out a laugh. "Same."

But my laugh dies in my throat when Miller continues, "Speaking of lovebirds, how are things with your boyfriend?"

My brain immediately flashes to the memory of kissing Joey under the stars, and a giant boulder lands at the bottom of my stomach with a force that threatens to take my knees out from under me. Miller eyes me curiously from across the bar, and I panic for a second before the synapses in my brain finally start connecting again and I can breathe properly.

However, my laugh is still a bit forced when I explain,

"I'm not dating anyone. I just told those idiots I was because they were being, well, idiots."

When Jeremy had been texting me trying to reconnect with Carter, my brothers lost their shit, so I told them I had a boyfriend to shut them up. Or maybe to throw it in their faces? I'm not sure which. Either way, it was just a ruse I'd forgotten about until Miller brought it up.

Miller snickers and continues wiping down the bar. Of all my brothers, he's the least overbearing, probably because we're so much closer in age. Over a decade separates me from Cash and Carter, and Denny is closing in on thirty himself. And while Miller still oversteps sometimes, I tend to be more open with him about most things. I think our bond is due to our shared feeling of missing out on way more time with our dad than our older brothers did.

"Well, they won't hear it from me," Miller promises with a click of his tongue ring against his teeth.

I smile in response as Miller reaches for his clattering phone on the bar top to see who's calling. When I catch his expression before he answers, I know it must be his girlfriend, Maisy, so I excuse myself down the bar to give him privacy.

Without my permission, my thumb glides over my own phone screen, waking it to reveal the same texts I've read over a dozen times already.

> JOEY:
>
> I'm sorry.
>
> JOEY:
>
> Can we talk? I'd really like to apologize and explain.

And the last one that's had me in knots…

JOEY:

Adam Duritz is a poet.

Because Adam Duritz, the lead singer and lyricist of the Counting Crows, is indeed a poet. And Joey remembers the song I said I loved. The same one that played while we shared our first—and only—kiss.

Dammit!

"Maisy and Bear are bringing lunch over before we open." Miller pulls my attention from my phone, and I quickly shove it into my back pocket.

"Awesome," I reply, telling the truth. I adore Maisy and her little brother, Bear. He's a riot.

"No traumatized burritos who've seen too much."

I muster a smile for Miller. Who needs men when I already have so many awesome people in my life?

Not me. Nope.

CHAPTER
TEN

HOT DOG POWER TRIPS AND
OTHER MISADVENTURES

JOEY

This is stupid. If she wanted to see me, she would have responded to my texts. Yet that fact isn't stopping me from spying on Lynn from behind a concrete pillar in the main concourse while Gunner covers for me down in the clubhouse. It's our pregame downtime, so I'm not technically doing anything wrong by being here, but it's customary to stick to the clubhouse until we hit the field for pregame warm-ups. Instead, I'm out here acting like a stalker.

It took fifteen minutes to hit all the concessions until I found the one where Lynn is stationed tonight. Her dark hair is pulled up into a high ponytail just like the first day I met her, and she's wearing her red apron over a tight T-shirt and jeans while she smiles at customers and hands over nachos and sodas. The crowd is sparse since it's still an hour until game time, and if I don't get my ass out from behind this pillar, I'll lose my shot.

Just as my feet start taking me her way, though, Lynn

exits out a side door and starts walking toward me, her eyes trained on the phone in her hand. I stop so I don't run head-first into her, and I catch her with a hand to her elbow as she practically trips over me.

"Oh my gosh. I'm so sorry! I wasn't looking where I was —" Her words halt on her lips as soon as her eyes reach my face. "Joey?"

"Hey, Lynn." She's even more gorgeous than my memories made her out to be. There's a deeper tan to her skin, highlighting a spray of freckles across her nose and bringing out the intense caramel tone of her eyes. She's sun-kissed and beautiful, and all I want to do is lean down and capture her lips with mine.

"Hey." She glances down at her shuffling feet.

I know I don't have any more time, so I get down to business. "I wanted to find you to explain what happened last week." When she doesn't run away or punch me, I hurry on. "That stupid bet—I'm so sorry—it was just José trying to prove to Paulie that the only reason he gets dates is because he's a ballplayer. That's it. The only reason I had anything to do with it is that I realized they were going to use you to prove a point, and I wanted to keep them away from you."

When her eyes lift to meet mine again, it's clear she's searching mine for the truth. I hope she finds what she's looking for.

"So why did Paulie say you won?" Her gaze still holds some doubt.

"Because they saw me get your number. That's it. I didn't win anything." I put both palms out as if to prove I'm holding nothing back.

"And you're being straight with me?"

I make an X over my heart. "I swear on Smegma's grave."

The corner of her mouth quirks, and I hold my breath, hoping I've fixed things enough for her to give me another shot.

Lynn watches a few passersby before bringing her eyes back to my face. "And what about the age difference?" There's a challenge to her tone, and it makes me want to smile. She's nothing like the cleat chasers I've wasted time on in the past. They act like demure little kittens and agree with everything you say, to the point of hiding their entire personalities sometimes. Not like Lynn, who wouldn't dare to hide her opinion.

I wisely shake my head, remembering my chat with Gunner. "Age is just a number."

"You're damn right it is," she responds, this time allowing a half grin to form on her lush lips. But her grin drops as she glances back at the concession stand. "Look, can we chat later? I only have a fifteen-minute break, and I heard the athletics team will be wrapping things up downstairs. I want to see if I can intercept someone."

"Absolutely." She heard right. They'll be gathering in the hall downstairs like they do every night while the team dresses and warms up. It's the ideal time to chat someone up. Maybe I can even introduce her to Amy, a therapy assistant I worked with a couple times. "I'm headed that way too. I'll walk you."

She smiles up at me again, and it's like the sun made its way inside Ardent Park to shine on me.

"New girl!" We both turn at the shout coming from the concession stand to see her asshole boss glaring at her. The guy is maybe five-eight with a receding hairline and a bony frame, likely one of those guys who gets off on treating other people like shit because he's not getting laid. "Get your ass back here! We need more hot dogs for when the rush comes!"

I open my mouth to give him a piece of my mind, but Lynn beats me to it. "I'm on break, Ennis. I'll be back in a few."

"No breaks! Hot dogs take priority!"

Lynn mutters something under her breath, and I can feel the adrenaline start coursing through my veins at his tone. This guy is out of his mind. It's like he's on a hot dog power trip.

And when he opens his mouth to bellow, "Now!" I lose my cool.

Before I know what I'm doing, I stalk over to the counter and lean in, towering over this asshole. "Hey. Pipe down!" When he rolls his eyes at me, I put a finger in his face and drop my voice. "First of all, she has a name. It's Lynn. Not *new girl*. *Lynn*. Second, she already told you she's on break, so why don't you get off your ass and roll some hot dogs yourself until she gets back? Third, stop treating your employees like shit. You got that?"

His expression doesn't change, despite the fact that I'm in his face and could easily reduce him to nothing but a blood-stain on the concrete floor. Not that I would, but he doesn't know that. "And what are you going to do about it?" he asks with a greasy sneer. "Some of us are here to work. Stop hitting on my employee, go buy another Miller Lite, and watch the game, you loser."

My nostrils flare at that, and I briefly reconsider the importance of remaining employed and staying out of prison. But this guy isn't worth it. Still, I'm not about to let him continue treating Lynn this way. That's not up for debate.

"Uh, Ennis," a young blond guy says from beside him.

"Not now, Remy," Anus—that moniker is beyond fitting—bites back.

I take a breath to tell this asshole where to go again, but the blond kid interrupts, saying, "Ennis, that's Joey Martel. Shortstop for the Arrows," in a stage whisper.

Ennis's eyes widen for a split second, and I almost laugh before he schools his expression and pastes the sneer back on. But he's not looking at me anymore. His eyes are trained over my shoulder. "Trying to go over my head to tattle, new girl? Stupid move. My uncle is the Director of Operations for Ardent Park. Looks like you're barking up the wrong tree, girlie."

When I turn again to reassure Lynn that I've got this, the only thing I see is her back as she darts down the concourse and away from all of us.

I take off after her, yelling over my shoulder at the douchebag, "We're not done here!"

"Lynn!" I easily gain on her as she takes the stairs up to the mezzanine. "Wait!"

"Just leave me alone!" she calls behind her.

I draw even with her, but she keeps running, taking the stairs like she regularly trains with our team. "No! I can fix it!"

"You've done enough already," she spits as she pivots on the landing to reach the next set of stairs. When I grab her arm, she skids to a stop, whirling on me. "I told you I can take care of myself, Joey!"

"He was treating you like shit. I was just trying to help."

A few fans in Arrows gear stare as they pass by, but I'm beyond caring.

"No, you were trying to take *over*. I never asked you to do that, and now I'm probably going to lose my job!" She rips her arm from my grip, and I let her go. Shit.

"I'm sure I can fix it." I don't make a habit of using my status to pull strings, but I won't hesitate in this case. Hell, all it would take is a word from Gunner to Elizabeth's bestie, Skye, and Lynn could have any job in the stadium she wanted. Within reason, that is. Skye's boyfriend owns the entire Arrows franchise, and word on the street is that Bronte Hughes will do absolutely anything for his woman.

"Don't do anything. Please," Lynn begs, and my jaw locks at the hurt look on her face. I did that to her. Again! "Just leave it alone. Just leave *me* alone."

I'm fucking everything up. Dammit!

"Lynn," I plead. "I couldn't just stand there and listen to him talk to you that way." She's got to understand.

She closes her eyes and exhales, and when she opens them again, I can see her slipping through my fingers. Her calm, matter-of-fact tone seals it. "I don't need you punching anyone in the face or stringing anyone up by their nuts because you're offended on my behalf. That's not your right. It's mine, and I was handling Ennis just fine on my own until you stuck your nose into it."

"I'm sorry, okay?" What else can I say? My intentions were good, weren't they? She's got to see that.

But her head is still shaking. "This isn't going to work."

Panic seizes hold of my chest, even though I knew this was coming. "How can you say that?"

She exhales again with a sad smile. "Because it's not supposed to be an uphill battle, and I feel like we've been fighting longer than we've even known each other. Just…let it go. It's not meant to be."

"But…" I step closer, but she backs up out of my reach.

"Goodbye, Joey. Please don't text me, and please don't track me down again."

"I…"

She clasps her hands in front of her chest as her brow furrows. "Promise me."

She looks so earnest and distraught—and still so beautiful. This is *my* fault. And since nothing I do seems to be right, I figure the least I can do at this point is precisely what she asks.

I take a deep breath and let it out. "I promise."

Lynn hurries up the rest of the staircase and disappears around the corner before I can say another word.

PART TWO

ONE YEAR LATER

LYNN

"They showed up again?" Miller licks the melted marshmallow off his finger and goes in for another bite of his s'more.

"Yup," I reply, turning my stick to get just the right shade of brown on all sides of my mallow as I hold it over the campfire.

"Why isn't Lynn's burned like ours?" Bear asks from his seat on a stump next to Miller.

"Because Lynn is patient," his sister, Maisy, explains while she shakes her head at my brother. "And Miller is… not." Understatement of the century.

Completely unbothered, Miller smiles wide, mouth full of gooey chocolate and sugar, making Bear laugh. What can I say? The kid is ten; he's easy to impress.

"Here, Bear, you can have this one." I hand over my stick with its perfectly toasted marshmallow on the end as I watch Bear's eyes widen in the firelight. It's a small sacrifice to make for being invited on this Bigfoot-hunting trip.

And by that, I mean the mandatory camping down the way from our house that Bear insists on every time he visits. I'm convinced the Bigfoot hunting is just an excuse to eat s'mores and stay up past his bedtime. Still, I've missed these goobers while I've been away at school this past year. Not much changes around here, but it's good to be home.

Miller swallows and gets back to the original topic. "Why can't these people take no for an answer?" He's referring to the various developers who knock on Mama's door every so often, trying to get her to sell her property. The house itself is nothing to write home about, but the land is part of a big three-lot collection up in the mountains to the east of Asheville. Our lot backs up to the state land that holds the Blue Ridge Parkway.

"I don't get it," Maisy says. "There's no view from the properties. Isn't that what developers want?"

She's right. The only thing to see from Mama's house is trees, and the drive can be treacherous when it snows or storms. "These people have bucket loads of money to throw around, so they'll buy anything," I speculate.

"Well, I hope you told them we're never selling," Miller says, holding a graham cracker for Bear while he constructs his new s'more.

"Do I look like a moron to you?" I frown at my brother. Of course I told the woman to get lost when she came driving up in her fancy-ass Lexus and knocking on our door. Mama would never sell her and Dad's house, and neither would our neighbors Wes and Adrina to the right or old Winston to the left. Everybody is here to stay. Let the developers buy someone else's land to build a gazillion-dollar house on.

"Don't ask if you don't want an honest answer," Miller

replies with a smirk, earning himself a raw marshmallow to the head.

"Food fight!" Bear yells, dropping the perfectly toasted marshmallow onto Miller's lap and diving for the chocolate bars. "Imma smoke y'all's butts!" He beans Maisy in the boob with an open chocolate bar.

She looks down at the fresh brown stripe on her white T-shirt and chases after Bear as he runs for cover behind a tent. "Oh, it's on, little brother!"

"I see nothing has changed since last summer," I say, grinning at Miller.

"Nah. Maisy misses Bear when he's at his dad's, but we're all doing good." He wipes his sticky hands on his jeans and rests his elbows on his knees. Maisy used to spend a lot of time protecting her brother from their mom's neglect until Bear's dad came to the rescue last year. "Mama's happy you're home. Adrina's driving her crazy with wedding plans. You might prevent a homicide while you're here."

This is unsurprising news. Our brother Denny is marrying Adrina and Wes's daughter, Rosie, later this summer, and you'd think they're the first two people in the history of the world ever to get married with the way Adrina is flipping out over every detail.

"They should seriously just elope," I offer, spearing a new marshmallow with Maisy's abandoned stick.

Rosie's dad, Wes, would probably second that idea. He was out of work for a good while after being laid off a couple years ago. And, while he's working now, I have to imagine their savings took quite the hit. Hell, Rosie was even sending them money from her side hustle while she was in college. No way does he want to drop money they don't have on a big wedding.

"It would end up being the shortest marriage on record if they did, considering that Adrina would kill both of them the minute they stepped off the plane."

I snort at that. Adrina is a true Italian mom, and she takes her job very seriously, meaning that she requires every one of us to take *her* seriously. And if Adrina wants white doves and ruffled tuxedo shirts, that's what she's getting. Luckily, Rosie is used to her mom, so she's not letting herself get bent out of shape about it. At the end of the day, she just wants to marry my brother and doesn't care all that much about the manner in which that comes about.

Maisy steps back into the firelight and collapses onto her camp chair. "That little fart varmint just outwitted me. I threw two bars of chocolate at him, and now he's hiding somewhere, chowing down."

"Smart kid," I say, turning my stick. "I hope he can sleep after all that sugar because he's my tentmate, and I need to hit the hay soon. I've got to be down at the ballpark early."

"Is it an early game tomorrow?" Maisy asks, tucking her dark hair behind her ear.

"Lynn's graduated from concession work, didn't you hear?" Miller grins over at me. I love that big dummy.

When Maisy turns back to me, I explain, "I get to shadow the athletics and rehab team this summer. It doesn't pay, but I saved up during the school year with my side job—and Cash and Cart are giving me some hours this summer." I make the sign of the cross, and Maisy laughs. She's been witness to a few of my brothers' shenanigans, so she knows the risk I'm taking working for them. "It's my first day, so I don't want to be wiped out before it starts."

I'm ridiculously excited, so the truth is, I probably won't sleep a wink.

Working for Ennis last summer was unbearable, but it was worth it—even if he had me cleaning grease traps and fryer tanks to make up for what he called my "insubordination." Honestly, if his big-wig uncle thinks so highly of him, why does he have his nephew overseeing a handful of hot dog stands in ninety-degree heat all summer?

But my fortitude paid off, and I did what I set out to do by finagling conversations with therapy team members and some other athletics staff throughout the summer. They even gave me a tour of the facilities and some advice on applying for internships and such.

And while I'm still not eligible for a real clinical internship until I enter the PhD phase of my program, I somehow managed to score this shadowing opportunity this summer. I won't get to do anything hands-on, but I can still learn a ton just from watching. My department head was thrilled for me, and she's waiting for all my feedback once I get back to school in the fall. I'm determined to be a complete sponge. Just call me Bob.

"Congrats. That sounds awesome," Maisy says.

"Thanks. I hope I get to see an Achilles rupture or an ACL tear this summer." Not that I wish any of the players ill or anything, but I need to see some gore, people.

"That's... disgusting."

I grin at her with a raise of my eyebrows. "I know, right?" My marshmallow masterpiece is finished, so I pull it from the stick and pop the entire thing into my mouth. Yum.

"Hey, Bear! I'm going to bed!" I shout into the darkness as I stand and head to the tents. "If you want to hear stories about college girls, you'd better come with!" That kid may be ten, but he sees himself as quite the Casanova and collects girlfriends like his friends probably collect Pokémon cards.

Rosie was the love of his life last summer, so it'll be interesting to see how he takes the whole wedding thing.

As I knew he would, Bear appears at the entrance to our tent a nanosecond later, his face smeared with chocolate and his expression eager. "Are any of them volleyball players? I have a new appreciation for volleyball after seeing it on TV."

I can hear Miller choke out a laugh.

"Every single one," I lie, dropping a hand to Bear's scrawny shoulder and guiding him into our tent.

CHAPTER
TWELVE

OF ALL THE CLINIC ROOMS IN ALL
THE WORLD

JOEY

This day is not going to plan at all.

"Here, take my shoulder," Diego Sanchez, our third-base coach, says as I favor one side on our walk through the tunnel to see the team doctor.

I brush him off and try not to wince each time I put pressure on my left foot. "I told you, I'm fine."

"Your opinion isn't the one I care about right now. We'll see what Doc has to say." His tone reminds me of my dad's when I used to forget to take out the trash as a teenager.

Taking the lessons I learned back then, I keep my mouth shut and slowly shuffle the rest of the way to a treatment room. Thank God we're only in warm-ups and the game hasn't started, because there's no way I'm missing a game.

"So, what do we have here?" Doc asks as soon as we clear the doorway.

"It's nothing," I reply. "Jackson's cleat caught me in the leg, and I went down a little wrong on my left foot. I can walk it off, but Coach is feeling maternal today."

Doc points to a padded table, and Sanchez hovers over me until I hoist myself up on it. He even insists on pulling off my cleat and sock for me, the mother hen.

I get poked and prodded for a couple minutes before Doc declares, "We'll get some ice on it and check your mobility and swelling in twenty." He walks to the door on the other side of the room and opens it. "Can we get some ice for a contusion?"

"Coach, I got it from here," I tell Sanchez, hoping he takes the hint and returns to the field.

He nods. "I'll send somebody back down to check on you in a few. Gotta go talk to Coach Gibbs about the lineup."

A surge of panic has my back straightening at the mention of our head coach. "Don't let him scratch me, man! I promise I'm fine."

"I got you," Sanchez reassures before exiting, but it does little to make me feel better.

I use my nervous energy to replay last night's game in my head. My control was a little off at the plate in the ninth, and I need to make sure my focus is on point all night tonight. Rice, the Rovers's star pitcher, has a nasty inside sinker, and if I swing at it again tonight, I'm screwed. We might have won last night, but it was no thanks to my batting in the last couple innings.

"Hello there," Amy, the PT assistant, says as she sweeps through the open door that leads to the adjoining therapy room. She's wearing the standard black scrubs the entire athletics and rehab staff wears, her tortoiseshell glasses perched on her nose.

"Hey, Amy." We've met a few times, and I've always found her efficient, if not overly friendly.

She props my foot up with a couple pillows to elevate it as she takes a look. "I've got ice on the way."

"Can you do me a favor and tell Doc I'm fine? Sanchez is making a big deal out of nothing."

Her warning glare has me giving her my palms and lying back down. "I'll shut up now."

"Smart man." She grins as she pokes the top of my bare foot. It barely hurts.

"Here you go, Amy." We both turn at the new voice, and I worry for a second that I've sustained a brain injury instead of a turned foot.

"Lynn?"

I can't believe the girl who's taken up rent-free residence in my mind for the last year is standing in front of me. In the flesh and looking so beautiful, it hurts. Her hair is a little shorter than last summer, but everything else about her is the same, from her tan skin and freckles to her long legs and white low-top Chucks.

Lynn's eyes flash from Amy to me, widening almost comically at the sight of me reclining on the treatment table.

"How do you two know each other?" Amy asks casually as she retrieves the ice pack from Lynn's hands and focuses her attention on arranging it over a towel around my foot.

"Um," Lynn recovers first. "I worked at the stadium last summer, and we ran into each other a couple times."

Apparently satisfied with her answer—or, more likely, not caring all that much—Amy gives the ice pack one more tuck before stepping back. "Just sit tight for twenty, and I'll be back to unwrap you."

With her usual efficiency, she quickly retreats through the doorway, calling out, "Come on, Lynn, I'll show you the paraffin bath."

Lynn opens her mouth, as if to report something urgent, but shuts it again without another word, following Amy through the door and leaving me to wonder if I dreamed the entire thing.

When Amy returns twenty minutes later, Lynn is nowhere to be seen. Doc gives my foot a once-over and declares me good to go, instructing me to keep an eye on it and let him know if the pain worsens.

I need to clear my mind and maintain one hundred percent focus on the game, not a pretty girl whose picture hangs in my mind under a plaque reading "The One That Got Away." This is about baseball. My job. So I do what I have to and brush all thoughts of Lynn aside as I jog up the tunnel and hit the dugout.

THE HOT WATER rains down on my tired body, and I hang my head to keep it from my eyes as I prop a hand on the tiled shower wall in front of me for support. Damn, I am wiped. My foot is throbbing a little, but if I ice it at home tonight, I should be good to go tomorrow. We pulled out another win over the Rovers, and we'll be off to their neck of the woods tomorrow for the back end of the series. I managed to keep my head on my shoulders and not let Rice tempt me into swinging at his inside sinker, so I'm pleased.

"You coming out tonight?" Paulie asks from the shower next to mine. "Some cleat chasers are taking Riley and Finch dancing, if you can believe that." He laughs.

"Nah, I'm beat."

I'm also distracted now that the game is over and thoughts of Lynn have begun rushing back in like high tide.

Paulie shuts his water off and throws a towel around his neck. "Okay, man. See you in the a.m."

I nod my chin without turning. The pounding water feels way too good on my back to move, and the mental image of Lynn's wide eyes at seeing me earlier is too good to lose.

To be fair, I shouldn't have been all that surprised to run into Lynn in the athletics rooms, but I was preoccupied with my foot and my worry about being scratched from the starting lineup.

I kept my promise last summer not to go looking for Lynn again, but that doesn't mean I wasn't still cut up about the way we left things. I ended up talking to Gunner and asked him to pull a couple strings with Skye to get Lynn an invite for a walk-through of the treatment and training facilities. It was the least I could do after fucking things up with Anus, the hot dog heir. And, okay, maybe I followed up to ensure it happened and Lynn didn't lose her concession job too. But that was as far as I was willing to go. She clearly didn't want my interference in any aspect of her life, so I took it seriously.

In my book, getting her a meeting and making sure I didn't get her fired wasn't really interfering.

It wasn't my fault that when I went out for drinks with Gunner, Elizabeth, and Skye during spring training this year, Skye asked about my mystery girl and if she could do anything else to help me mend fences. From the little I know about Skye, it's clear she enjoys a good dose of drama when she can get it. I mean, I've never seen the woman in anything but stilettos and cleavage-baring dresses, so low-key is not a word in her vocabulary.

But I don't even know Lynn's last name, so it's not like I passed her resume to Skye or anything. I just said it could be cool if the rehab staff kept her in mind if they had anything going on she could participate in. With Lynn doggedly withstanding a summer under her horrible boss just for the chance to connect with rehab, I assume she took advantage of her conversations and tour to drop her contact info with them.

So, yeah, I knew Skye would probably whisper in some ears. Nobody at the table that night missed the fact that it had been seven months, and I was still into this girl who'd dumped me.

Either Skye followed through or Lynn hustled like a champ to get herself a gig following Amy around as she imparts her wisdom. Good for her.

I tilt my head back, letting the water pelt me in the face as my lips tip up. Lynn made me promise not to track her down, but it wasn't me seeking her out today. She was stepping on my home turf this time, and believe me, I'm more than happy to roll out the welcome mat next time she has the urge to stop by.

CHAPTER
THIRTEEN

SO NOT CONVENIENT

LYNN

Seriously? My first day?

I knew there was a chance I'd run into Joey Martel at some point this summer, but God has a seriously fucked-up sense of humor to plant his hot ass on a treatment table on my first day.

I wasn't ready to see him. I hadn't had a chance to work up an ultra-smooth greeting that hit the ideal mark between aloof and look-how-happy-I-am.

Thank God he only required an ice pack for a few minutes before being discharged to the field to do whatever he does up there. I know from Wikipedia that a shortstop fields a lot of hit balls and throws a lot of players out, so I'm sure that's what he was doing—with great skill and agility if Mother Nature has followed through on her job where he's concerned.

"You can collect all the linens and drop them in the hamper," Amy suggests.

Of course, I take it as more of an order because I'm not

stupid. I'm here at the whim of the staff, so I plan to make myself so indispensable that they'll ask me back next year. Turns out shadowing is code for gofer-slash-maid, but I don't mind. Amy showed me pictures of a gnarly contusion one of the players had last week, so I consider that payment enough for the day.

It's a skeleton crew here during the evening game, with only a team doctor and a PT assistant, but the head physical therapist, Nora, was here earlier today, and we had a chance to chat. I know I'm going to learn a ton this summer, but not if I let myself get distracted by a certain ballplayer. I truly hope he keeps his distance because I don't need anyone thinking I'm using my access to flirt with players. The Arrows' star shortstop holds way more value to the team than some chick who's following the PT staff around like a puppy with an unhealthy interest in gruesome sports injuries.

While things are quiet during the game, we get a couple players coming in for stretches and ice afterward. I keep busy doing whatever small task Amy wants until it's time to pack it in for the night and head home. It's almost midnight by the time I make my way to Priscilla in the parking lot. She's named after Priscilla Presley because that woman has been *through it* and is still truckin'!

As always, I grip my car key between my index and middle fingers as I walk, ready to stab any would-be kidnapper. But nobody bothers me, and I'm soon headed up the mountain toward Mama's house without incident.

It isn't until my tired butt is tucked into my childhood bed that I allow myself the tiniest bit of regret that Joey didn't try to find me after the game.

God, I hate it when I'm a cliché.

IT'S BEEN a week since I started my new position as what I now refer to as a "rehab puppy," and it couldn't be going any better. Amy even let me touch a relief pitcher's elbow the other day to feel the sac bulging out of it from his bursitis. It was awesome.

But the team is back and forth on the road all the time, and they'll be away for the next few games—what I've learned is called a series—so I'm working at Blue Bigfoot whenever they're gone. I, understandably, don't get to travel with the team, despite volunteering to ride inside Nora's suitcase.

"Table in the corner needs busing," Cash says as he clomps by me on the taproom floor.

It's a weekend night, which means it's busy. It's also loud because of both the big crowd and Maisy's band playing up by the patio. She plays piano like a wizard, and the couple who sing are so good I keep telling them they need to make a record. Grady, the guitarist and lead singer, said cover bands don't usually make records, but whatever. I'd buy it.

"On it," I tell my brother. Cleaning up after drunk people is almost as glamorous as wiping sweat from treatment tables, but it pays my phone bill and keeps my car gassed up, so I can't complain.

Kelsie, a waitress with amazing purple hair and a killer tattoo of a dinosaur dressed like the pope on her left arm, scoots up beside me where my bus tub rests against my hip. "Do *not* look, but one of the Arrows players is checking you out by the back wall."

My eyes immediately swing to the far side of the

taproom to find none other than Joey Martel watching me from under a nondescript blue baseball cap. Damn.

"I said don't look!" Kelsie practically screeches. "You're terrible at this, you know that?"

I glance at her before swiping up an empty pint glass from the table beside me. "We already know each other."

Her eyes widen before a smirk settles on her lips. "This just got interesting." When I roll my eyes, she only cackles and takes off to fill an order at the bar.

I knew this was a risk. After all, I've seen him here before. Did some part of my subconscious plan this? It's unlike me to take my brothers up on a job offer. In fact, last summer, I avoided this place like the plague. My ovaries start singing Ricky Skaggs's "I'll Take the Blame," and I steel myself as Joey rises from his chair and picks his way through the crowd toward me.

Well, shit.

He looks good. I mean, *really* good. His thigh muscles bulge under the denim of his jeans as he walks, and I'm pretty sure he's close to ripping the arms off his T-shirt with those guns. Dark hair peeks out from beneath his cap, his strong jaw carrying a new dusting of stubble that promises to offer some lucky girl's inner thighs quite the beard burn.

Come on! Exactly how strong does the universe expect this woman to be?

"Hey, Lynn." His familiar gritty rumble has my knees forgetting we disapprove.

"Hi, Joey." I shift my weight to my left hip so I can support the heavy bus tub.

He delivers one of his lopsided grins, and it's like those damn pterodactyls in my belly have taken memory lessons from my knees. They're dragging me right back under the stars at the side of a country road.

Even over the din in the bar, I can hear his deep rumble. "I swear I didn't know you'd be here tonight." He glances down at my tub, still grinning. "In fact, I had no idea you worked here."

Now that the cat's out of the bag, it's not like it's worth hiding anything. "My brothers own the place. I'm working for them part-time this summer."

His grin drops, and by his responding expression, I could knock him over with a pterodactyl feather (wait, do they even have feathers?). His eyes dart to the bar where Cash and Miller are waiting on customers. "Hang on." When his gaze darts back to me, every bit of white around his dark irises is visible. "Cash, Carter, and Miller are your *brothers*? The ones you told me about?"

Well, hell. I didn't see this coming. "You know them?" Exactly how often does he drink here?

"Yeah, I know them. I come here at least once a week in the offseason and maybe half that during the season."

I swear, this town is *way* too small.

I raise my voice to be heard over the music. "Well, that's…" I have no clue what word I'm looking for.

"Convenient." Joey chooses for me. I frown at him, but it only makes him laugh. "Or maybe not. Sorry."

It's obvious I need to get over myself because Joey and I are going to run into each other this summer, whether we mean to or not. And he's not a bad guy. Just not the kind of guy for me. And that's fine.

"It's good to see you, Joey. From what I hear, you guys are having a good season."

"Do I hear a hint of a developing interest in America's

favorite pastime?" I gotta hand it to him; he gives good sarcasm.

"Let's just say I'm not petitioning Congress to have the sport banned."

There's that lopsided smile again. "The team looks good. My foot isn't causing even a twinge, so I'm all set there. Now if I can just improve my batting stats, I might still have a job next year." My brows lift in alarm at his words, and he coughs out a laugh. "I'm joking. Well, kind of. Players get traded all the time, but I'm fine." He throws a thumb over his shoulder toward his table. "Besides, our left fielder, Gunner Nix, said he'd stage a sit-in if they ever try and trade me. Not sure what that would look like, but it could be amusing."

My gaze flashes that way and I see a handsome bearded guy with short brown hair and an eye not so surreptitiously trained our way. Mother magnolia.

"It's good to have backup."

As if hearing my comment and taking it as an invitation, Cash appears at my side, both hands perched on his hips. "Table in the corner needs busing, Lynnie," he repeats. His voice is neutral, but his eyes stay narrowed on Joey to such tiny slits it's a wonder he didn't trip over a table on his way over here.

Sigh. Here we frickin' go again.

JOEY

"I said I'm on it," Lynn replies to Cash, who's looking at me like he can't decide which of my appendages to rip off first. I can't believe the Brooks brothers are the same brothers Lynn was going on about last summer.

Cash inches a step closer to me.

Or maybe I can.

This entire week has been full of surprises, so I'm half expecting to go home tonight to find an orphan I never knew I fathered waiting at my doorstep. It might throw me for less of a loop than my two run-ins with Lynn and this news about her brothers.

At least now I know her last name.

"Hey, Cash." I extend a hand to her brother, knowing he won't be able to refuse it, no matter how bent out of shape he is. I could tell him he has nothing to worry about where Lynn is concerned, but that would be a lie since I've spent the last year having the dirtiest thoughts imaginable about his little sister—and I can't see that stopping anytime soon.

She may not be interested in me, but my dick hasn't gotten the memo, even after all this time.

Cash accepts my hand with a grunt. "Martel." It takes all I've got not to laugh when he squeezes my hand like he's hoping juice might come out of it.

"Lynn and I were just chatting about things down at the ballpark," I say, letting him interpret that how he wants.

"Joey had a foot injury the other day, so we saw him in rehab," Lynn explains before sighing and hefting her black plastic tub into both hands. "I'm off to bus some tables." Her smile is fake as hell, but Cash doesn't seem to notice. He watches her snake between customers and tables before returning his eyes to me.

"Don't even fuckin' think about it," is all he says before turning on his booted heel and stalking back to the bar.

I tip my head back on a sharp laugh because that shit was hilarious.

"What was that all about?" Gunner asks when I park my ass back in my seat.

"Get this. Lynn's last name is Brooks. As in Blue Bigfoot Brooks. Cash and the guys are her older brothers."

"Come again." He cups a hand behind his ear in an exaggerated gesture.

"You heard me."

Gunner takes a sip of his beer and squints at the bar before finding Lynn in the crowd and watching her for a few seconds. "I guess I can see it. I mean, she's way better looking, of course. And she's got a better rack."

When I frown at him, he smacks the table and laughs, so my only choice is to respond, "Elizabeth's isn't too shabby either," which turns his smile into a scowl, precisely as I intended.

It's just the two of us tonight. We stopped by for one beer and are making it an early night since we've got a flight to Philly in the morning. Don't get me wrong, I like hanging out with all the guys, but Gunner and I are tight in a way I'm not with anybody else on the team.

"So that explains why she's here," Gunner says as we both watch her make her way behind the bar with her full bus tub. She's wearing a pair of cut-off jeans that make my eyes cross. "I thought for a second that maybe the tables had turned and she was stalking *you*."

"I never stalked her." I lower my voice and lean into my elbows on the table. "Jesus, man, you can't say things like that these days. You trying to get me fired?"

He mimics a zipper over his lips, and we both sip our beers while the band plays a Journey cover.

"At least she doesn't seem to hate me anymore," I finally say.

His zipper is about as secure as most invisible things because he immediately replies, "I never understood what the big deal was anyway, but if Elizabeth says it was, then I've learned not to argue."

Yeah, I got a lecture last summer about boundaries that I'm unlikely to forget anytime soon. That and an unsolicited subscription to *Ms.* magazine's daily newsletter. Elizabeth swore she didn't know that giving them my email would result in the onslaught of online ads featuring feminine hygiene products and IUDs that blanketed my screen every time I glanced at my phone the following six months. Hell, I've just now stopped getting promotions featuring tips on how to treat my PMS symptoms homeopathically.

I'm optimistic I've learned my lesson, but the proof's in the pudding, and I haven't exactly put myself out there recently to test the waters. *I've been busy, okay?* Never mind, I had four months of offseason to do whatever I pleased. Turns out I was pleased to binge-watch *Bojack Horseman* on Netflix and develop a Twizzlers addiction. There are worse things.

"Just tread carefully, my man," Gunner advises, raising his glass to toast mine. And since he's one of the only guys I know in a happy relationship, I decide the smartest thing I can do is listen.

OW.

Fuck.

OW!

FUCK!

"Martel!" somebody shouts, but it sounds like an echo. I have no idea where I am. All I know is my left arm feels like it's been wired for electricity, and my head is pounding.

"He's back!" another voice yells, and this time I try blinking to see who it is. My eyelids immediately slam shut again at the bright light.

"Joey, can you hear me?" Yet another voice.

I groan and try grasping my arm with my right hand to ease the tingling, but I can't reach it. I try opening my eyes again, and the light is less intense now, so I blink a few more times. All I see are a bunch of heads thrown into silhouette by the stadium lights above.

"My arm," I croak, reaching for it again as I realize I'm on my back on the field with my head immobilized by a stiff collar.

A hand stops me, and I recognize Sanchez's voice over

the half-hushed buzz of the crowd. "You and Niederman collided real good. Knocked you out and banged your arm up."

"Okay, everyone, back up!" Three pairs of hands lift me into the air, and I realize I'm on a board. The whir of an electric engine sounds before a cart propels me toward an opening to the tunnel, and I'm whisked away to the buzz of swelling cheers from a stadium full of fans.

But I don't see what there can possibly be to cheer about. I'm a professional baseball player who just fucked up his arm and head—and maybe my whole future.

The next thirty minutes are a blur of questions, flashing lights in my eyes, and pain. I finally get a few moments of blessed silence as the emergency medical team confers with Doc on the other side of the room. And now that the pain meds are starting to kick in, I can draw in my first full breath since I opened my eyes on the field.

Hard as I try, I can't remember it happening. The last thing I can recall is catching the line drive off Moreno's bat and turning to throw the ball to Paulie at second. That's it. I don't even remember seeing Paulie catch the ball or Niederman rounding second. Best I can figure, Paulie flubbed the catch, and Niederman hauled ass to third— plowing into me in the process.

I lift the ice pack from my arm to get a peek. There's already bruising around my elbow, and—*fuck*—my wrist is swollen to the size of a baseball.

Doc and the EMS crew return to the stretcher, where I'm resting. "Okay," Doc begins, "We're sending you to the hospital. The concussion is a bit worrying. I'll meet you there, and we'll get an MRI of that arm and an ortho consult. See where we go from there."

"Doc," I grunt.

He doesn't make me wait. "My best guess is a ligament tear—it doesn't feel broken. We'll know for sure after the pictures."

I let out a breath. Okay, not as bad as it could be, I suppose. Benny Duvall from the Black Dogs had a partial ligament tear in his wrist last season, and he was out for four weeks. Still, that's a hell of a long time in baseball days. At least it's my left, not my throwing arm. However, a broken nose from Neiderman would have been preferable since I still need my wrist for catching and batting.

"Don't worry, son." Shit. Should I be extra concerned he's gone all paternal on me? *No, don't read into it, Martel.* Deep breaths. "We'll have you back on the field as soon as possible."

His mouth to God's ear, as my dad would say. Because without baseball, I have no idea who I am.

LYNN

"They're bringing up somebody from the farm team, I'd imagine," my brother Denny comments to no one in particular, as far as I can tell. I zoned out as soon as they started talking about RBIs and ERAs. I've gleaned enough from my hours at Ardent Park to know they're talking about baseball, so that's progress, but I'd still rather read my book than talk baseball over breakfast.

"Anybody want more eggs?" Mama asks from the stove.

"You sit, Mama. I got this." We all freeze and lift our eyes at Cash's words.

Denny is the first to break. "Since when do you cook?"

"Since the vet suggested Betty might benefit from a homemade diet," Hollis responds with a barely concealed smile from her seat next to me at the kitchen table. "That big baby gets a gourmet meal twice a day."

"She's lacking opposable thumbs. What am I gonna do, let her starve?" Cash challenges with an incredulous expression as he takes the skillet from Mama's hand and surveys the gathered ingredients on the counter.

I grin at Hollis, and she rolls her lips between her teeth to keep from laughing. Those two need to have a baby or something so Cash can put all his mothering to better use. Actually, that's a brilliant idea! He wouldn't have time to interfere in my business anymore if he had a screaming baby. Of course, that would still leave the rest of these nosy Nancies. Now that I think about it, I'm not sure if it's safe for any of them to procreate. I'll have to reconsider things later.

It's a full house this morning, which is unusual these days. Everyone must have been starving because they all descended on Mama's house after her early morning text offering French toast and made-to-order eggs for anyone who showed up. Some of the family has spilled into the den to eat, and Bear is sharing his breakfast with Mango out on the back porch.

"Did you register for cookware, Rosina?!" Adrina rushes in from the den, a degree of urgency in her voice suggesting my brother and his bride will be solely responsible for nourishing a small, developing nation from their apartment kitchen after the wedding.

"Yes, Mamá. I registered for that set at Costco, remember?"

"I didn't know we could register at Costco." Denny's eyes light up. "Can we sign up for one of those giant seventy-pound parmesan cheese wheels they had last time we were there?"

"We're not registering for cheese, Denver Brooks." Rosie eyes my brother.

He looks around for backup as if his fiancée is the crazy one.

Rosie's brother, Luca—who's basically family like the rest of the Carmichaels—throws Denny a chin lift from the doorway. "I got you, man."

"Two scrambled eggs, just how you like them." Cash presents Mama with a skillet of half-cooked eggs, and she smiles up at him like he just single-handedly built the Taj Mahal. I can't help but roll my eyes. Looks like I might need that surgery sooner rather than later.

"Thank you, sweetheart, but I think *you* should eat them. You look hungry." Mama is a genius.

Cash shrugs and grabs a fork, digging into the awful eggs straight from the pan. Hollis mumbles something about good taste under her breath, and I laugh out loud.

"So, how long is he out? Do we know?" Miller asks, but I've lost track of the six conversations going on around me, so I drop my nose back into my book. It's a vampire rom-com that offers everything I'm looking for in a summer read: a funny hero, plenty of steam, and absolutely nothing serious. Vampire rom-coms I can take. A vampire movie, on the other hand? No thanks. It's not the gore that bothers me; it's the jump scares. They get me every damn time, making me literally pee my pants. Okay, so it only happened once, but it was very memorable.

"No idea, but a sprained wrist doesn't sound like it would take too long to bounce back from," Luca replies.

"Have you heard anything, Lynnie?" Cash asks.

I look up from my book and blink at him. "Have I heard anything about what?"

Cash holds his egg-laden fork in front of his mouth. "Joey Martel. His wrist injury."

My chair screeches on the wood floor. "*What wrist injury?*" Shit. I said that really loud, didn't I? I take pains to force a more casual curiosity into my voice. "What are you talking about?" Is my face red? Is my blood pressure rising?

"We've been talking about his wrist for the last ten minutes." Miller waves a hand in front of my face, and I bat it away.

"That's right—you're working with the rehab staff at the ballpark," Maisy comments from her spot leaning against the counter by the fridge. "Will you get to treat him or anything? That would be so cool."

"No," I answer distractedly. "When did this happen?"

"Away game a couple nights ago. Saw it on *SportsCenter* last night. The dude got knocked out cold on the field," Luca says before shoving half a slice of syrup-soaked French toast into his mouth.

Joey got knocked out? And he's out with a wrist injury? Oh god. He's probably so bummed right now.

"I guess I'll find out more about it later today," I say, trying to remain calm as I grip my coffee mug with both hands and force myself to breathe normally. The team is back in town, so I'm back to work today. And Joey is injured.

"Aha!" Denny reaches over the table, turning his phone screen to Rosie. "You *can* register for a giant cheese wheel. Excellent!"

"Is anyone going to help me here?" Rosie throws her arms out.

"Have you thought about eloping?" Maisy asks, sending Adrina into a fit of unintelligible Italian that lasts a good five minutes and has Rosie arguing back in English. Everyone else carries on drinking their coffee and cleaning their plates like this is just another Wednesday morning.

French toast and weddings are the last things on my mind, though.

I MAKE it a whole two hours before texting Joey. To be fair, I need to be at work in an hour, so I was running out of time to pretend I have self-control.

> ME:
>
> Hey.

I try not to read into the fact that his response is immediate.

> JOEY:
>
> Hey.

> ME:
>
> You okay?

That was stupid. Of course he's not okay. As usual, he's kind and doesn't call me out.

> JOEY:
>
> I've been better.

I close my bedroom door and settle on my stomach on the bed while I type my response.

> ME:
>
> I figured. What did the doctors say?

> JOEY:
>
> Some bruising, a partially torn ligament, and a concussion. Said I was lucky.

> ME:
>
> I'm sorry. Does it hurt?

JOEY:

Not if I take my pain meds. But I'm not a huge fan of the talking dead people who show up when I take it, so I might stop.

Oh my god! I jerk up to sit and grip my phone with panicked fingers.

ME:

Joey! That's not good. Have you talked to your doctor? Don't stop taking the meds, whatever you do, but they need to adjust them for you right away!

Should I call the team doctor? Amy? Crap. I don't have anyone's number!

JOEY:

Relax. I was joking. I'm on ibuprofen.

My jaw drops, and I fall backward with relief, my head hitting the mattress.

ME:

Anus.

JOEY:

I prefer asshole, if you don't mind.

I send him a devil emoji. But, hey, if he's joking around, that's a good sign, so I can cut him some slack.

ME:

Did they say if you need surgery or not?

Would it be tacky of me to ask him to text me the X-rays? Yeah, probably.

JOEY:

Looks like I'll dodge that bullet with it only
being a partial tear.

ME:

That's good then. Do they have an
estimated recovery time?

JOEY:

Best estimate is four to six weeks before I
can get off the IL.

I give myself a little pat on the back for knowing he
means the injured list. Learned that one my first day.

ME:

Wow! That's great!

JOEY:

Is it?

Yeah, I suppose it doesn't feel too great to him right now.

ME:

It could be so much worse. The time will
fly by.

I don't tell him Amy shared a story about a career-ending
injury she treated at her last job with another team.

JOEY:

Well, I'm guessing you'll get to see it
yourself tomorrow. They have me coming in
for the whole medical staff to poke at me.

Cool. Of course, I don't say that.

ME:

You can hack it. Can I do anything?

The ellipses come and go a few times, and I wonder if he's drafting a multi-page list of requests. But when the message finally pops up, all it says is:

JOEY:

Not really. Unless you want to send me a playlist.

Ooh, my favorite.

ME:

On it!

I scroll through my favorites on Spotify with a goofy smile on my face as I start making a playlist of upbeat songs that might make a dent in a miserable baseball player's mood. I throw in a little Crash Karma because he said he likes Canadian alt rock, and of course I add some Green Day because, *duh*. I pepper in a little of this and a little of that, only hesitating when my thumb hovers over the Counting Crows. I opt not to include any of their tracks, and once I'm satisfied, I copy the link and text it to Joey.

His responding text appears only a minute later.

JOEY:

Bizarre Love Triangle? Bold choice.

ME:

I had to pull out the big guns.

JOEY:

Thanks, Lynn.

There's a flutter in the vicinity of my heart, and I sigh out loud as I roll back onto my stomach on the duvet and work my thumbs over the phone screen.

ME:

Get some rest. It's the best medicine—until the PT team has you sweating your ass off, that is.

JOEY:

Can't wait.

And as messed up as it sounds, neither can I.

JOEY

"You're not coming to take care of me." I swipe the fingers of my good hand through my hair while I try getting through to Liv. My cousin is stubborn as hell.

She tuts through my earbuds. "Yes, I am. It's what I do."

I still with my head inside my refrigerator, where I'm looking for something to reheat for lunch. It's easy to get spoiled with all the catered meals being a ballplayer. "You're a veterinarian," I remind Liv.

"Yeah, so? Regular doctors only know how one species functions. Vets know dozens. That makes us better prepared."

I grab a string cheese and close the door. "Do you find that people often grow tails?"

"Haven't you ever seen *The Shaggy Dog*? *The Emperor's New Groove*? Kuzco was stuck in a llama's body for like a week!"

"Are we really having this argument?" I ask as I realize I can't open the cheese with one hand. I bring it to my mouth and tear the plastic loose with my teeth. They've got my wrist in some contraption for now, and I'm only allowed to take it off to ice and shower while I'm on a seventy-two-hour resting protocol.

"No. I'm coming Friday. Conversation closed."

"Liv."

"Joey." I can practically hear her tapping an impatient foot on her kitchen tile.

"I'm not going to talk you out of this, am I?"

"See, you're not as dumb as you look." Her voice is too cheerful.

All I can do is chuckle and take a bite of my cheese. Yuck. It's just not the same when you can't peel it. Maybe I'll stop in the clubhouse and eat there. "Please tell me you're at least bringing Brett so I have someone who understands my pain." I swallow and ditch the rest of the cheese on the counter, making my way to my living room instead.

"You're in luck. But he can only stay the weekend."

"Wait! You're staying longer? It's just a sprained wrist!" Not that I don't love Liv, but she's going to hover. I just know it.

"I've got the entire next week off. You're welcome."

"I think I hear my doorbell," I lie.

"Liar." She calls me out. "But I'll let you go anyway. Oh! Do I need to bring a bed for Tambo, or can he crash on your couch?"

My eyes dart to my practically new leather sectional as I position myself by the windows of my high-rise condo. "You're bringing Bo?" At least slobber wipes off.

"I thought you said the concussion wasn't causing any brain issues."

"Right. Sorry." Liv and that dog are inseparable. To be

fair to my concussed brain, though, somebody dog-sat him back in Greensboro last time they came.

"He'll cheer you up," she reassures.

"Or tear another ligament," I tease.

"You love him."

I watch the cars on the street below and grin. "I do. And I kind of love you too. I guess."

"Aww. Maybe we'll get on the road early. You sound like you need a hug."

"Bye, Liv."

She cackles. "Bye, cuz."

I've got to get to the ballpark. I can worry about my meddling cousin later.

As soon as we hang up, I scroll to the playlist Lynn made for me last night and hit play. No Doubt's "Spiderwebs" starts up right where I left off earlier. After that comes "Steal My Sunshine" by Len, which plays as I dress for my trip to the ballpark. There's a definite nineties theme going on here, which shouldn't surprise me based on what I already know of Lynn's music taste. By the time I'm in my truck on the way there, I'm hitting play on the first song on the list again and feeling more optimistic than I've felt since Niederman made roadkill of me.

"Tell me the truth. You just missed my face, didn't you?" Nora, the team's head physical therapist, bustles into the room behind Doc in her scrubs and no-nonsense cropped hair. I've been sitting on the treatment table for a few minutes while everyone gathers to inspect me like a science experiment gone wrong. Nora treated me last season for a mild knee strain that had me out for a couple games, and we clicked immediately. Either that, or she just gets off on busting my balls.

"You got me. I planned it all along." I'm not about to let my anxiety show.

There's no sign of Amy or Lynn, not that I'm looking. Okay, fine, my eyes dart to that connecting door every time I sense motion. I'm only human.

Doc removes my splint, and Nora bends close to peer at my wrist, not hesitating to prod it with her experienced fingers. Ow.

"Okay, we can work with this."

Doc moves my wrist here and there, asking about pain and discomfort. None of it feels great, but I grit my teeth and try to ignore the pain. I just need this thing to heal so I can get back on the field. They've already brought a guy up from Triple A to take my place while I'm on the IL, and I don't want him getting too comfortable.

"Here's the deal, Joey," Nora says. "We'll work on your range of motion and keeping muscle strength as it heals. It's going to be slow and steady, so you'll need some patience." At the look on my face, she grins and continues. "First, we need to decrease that inflammation. As we proceed, the important thing will be to prevent compensating for pain and weakness by using surrounding muscle groups improperly. That'll lead to more injuries in the future. Last will be muscle endurance and strength to return to full function. With any luck, we'll have you back at practice in a few weeks. In the meantime, continue your RICE protocol—rest, ice, compression, and elevation—until that swelling goes down."

"You heard her," Doc says. "I'll leave you to it."

"Come on," Nora beckons, grabbing my discarded splint and nodding to the connecting PT room.

My heart rate climbs as I hop to my feet and follow. Lynn is in that room. At least I hope so.

Sure enough, I'm greeted with a concerned "Hey, Joey," from just the girl I was looking for. She's wearing the same black scrubs as everyone else, and her wavy hair is pulled up into a high ponytail, showing off her delicate jawline. Her brow is furrowed, and I hate her worrying about me. But it feels good all the same.

I throw my good hand out to the side. "Do with me what you will," I offer, making Nora laugh and Lynn blush. I only realize how that sounds after the words are out.

"Come on, Romeo." Nora leads me over to a chair and has me prop my arm up on a padded table. "We're going to start with some very light gripping exercises."

The therapy is somewhat dull, and I find my eyes straying to Lynn across the room too often. She appears to be tidying up and taking inventory most of the time. Amy is in and out, the two of them poring over a tablet when she's there. When Lynn tells Nora she's fetching towels and leaves the room, I let out a sigh.

"You've got it bad, huh?" Nora grins down at my hand, where I'm holding a foam ball.

"What?" Busted. Thankfully, it's only the two of us in the room now.

Nora laughs. "You, my friend, are not subtle. I take it you and Lynn know each other—or do you simply default to flirt mode whenever you see a pretty girl?"

"Flirting in the workplace is unprofessional," I blurt out for some reason.

Nora dips her chin into her chest and snickers—which I totally deserve. "Lynn's not getting paid. She's free labor—in fact, she's here as a favor from the top dog."

Shit. "Does she know that?"

"Hell, no. Do I look stupid to you? Anyway, she's a smart girl, and she never complains. I consider it more of a favor to us than to her." Nora replaces the ball I was squeezing with a harder one. "Try this one now. Remember, don't push yourself too hard. This is a marathon, not a sprint."

Ignoring her instruction, I squeeze the ball tightly, pain radiating up my wrist. "Shit."

"Stop," Nora instructs. "Your poor mom."

"Huh?" Who brought my mom into this?

Nora glares at me. "Dealing with a stubborn athlete for the last couple decades."

I roll my lips in and decide to shut up.

She has me do a few more turns of my wrist to test my motion before declaring, "Okay, you're done for the day. Let's ice it up and get you on your way." My stomach chooses that moment to growl. "Maybe you should ask a certain assistant to grab a bite for lunch," she suggests.

I raise my eyebrows at her and nod once. "I might just do that."

Amy and Lynn choose that moment to reenter the room, a stack of folded towels in Lynn's arms.

"Hey, Lynn, you want to put ice on Joey over here?" Nora yells as she shoots me a wink.

Lynn's jaw drops briefly until she composes herself and straightens her spine. "Absolutely." She grabs a towel from her pile and goes to a standing freezer to retrieve a large, flexible ice pack.

"That's right," Nora says seconds later. "Place the towel securely around the arm first, and then gently mold the pack around before wrapping the whole thing in another towel." When Lynn does as instructed, Nora smiles. "Great job."

Turning to me, she finishes, "I'm off to lunch. Amy and Lynn will remove the pack and get your splint back on before you leave." She jerks her chin toward Lynn, a painfully obvious eyebrow lift accompanying it. Good lord. She could battle Liv for interferer of the year.

Lynn watches my covered wrist like it might jump up and strangle her if left unmonitored, and it has me fighting a smile. "I don't think it's going anywhere."

Her eyes flash up at me. "Sorry. I just want to make sure I'm doing everything right." She exhales, and I feel the warmth of her breath on the hairs of my arm. It has my dick going hard. He's so easy.

"Well, the ice feels good after the exercises, so I'd say you did it perfectly."

Her mouth shifts to the side. "I'm sorry you're going through this. I may not be the biggest baseball fan, but it's clear how important it is to you. It's basically your life, right?"

She doesn't know how right she is. I nod in response. Baseball is all I know how to do, and I'm damn lucky this injury wasn't worse than it is. "Well, I do eat and sleep, too," I clarify.

A grin breaks through her concern. "Right. And drink beer."

"That too." I smile back. "How's your internship thing going? Are you here the whole summer or just part of it?" I have no idea what Skye arranged.

"The whole summer. It's unpaid, but I'm fortunate to have it. I've already learned a lot, and it's only my second week. Nora and Amy are great mentors, so it's pretty much my dream job."

"Good. I'm glad you're not working for that asshole again this summer." Crap. I shouldn't have brought that up. It was, after all, the ultimate cause of my crashing and burning last summer.

But Lynn appears unbothered. "Me too." Her eyes widen, drawing my attention to their warm caramel color. She's not wearing any makeup apart from a swipe of lip gloss, as far as I can tell, and I'm struck a little dumb by her natural beauty. "I ran into a coworker the other day, and he said Ennis is on a rampage this summer. Something about the Nacho Olympics?" She shakes her head and laughs. "I have no idea. Poor Remy."

"I can't even begin to imagine what that might entail." I watch as she tucks a loose strand of hair behind her ear, and then I push ahead, needing to set things straight. "Hey, I want to apologize for last summer. You were right, and I overstepped. I'm really sorry."

Lynn tilts her head, and one corner of her mouth lifts. "Thanks. That's nice of you. I know you meant well, but I appreciate you taking the time to understand and take my boundaries seriously."

Wanting to lighten things back up, I shrug. "What can I say? Independent women are hot."

She busts into a laugh at that, and I sit here and bask in the sound. I don't know what made me think I could ever forget this girl. She's beauty and magic.

Amy comes over to watch Lynn remove the ice, and she replaces my splint while Lynn puts the towels and ice pack away. I find myself standing beside the freezer a minute later, waiting for Amy to walk away so I can talk to Lynn in private again.

I finally get my chance. "I have no food at my condo, so I was gonna go grab a bite for lunch. You want to come?"

Lynn glances at Amy and then at her watch before bringing her eyes back to me. "Sure." She shrugs. "Why not?"

It might not be much, but I'll take it.

JOEY

"Um…" Lynn watches me from across the table with pronounced wrinkles between her eyebrows.

"I didn't really think this through, did I?" I peer down at my giant burger and frown. How in the hell am I supposed to eat this one-handed? My eyes dart around the diner as if the answer lies somewhere among the Formica-topped tables and vinyl booths.

Taking pity on me, Lynn shoves her plate aside and hoists mine over in front of her, where she painstakingly cuts my burger into bite-sized pieces like the seasoned mom of a toddler—where I'm playing the part of toddler.

"This injury is turning out to be quite the humbling experience," I mutter as I watch her.

"This is nothing. When Miller broke his arm last year, he forgot he had to bag the cast before showering, and I had to rescue him—with my eyes closed! That's an experience no sister wants to have twice."

"No comment." I wouldn't mind Lynn helping me

shower at all. And, being the thoughtful person I am, I'd even soap her up in return.

She gives me a puzzled look and hands my plate back to me. "There you go."

"Thanks." I fork my first bite and bring it to my mouth, moaning when the taste hits my tongue. When Lynn looks up from her plate, I shrug. "I haven't eaten since yesterday," I explain once I swallow.

"Wow. Do you need to hire a live-in maid or something?"

"Unfortunately, I think I have one on the way." I spear another bite. "My cousin has decided I need a caretaker."

"That's sweet," Lynn responds as she picks up her club sandwich.

"Is it?" I tilt my head and eye her.

That makes her laugh. "Ah, I see. Maybe she and my brothers can bond over their overprotective natures." She takes a giant bite of her sandwich. Impressive.

"At least her boyfriend is coming too. He's more normal."

Lynn covers her mouth as she talks around her mouthful of food. "Normal people are so underrated."

"I couldn't agree more." We both chow down, clearly having been deprived of sustenance for a dangerous length of time. When I'm sure I won't die of low blood sugar, I ask, "So, how was this last school year? It's been a while."

"You know, normal college stuff." She shrugs, looking uncomfortable.

I lean into my forearms on the table. "Hey, you can talk about it. I want to know. That's why I asked."

"Yeah, I know. It's just…"

Shit. "That I treated you like a kid last summer?"

She wipes her mouth with her napkin and leans back in

her chair with a sigh. "I feel like I'm still punishing you for something in the ancient past. Sorry."

I shake my head. "Clean slate, okay?" When she nods, I ask again, "So, how was school?"

This time, she smiles. "Amazing." She goes on to tell me about the semester-long research project she did on exercise physiology and some independent study work she got to do with her department head.

"You really take this seriously, don't you?"

"Why else would I spend all this time and money on school?" She pops a fry into her mouth.

"I don't know. I mean, a lot of people go to college to party." I'll admit I spent way too much time partying and playing ball and way too little time in the classroom for the two years I was in college.

"Well, I didn't say I don't have fun." She sends me a half grin and straightens in her seat. "I've been known to attend a party or two."

"Oh yeah?" I ask around my straw. I've opted for water, and while I hoped Lynn would order Cheerwine, she's also drinking water.

"I even might have—gasp—indulged in an illegal beverage now and then."

I shove my drink aside in feigned disgust. "That's shocking. How dare you?"

She dips a couple more fries in ketchup and grins. "Well, the thrill of law-breaking is behind me now that I'm officially twenty-one. The misdeeds of my youth are a thing of the past."

"You might be the oldest twenty-one-year-old I've ever met, you know that?"

She only shrugs and shoves the fries in her mouth.

"Why is that?" I ask when she's done chewing.

"I mean, being the youngest of five, I guess I spent a lot of time wishing I were older. I was kind of in a hurry, you know?" I nod and she continues. "And then when my dad died, there was that realization that nothing is a given. Your sense of security as a kid that you'll always be cared for is tilted on its head. Don't get me wrong, my mom is a kick-ass mom and resourceful as hell. But I can't say it didn't cross my mind a time or twenty that she could suddenly die too, and I'd be left alone."

"You'd have had your brothers, though, right?"

"Yeah." A wistful smile crosses her lips. "I know I complain about them a lot, but I really do love those bozos. I'm lucky to have such a tight family."

"I'm happy for you."

Lynn watches me as she takes a sip of water. "You're not close with your family?"

"I am. It's just not the same living so far away. They don't get the whole baseball thing either, so that can be tough. When I left for college and then to pursue baseball, I never really went back, so it's basically phone calls and holiday visits now."

"I have no idea what it feels like not to have at least one family member sticking their nose in my business on the daily. Hell, my mama sends me pictures of Mango at least twice a week so I don't forget what he looks like."

"The skunk, right?"

She pulls out her phone and scrolls briefly before turning the screen toward me.

"Holy shit. That's a full-grown skunk." Displayed on the screen is a black-and-white animal that looks like a cross between a messed-up fox and a porcupine. I realize I've never seen a skunk up close.

"What did you think I meant?" Lynn snickers at my expression and takes another bite of her sandwich.

"I don't know. I guess in my head he was some combination of a cuddly kitten and Pepé Le Pew."

"The cartoon molester skunk?" She covers her mouth as she chuckles over her food.

I can only shrug because I'm an idiot. "You'll have to introduce us." Yeah, I'm using my blunder to try and win another date.

She grins over the table at me. "How's that burger? Need me to cut up your fries too?"

"Smartass."

We finish lunch, and when the check comes, I expect her to argue with me about paying. Instead, she allows it, commenting, "I've got the next one," which makes me happier than she can possibly know. Because that means I have another date with Lynn Brooks.

Finally.

CHAPTER
EIGHTEEN
NO PAIN, NO GAIN

JOEY

Since Lynn insisted on driving—apparently she didn't feel safe with a one-handed driver—we get in her ancient Mazda and head back to Ardent Park.

"You know I'm driving myself home after I work out, right?" I ask from the passenger side where I've moved the seat all the way back to accommodate my legs.

She looks over her shoulder before backing out and hits me with a sugary smile. "Yeah, but once you're out of my sight, I'm not responsible for you anymore."

"Who's being overprotective now?"

She at least has the grace to look a little guilty. "Touché."

When we get back to the ballpark, Lynn parks in the employee lot and moves to open her door, but I stop her at the last minute. I'm operating purely on instinct here, so when she glances over with a curious expression, I blurt out. "Can I kiss you?"

Something has her smiling, and I'm unsure if it's the fact

that I *asked* or if it's simply the notion of kissing me—either way, I'm good.

When she nods, I don't waste another second before leaning over the console and cupping her jaw with my one good hand. It feels so natural and right when our lips meet that I'm soon hauling her into me with the damn console getting in the way. I'm taken right back to last summer as her taste explodes on my tongue. This time, it's less Cheerwine and more Lynn—a flavor all her own and one I could easily become addicted to.

Her fingers twist in my hair, and the kiss ratchets up in record speed. Our tongues dance, and she moans into my mouth, making me stroke my hand down her back to her ass in her scrubs. Thank God for thin cotton pants. She surprises me by throwing a knee over the console and crawling across to straddle my lap. Now, this is what I'm talking about.

"Fuck," I groan as I release her lips and trail my mouth on a path down her throat. Her head drops back to give me more access as I shamelessly thrust my hips up and grind into her. She returns the favor by nestling her crotch against my cock and sending it on an upward trajectory it might never come back from. Her skin is salty and sweet on my tongue, and when I nip her earlobe, she jumps in my lap and comes back down to press her tits into my chest and her pussy into my cock. Full-length contact from shoulders to privates, just how I like it.

"Joey," she murmurs, and it sounds like a plea. My fingers reflexively tighten on her ass and urge her to grind on me. I could come just from this, and I want nothing more than for her to do the same. Right fucking now. To that end, I capture her lips again and slide my hand under both her scrubs and underwear to feel the smooth, silky skin of her ass. Damn, I wish I could use both hands. As it is, I'm holding my left hand awkwardly to the side and trying to ignore it.

"God, you feel good." I break the kiss to get the words out and pull in another breath before going back in. The last thing I want is to pass out from oxygen deprivation.

"Joey," she repeats my name, and I squeeze her ass one more time before sliding my fingers to the skin of her hip.

"Back up a little. Let me make you come," I pant.

When she lifts her head, she looks utterly drunk and entirely beautiful. Her hair is wild, her cheeks flushed, her lips swollen and red, and her eyes unfocused. I could stare at her all day.

When she doesn't speak, I let my fingers slide around her hip and delve inside the front of her pants. When my fingers touch smooth skin and brush against a tiny patch of hair, she closes her eyes. Her lips part, and I beg my dick to hold on and not embarrass me. But just as I inch down to the promised land, a car horn blares loud and long, and we both jump in the seat, Lynn smacking her head on the roof.

My hand jerks out of her pants like I'm a teenager who's just been caught jerking off by his mom. Lynn's hand goes to her head as her gaze shoots this way and that, as if she's trying to orient herself. Once the reality of our situation hits her, she yelps and scrambles off my lap, kneeing me in the dick on her way back to the driver's seat.

I gasp before letting out a pained *"Oof!"* and my body locks in agony.

Lynn's gasp is right on mine's heels as she claps a hand over her mouth. "Oh my god! I'm so sorry!" she yelps from the driver's seat, where she's half upside down from clambering off me so fast.

"It's okay," I manage in a strained groan.

And, honestly, if I had to choose to do it all over again knowing how it would end, I absolutely would every time.

LYNN

"You might want to be careful," Amy says as I balance a sanitizer container over the sink.

"Okay. Got it," I reply without looking her way.

"I wasn't talking about the sanitizer."

When I shoot her a puzzled look, she crosses her arms over her chest and says, "It's frowned upon to fraternize." It takes a second for her words to sink in, but as soon as they do, every ounce of blood in my body crashes over my face like a humiliation tidal wave. *Oh my god*. Did she see me making out with Joey in the parking lot the other day?!

"Oh," I finally manage to eke out. What else am I supposed to say? Even if she didn't catch us attacking each other in my car, it's obvious Joey and I know each other—and, yeah, we've both been flirting with abandon when he comes in for his appointments. It's hard not to after my car—and with how he's mastered the art of being both adorable and hot as sin at the same time! At this point, I can't even remember why I was mad at him last summer. He's *such* a good guy, I could almost cry.

"Just a little friendly advice if you want a future here, that's all." Amy's tone isn't nasty or vindictive; it's matter of fact, so I can't exactly be mad at her for setting me straight.

Shit. Shit. Shit.

"I do!" I hurry to assure her. What was I thinking? Of course it's unprofessional to flirt with a patient—or stick your tongue down his throat! Jesus, Mary, and Jolene! I'm an idiot! "Thank you. I understand."

Red-faced, I make an excuse and take off down the hall for the women's bathroom. My reflection shows a sheen of sweat on my pink cheeks and a wildness in my eyes that's new. I can't fuck this up—it's part of my plan for a kick-ass future in sports physical therapy, and I'm not about to throw it away for a guy. Even one as great as Joey. Guys come and go, and I can't let this one throw me off my game just because he turns my panties into Splash Mountain!

With no games to play and limited workouts available to him, Joey is going out of his mind with boredom, so he's taken to texting me at all hours. I'm trying to chalk it up to boredom instead of something more panic-inducing, like a concerted effort to make me his girlfriend or something. When we texted last night, I agreed to go out for drinks with him and his cousin, who arrives in town today. I was really looking forward to it—and to maybe kissing him again—but now there's no way I can go.

I pull out my phone with trembling fingers.

ME:

Hey, looks like I can't make it for drinks after all. Sorry.

He immediately answers. See, he's just bored.

JOEY:

Oh no. Everything okay?

ME:

Yeah. Turns out I have to work.

It's a lie, but I'm incapable of explaining things right now
—especially not over text.

JOEY:

It's an afternoon game.

Of course he knows the team schedule. Duh.

ME:

I've got to fill in at Blue Bigfoot.

Cash did ask if I could fill in for Jodi if they got busy, so
it's not really a lie. Except that I told him no since I was planning on drinks with Joey and his cousin. Looks like I'll need
to fix that.

JOEY:

Damn. And here I was hoping you could
save me from Liv.

*Don't engage in banter with the sexy man, Lynn. It can't go
anywhere good.*

ME:

First you make me cut up your food, and
now I have to protect you from your cousin?
Wow.

JOEY:

You haven't met her yet. She's very
frightening.

ME:

Maybe next time.

Or never. Why do I want to cry?

JOEY:

Okay. Don't work too hard. Talk soon.

See, he's not even disappointed. Like I said, he's just
bored.

When I return to the clinic room, Amy is nowhere to be
found, so I finish refilling the sanitizer containers and then
file exercise instruction sheets before finishing the day. It's
little comfort when Cash falls over himself to thank me for
covering for Jodi. But a girl's got to do what a girl's got to
do. Right?

CHAPTER
TWENTY

BOUNDARIES: MY LEAST
FAVORITE SCRABBLE WORD

LYNN

"I didn't know you were working tonight," Miller says when I slip in the back door of Blue Bigfoot and drop my stuff in the office.

"Yeah, Cash wanted me to fill in for Jodi if y'all get slammed."

He nods and fiddles with one of his gazillion earrings. "Good, because Maisy is playing tonight, and it's already packed out there."

I glance at my watch. "It's not even seven."

Miller grins. "I know, right?" He takes off down the hall toward the taproom, calling behind him, "Bear and Mason are here tonight. Make sure you stop by their table so Bear can flirt with you."

I bark out a laugh and secure my apron around my waist. Miller has changed a lot in the last year—for the better. He used to not care much about anything and only gave token effort to most endeavors. Now, he's taking pride in his job at the brewery and stepping up in a big way with Maisy and

Bear. He's also earned the respect of all our brothers, which is huge.

I'm low-key bursting with pride, to be honest, not that Miller's ego needs it. He's even admitted that the car crash that broke his arm last year was probably driver error—something Cart is now annoyingly smug about since it was *his* car that got totaled. Miller kept claiming something was wrong with the brakes, but his track record spoke for itself. All that was left was for him to cop to it. In the last year, though, Miller hasn't had so much as a fender bender or even a conversation with a member of the Asheville police force. That's considered progress in our family.

I shove my phone in the back pocket of my cut-offs and follow my brother to the taproom. Even if Cash doesn't need me, I need something to do or I'll drive myself batty thinking about this thing with Joey. Damn, I really like him.

As if the universe is messing with me, the first person I lay eyes on when I step out onto the crowded floor is none other than Joey Martel. Looking incredibly hot and… a bit guilty.

"Hey." He approaches, a sheepish grin on his full lips. "So, I figured if you couldn't join us, maybe we'd join you?"

My immediate reaction is to smile because, damn, that's sweet. But panic soon follows and has me biting my lip. Joey appears only to notice the smile, though, because he ushers me over to a nearby table where a petite Asian woman and a bearded white guy sit enjoying some drinks. They both smile up at me.

"Lynn, this is my cousin Olivia and her boyfriend Brett. Guys, this is Lynn."

Hellos are quickly exchanged, and Brett even stands to shake my hand.

"You can call me Liv," Olivia says. "This place is great! Joey said your family owns it?"

I nod. "Yeah, my brothers do. It's a labor of love, you could say." I raise my voice to be heard over the music and conversation.

"Very cool," Brett responds, looking around the busy taproom. "I don't think I could own a bar, though. I'd sample too many goods and go out of business."

"Sorry to crash your job like this," Liv says, eyeing her cousin in a way I can't quite interpret.

"Oh, it's fine." I muster a smile before glancing behind me to see if I've been spotted by Cash yet. The last thing I need is another scene in front of Joey's cousin.

Joey misinterprets my movements, saying, "Oh, hey, sorry. You probably need to get back to work."

I take the out to make myself scarce. "Yeah, sorry. It was nice to meet you guys." I keep the smile pasted on and buzz over to the bar to grab a bus tub. Cash must be next door at Hollis's dog salon or in the brewhouse with Carter because he's nowhere to be seen. Looks like I got a lucky break.

I bus a couple tables and stop by to see Bear and his dad where they sit on the far side of the room. The band is in the middle of a set, and they're playing one of my favorite oldies, "Sister Golden Hair" by America, but I'm finding it hard to enjoy it tonight. Even Bear's Casanova antics aren't making a dent, although I can't help but smile when he tells me my cowboy boots are "tight."

By the time I make it out to the patio to bus the picnic tables, the labor and stress of the day have caught up with me, and exhaustion is setting in. I sigh at the relative quiet and drop my tub on a nearby bench seat to rest out of sight.

It doesn't take long for the universe to resume its game and send Joey out to find me.

"Hey." He's got his good hand shoved in his jeans pockets and the bad one dangling at his side. No splint tonight, I notice.

"Have you been keeping up with your icing?" I ask. It's not like I can turn and run away or something. I know we need to have a conversation.

He ignores my question, instead asking one of his own. "Did I overstep by coming here tonight?"

Oh, god. Joey. You're such a good guy. Even now, he's got my boundaries at the forefront of his mind.

"No." I shake my head, and he's visibly relieved. "I just… I need to talk to you about something."

"Okay. What is it?" He steps closer to where I'm leaning against the outside wall of the building.

"This…" I wag my finger back and forth between us. "I may be way off base in assuming there's something going on here, but—"

"No," he interrupts, taking another step toward me. "There's absolutely something going on here."

I draw in a shaky breath because his proximity, combined with those words and the confident way he said them, have my knees threatening to give out. This is way harder than I thought it would be.

"Joey."

"Lynn." Oh, damn, that rumble. Now my panties are wet.

"I'm not allowed to fraternize with the players, and I can't afford to lose this job," I force myself to declare.

His brow immediately furrows. "Your brothers are going to fire you if you date me?"

"No." I can't help my grin, despite the pain in my chest.

"Although, that might be true too." I shake my head. "The rehab job. I'm going to get fired if we date, so we can't date."

"Oh." He tilts his head, causing his dark hair to flop over his forehead. "Really?"

"Yes. I was directly told it's 'frowned upon,' and everyone knows what that means."

"Wow. That wasn't the impression…" He trails off, and it's my turn to tilt my head. "Never mind." He takes a deep breath and glances around the patio before bringing his eyes back to me and shrugging those broad shoulders. "We just won't tell them, then."

"Joey!" I cross my arms over my chest.

"What?"

"You're not taking this seriously."

"Lynn, they shouldn't be able to dictate what you do in your free time."

I frown up at him, both frustrated that he's making this harder and thrilled it's important to him at the same time. "You flirted shamelessly with me during your appointments this week—in front of everyone!"

"So did you!"

Guilty. "Yeah, well." It's all I've got in my defense.

He dips his chin and reaches out to touch my arm. Just that light contact has lightning bolts shooting up my arm and down to my clit. God, I'm easy. "Okay, I'll try to resist flirting with you at your work. It'll be difficult, though, if you keep wearing those scrubs."

My nose wrinkles. "You are seriously messed up, do you know that?"

His lopsided grin does more things to my insides. "What can I say? I've got a thing for shapeless garments that make me imagine what's underneath."

My face flames, and I roll my eyes. "Mother magnolia."

Grabbing his chest like he's in cardiac arrest, he groans, "And those Sunday school expressions. You're really hitting me with both barrels, aren't you?"

"Shut up." I move to shove him as I try and fail to fight a smile.

He grabs my hand and erases the last of the distance between us. "Lynn, I want to see where this goes."

My hand trembles in his, and I don't understand why.

"It's not that I don't. I just… this job is important to me." I ignore the whisper in the back of my mind that says seeing where this goes would be utterly terrifying and we're much safer without the temptation of Joey.

He opens his mouth to say something, but appears to think better of it.

I take advantage and ask, "Can we be friends?"

A choking noise comes from his throat. "Friends? You're killing me here."

"Yes. You've heard of it, right? When two people sometimes hang out and are generally nice to each other." When all else fails, sarcasm is the best way to go.

He watches me for a few seconds before a naughty twinkle hits his espresso eyes. "Are there any benefits to this friendship thing?"

"Yes. I'll cut your meat for you."

His head drops back so fast, I'm concerned he's given himself another injury. "Fuck, Lynn."

"I know." I swallow. "But I need to do this."

His eyes come back to mine, and he squeezes my hand. "Boundaries," he murmurs.

I nod, feeling like an asshole that I've brought us right

back to the same place again—except this time we both know what it feels like to dry hump each other.

"Okay." He lets my hand go and takes a step back. I'm glad the wall is there to hold me up.

I did it, though. It's done.

But the universe isn't finished with me yet because, as Joey walks back into the brewery, he glances over his shoulder one last time and declares, "For now," before disappearing inside.

Jesus, Mary, and Jolene!

JOEY

"Well, that's disappointing."

"Liv," Brett warns, but there's no stopping my cousin.

"Friends, huh?" she continues, placing a finger on her chin. "Sounds strangely familiar."

"That's because you were dating that asshole when we first met. I had no other choice," Brett declares with a scowl, grabbing my TV remote and pressing pause.

Yeah, that asshole was my best friend and teammate before he fucked over my cousin and I broke his nose. Good riddance.

I fall back into my couch cushion, deflated. "She takes her future seriously. What can I do?"

"My advice?" Brett asks, taking a gulp of beer from the bottle in his hand.

"Anything."

"Bide your time. Embrace the friend zone and put yourself in her orbit as much as possible. She'll fold eventually;

they all do." He doesn't even try to hide his smug grin as he turns to Liv.

"You weren't always this cocky. Is this my fault?" she asks as she absently pets her giant dog's head.

"Absolutely," is Brett's immediate reply.

He does have a point, though. Personally, I think the no-dating thing is bullshit. I mean, Nora talked about it like she thought it was damn near adorable. I wonder what changed. But it's not like I can tell Lynn I talked to Nora about her—that would not go down well. I'll just have to follow my newfound feminist side (thank you, Elizabeth) and respect her boundaries. She'll finish this internship at some point, and then I can get back to the business of wooing her.

Yeah, I said wooing.

"And you couldn't just, I don't know, date in secret?" Liv suggests. There's a reason we're related.

Brett gives his head a hard shake like he's Tambo after a bath. "Lies always have a way of coming out."

Brett is a wise man, although I'd be willing to risk it for another of those make-out sessions with Lynn. I thought my dick was going to kill me after that—for multiple reasons.

"Maybe I should sit down for some girl time with Lynn," Liv muses, attempting to imbue her tone with an innocence she simply doesn't possess.

"No!" Brett and I respond in perfect unison.

"Fine. Jeez. It was just an idea." Liv looks at Tambo, where he's taking up half the sectional. "Nobody likes my ideas, Bo." His only response is a yawn wide enough to fit a human head.

Brett unpauses *SportsCenter*, and we settle back to catch up on the day's games. Since all three of us are giant sports nuts, it's always easy to agree on what to watch on TV. Liv falls asleep with her head on Brett's lap an hour later, and he carries her to my second bedroom.

"Hey," I call after him. "This is *my* house, so it's *my* rules." When he sends me a questioning look, I finish, "No audible funny business. I don't need any more therapy bills."

"Ah. Got it," Brett answers with a smirk I don't like all that much.

I turn off the TV and carry my empty beer bottle to the kitchen. It's been a long day, and despite not playing today, I'm beat. But my brain refuses to relax; it keeps replaying my conversation with Lynn from earlier.

I wander down the hall to my room, and before I can think too hard about it, I pull out my phone and open Words with Friends as I climb into bed. Once I'm settled against my headboard, I click the plus sign to start a new game and type *lynnqqueen* in the search bar. Yeah, I still remember her username like it's been seared into my hippocampus for eternity. When her name comes up, I select it and invite her to a new game before the board pops up with all my tiles in a row.

It takes a few minutes to decide, but I finally settle on a starting word and spell, "HOT." One of the worst words points-wise, but it's strategic. I grab my remote and switch on the bedroom TV to channel surf until I get tired. But the game notification alerts me a couple minutes later that it's my turn.

When I look at the WWF board, I see Lynn has not caught onto my plan, instead having spelled "DEPOSITS" off my "T" and earning herself a massive head start with a fifty-point bonus for using all her tiles. I'm not about to give up, though.

I respond with "KISS" off her "S" and sit perched on my

bed like a six-year-old on a weekend night when the babysitter has fallen asleep.

Lynn finally gets with the program, going with "KNEE," which has me laughing out loud. I send her a frowny-face emoji before responding with "OUCH," which draws a laughing emoji from her.

She comes back at me with "SORRY," and we continue back and forth until it's one in the morning. I fall asleep waiting for Lynn's response to my play of "SOMEDAY."

Yeah, I can do this friends thing. For now, at least.

TWENTY-TWO

CHARM SCHOOL DROPOUT

LYNN

"Wait, what do you mean he saw Larry?" The sole of my shoe squeaks on the finished concrete floor of the brewhouse that takes up the back portion of the Blue Bigfoot's unit.

Carter looks up at me from his crouched position beside one of the fermenters. His dark hair is ruffled, and he's wearing his usual uniform of jeans, boots, and his brewmaster apron. While a full apron has the potential to make some men appear more feminine, my brother's scowl and general grumpiness won't allow it—that, and his muscles. "I didn't say he saw Larry. Miller just commented that a customer came in on Friday and mentioned he saw a similar sculpture at a gallery in Raleigh."

"Yeah, but couldn't it be Larry?"

"No." He stands to his full height, which is an entire head taller than me. "You're one of the practical ones in the family. Why are you getting your hopes up about this?"

"I'm not," I lie. Not knowing who broke into the brewery

last year nags at me sometimes—just like half the other shit that went down last year. Simply because things have been quiet for the Brooks family these past few months doesn't mean I don't think about it. And Larry was Dad's. I want him back.

"I wouldn't have said anything if I thought you'd read into it. Morton Frye has made a lot of sculptures. He probably has a whole series that looks like Larry. Besides, galleries don't just buy stuff without authenticating it first. It's not Larry." Carter turns a few knobs, bringing his focus back to beermaking.

"I guess." Still, if I broke into someone's business and stole an expensive piece of art, I'd probably fence it. What good is having it instead of the money if you're the breaking-and-entering type? Larry has got to be somewhere. Why not Raleigh? Surely, you can fake authentication. I plan to quiz Miller about it as soon as I can.

"What are you doing here anyway?" Cart asks the fermenter. "We don't open for hours, and you're not on shift today, are you?"

I dig the heel of my shoe into the brewhouse floor and adopt a more cheery manner. "Can't I spend a little time with my brother?"

"You can. You just usually don't."

My jaw drops open. "That's totally untrue." Isn't it? Oh, god, am I being a bitch to my family? "I only avoid you when you're trying to run my life. Besides, the Arrows are out of town, so I don't have work today." And I'm trying to avoid giving in and calling Joey, I add silently.

The temptation is strong, especially when I know his cousin has left town and he's all by himself in his condo. A good friend would probably call and ask him to go do something to take his mind off missing out on all these games.

But I've been trying my best to establish some distance. Even though we still text and play Words with Friends, I've made myself scarce in the treatment room when Joey comes in for his appointments. It hasn't gone unnoticed, and the approving looks I've gotten from Amy reassure me that I'm doing the right thing. It's all I've got to hold on to at this point, especially when Joey shows up with his hair sticking out every which way like he's been running his fingers through it all morning. My pterodactyls begin to stir, and I tell them to go back to bed.

"As long as you're here, do you think you can bring me a stack of pint glasses from the taproom?" Carter requests, interrupting my thoughts.

"Sure thing, big bro." I need to shed the negativity around my brothers.

I mosey out to the bar and stack up a half dozen glasses, running into Miller on my way back to the brewhouse.

"Yo," he greets me, looking half asleep with his dirty-blond hair falling in his face.

"Hey! Just the man I wanted to see."

"I didn't do it," is his immediate response, but I ignore it.

"Cart told me about that customer who thought he saw Larry," I prod, going more for casual interest than rabid anticipation.

"Oh, right." Miller shrugs. "It's probably nothing. I gave him a call to follow up but didn't catch him. I was gonna try again today or tomorrow."

"You mind if I do?"

My brother tilts his head and looks me over. I smile

sweetly in return. "You know, if you need help, I can teach you how to relax," he offers.

I scowl, forgetting my sweet little sister act. "I like staying busy."

"Yeah, that's not normal." He yawns. "Most people like kicking back now and then, sis."

Yeah, when you have someone to kick back with, maybe. I don't give voice to my thoughts.

"Well, I'm not most people." I balance the pint glasses in both hands and try the little sister smile again. "Can I have the number, please?"

"Have at it." Miller shakes his head before pulling out his phone and forwarding me the contact info. "Just don't be too intense, okay? He's a customer."

"I'm charming as hell," I scoff.

"Is that what we're calling it?"

I stick my tongue out at Miller like the mature woman I am and head for the brewhouse with the glasses.

Not bad, if I do say so myself. Looks like I just got myself a little project to take my mind off the hot guy trying to steal my attention.

TWENTY-THREE

YOUR MANIFESTING NEEDS WORK

LYNN

"So, wait, this is the same guy from last summer?" Sadie asks through my earbuds. "That's a curveball."

Dammit! I still with one leg stretched in front of me and my head bent toward my knee as I try to complete my post-run stretches on the front porch. I didn't mean to bring Joey up. I just called my friend to catch up, and he kind of... popped out. "Yeah," I mumble before hurrying on. "Hey, what's up with your boss? Didn't you have some flirtation going on the last time I talked to you?"

"Nice try. We're still talking about you." My former dorm big sis cuts me off. "Why do I get the sense we don't hate him anymore?"

I straighten at that. "I never hated him. I just found him a little too similar to my overbearing brothers, that's all."

"But he made a bet about you, right? Yuck."

"No! That turned out to be a misunderstanding." I jump in to defend Joey. Why do I ever open my big mouth?

I can hear her trying to stifle a chuckle. "This is quite the turnaround. I didn't think I'd hear you coming to this guy's defense after last summer."

Since I know I'm busted, I sigh and start stretching my other leg. "Yeah, well."

"So, we like him now?"

"No!" Maybe I should just smash my phone on the ground and pretend I got hit by a truck.

"Wait, I'm confused." I can picture Sadie's kind eyes and her forehead scrunched up under her gorgeous red waves, and I give in.

"Sadie, I'm not allowed to like him. He's a baseball player for the team I'm interning with. I'm going to get fired."

"I thought they weren't paying you."

I straighten again and exhale as the sun tries to blind me. "Well, they're not. But still."

"Okay, I get it. It's important for you to keep your eye on the ball and protect your future. Very smart. Good job." There's an authority in her voice that reminds me why I dialed her number in the first place.

"So, you're saying I'm doing the right thing." Yes. Excellent.

But she laughs in my ear, turning the corners of my mouth southward. "Oh, girl, I see what's happening here. You're looking for me to give you an excuse to bang this hottie."

"No, I'm not!" When did I become such a liar? "I just… think I like him."

"Well, I think it's sweet. Does he… think he likes you too?" I so deserved that.

I sigh again. "Yeah. He kind of told me this friend-zone thing isn't going to last."

"Ha! I like this guy. To think he could be the man who finally captures my little sister's heart. I might swoon just at the thought."

"Sadie!"

"What? Is it so out of left field to think you could fall in *lurve*?"

"You're doing this on purpose."

"Probably, but to what are you referring?"

"Curveball? Out of left field? Eye on the ball? Your baseball idioms are too on-point to be unintentional."

"No, I swear. You're way off base."

A laugh bubbles up my throat. "I've created a monster."

"Like I always say, if you're not willing to swing for the fences, why play at all?" When she's done laughing at her own joke—okay, I laugh along—she sobers. "Hey, you deserve to have someone love you up, honey."

I make a noncommittal noise in response and ask, "Have *you* ever been in love?" Sadie was always focused on academics when she was at school, which is probably why we bonded in the first place.

"Sadly, no. Although I thought I was in second grade when Darren Valentine gave me a dandelion at recess."

"Aww. His name was Valentine?"

"I know. Adorable, right?"

"So what happened to this blooming love affair?" I ask as I settle on the top step of the concrete porch and cradle my water bottle in my hands.

"He told me it was a weed, and it was dirty like me."

I gasp. "That little asshole!"

Sadie laughs, clearly over her heartbreak. "It all turned out okay, though. My cousin Ruby threatened to punch him if he didn't apologize, so he ended up having to apologize in front of half the class. Two other boys asked me to 'go' with them the next day, and thus began the phase I like to call my slutty years."

I giggle. "You are really something, Sadie."

"That sounds like what someone says when they don't want to insult you, but they also don't want to lie about how awesome you're not."

"Ha! I learned it from my mama."

"Fair. *Anyway*, if you want my opinion, maybe you should give this Joey guy a shot—after the internship, if that makes you more comfortable."

I squint at an unfamiliar sedan in our neighbor Winston's driveway and consider her advice before responding, "I'll be back at school. Forget I said anything." It's better to leave it alone.

But Sadie's not buying it. "And this baseball player can't drive an hour? Especially in the offseason?"

Hmm. "It would be weird…wouldn't it?" This is dumb. I don't even *want* a boyfriend.

"Only if you make it weird. Look, babe, what's the worst that could happen?"

My heart could get smashed to smithereens. I don't say that, though, instead going with, "He could dump me, and it would be all over social media, making me a laughingstock across campus and the entire state."

"Lynn!" Sadie huffs. "Remind me to work on your manifesting skills next time we see each other. I don't think you understand how this shit is supposed to work."

CHAPTER
TWENTY-FOUR

FRIEND ZONE, SHMIEND ZONE

JOEY

She's avoiding me.

It's okay, I was prepared for it. In fact, the speed with which she scuttles out of the therapy room the minute I walk in each morning is kind of hilarious.

I'm taking Brett's advice and biding my time—and it appears to be working because, at night, when Lynn is tired and her guard is down, she texts me. It's almost like we're long-distance dating, something I've never done before. The benefit is that we're getting to know each other; the drawback is that I don't get to touch her or look at her pretty face.

But I do know how she likes her eggs (over easy if she has toast or potatoes, scrambled if not) and that her life's aspiration as a child was to become a zookeeper until she found out how much poop is involved. I've shared things about myself with Lynn too. I even confessed my most embarrassing moment—the time I ate the donut of the customer sitting next to me, thinking it was mine the whole time and glaring back at him when he kept glaring at me. And Lynn still texts me!

I'll admit there are nights after she texts me goodbye that I jerk off to thoughts of her. It's impossible not to.

I want more, but I can't push for it just yet. She needs to be the one to come to me and cross that line—to give me reprieve from the dreaded friend zone. Brett had better be right about this. I'm going to kick both him and myself if Lynn starts dating someone else. I need to keep putting myself in her orbit, even if it's mostly electronically for now.

As if she knew I was thinking about her, a text pops up on my phone.

LYNN:

I'm going gumshoeing.

I stare at my screen for a few seconds and lean forward on the couch to rest my elbows on my knees.

ME:

I'm sorry. What?

LYNN:

Maybe it's not a word. Let's go with sleuthing instead. Although that sounds boring in comparison.

ME:

Are you a closeted Hardy Boy?

LYNN:

Nancy Drew, thank you very much.

ME:

So what is this about, Nancy?

I mute the game on TV so I can focus on Lynn.

LYNN:

My dad had this valuable Bigfoot carving
that my brothers kept by the register at Blue
Bigfoot until last year when somebody
broke in and stole it.

ME:

Wow. That sucks.

LYNN:

Yeah, but a customer came in last week and
told Miller he thought he saw it at a gallery
in Raleigh. I just talked to the customer
today and got more details. But since the
gallery doesn't have a photo of it on their
website, I'm going to drive to Raleigh and
check it out in person.

ME:

Can't you just call the cops?

LYNN:

They won't do anything with a third-hand
possible sighting. I need to make sure it's
really Larry before I do anything.

ME:

Larry? And I thought Priscilla was a fluke. I
see naming inanimate objects is a family
pastime.

LYNN:

You'd understand if you saw him.

ME:

When are you going?

LYNN:

Tomorrow. The team isn't back for a couple
more days, and I'll make an excuse to my
brothers.

The team is in Colorado, and I'm not sure if I'd rather be here or out there. Either way, I'm not playing. The pain in my wrist is lessening each day, and I'm starting to do some actual strengthening exercises with Nora, so at least it feels like I'm making some progress. She even let me ditch the splint for good, which makes almost everything easier. It hasn't stopped me from watching my replacement's stats like a hawk, though.

ME:

Why aren't you telling your brothers? Wouldn't they want to get the carving back as much as you?

LYNN:

I sort of want to get a leg up on them. They've boxed me out of a few family fiascos, so I'm taking the lead on this one. I figure if I find Larry, I can run a victory lap around the taproom.

ME:

Your family is kind of messed up, you do know that, right?

LYNN:

Nah, we're totally normal. I promise.

She has me grinning with that one.

ME:

Right...

ME:

Okay, I'm in.

There's no way I'm sitting here on my couch while Lynn is traipsing across the state looking for stolen goods. Not that

I think she's in any danger; I'm just bored as hell, and I want to spend time with her.

> LYNN:
>
> ???

> ME:
>
> I'm coming with you.

> LYNN:
>
> Uh, no.

I laugh out loud because I can perfectly picture her expression right now.

> ME:
>
> Why not? It's not like I have anything else to do.

Yeah, it's a little sketchy playing on her sympathies, but I'm going stir crazy.

> LYNN:
>
> I don't know if it's the best idea.

> ME:
>
> Are you saying you won't be able to keep your hands off me if I come along?

> LYNN:
>
> Somebody thinks a little highly of himself.

> ME:
>
> See, then you have nothing to worry about. I'll even let you drive my truck.

Clearly, I'm desperate.

LYNN:

Hmm.

ME:

A good friend never lets a friend road trip alone. It's in the handbook.

LYNN:

You might have a point.

Hell, yes.

ME:

Sounds like we're going on a road trip, Ms. Brooks. I'll make a playlist.

LYNN:

Leave the playlist to me, Daft Punk.

ME:

Deal

And that, ladies and gentlemen, is how it's done.

I settle back on my couch and smile to myself. All right, I suppose it wasn't such an accomplishment considering how easily she gave in. Who knows? Maybe she's already reconsidering the friend thing. Fuck, I hope so.

I picture her lying in her bed at her mom's house, and my cock is so easily swayed, it gets half-hard at just the words "Lynn" and "bed" residing in the same sentence.

The TV goes black, and I toss the remote on the couch and head down the hall. My condo sits on one of the top floors of a downtown high-rise with views of the town and access to a rooftop pool. It's decently sized, with two bedrooms and an office, but my favorite part is the gigantic whirlpool bathtub in the master bath. That thing is worth its weight in gold after a rough game or a doubleheader. It's big enough for three people, not that I've ever tested its limits. But it's what sold me on this place—that and the building is an eight-minute drive to Ardent Park.

I consider the tub for a few seconds and then decide I'm not a guy who wants to swim in his own spunk unless there's a woman on top of me. So I flip on the tap in the shower and shed my T-shirt, shorts, and boxers before getting in. The shower is oversized too, with two shower-heads and a tile bench seat. I picture myself sitting on the seat with a naked Lynn straddling me, and my cock goes from half-hard to full-staff just like that.

As the hot water hits my back and steam starts to billow around me, I take my cock in hand and begin to stroke myself, imagining Lynn's Cheerwine-red lips pulling me in so deep my balls hit her chin.

I close my eyes, and my head drops back on a groan. Lynn's delicate fingers wrap around my base as she releases me from her throat and strokes my length before sucking me back in again. Fuck, I'm not going to last long. She releases me again to let her tongue rasp against the engorged head of my cock as she pumps me with one hand and cradles my balls with the other. When the vibration from her moan blazes from the head to my balls, I get impossibly harder and take over.

"I want more," she begs, and who am I to say no?

My hands cradle her wet hair, and I watch my cock drive into her mouth and past her tongue. She moans again until she's cut off by my cock down her throat. I hold it there, almost passing out from the squeeze for a couple seconds before pulling back to allow her a breath. Then she's got my ass in one hand while her other slides down between her legs to stroke herself. The hand on my ass urges me forward again, and I fuck her mouth while she gets herself off. When she moans her pleasure on my dick again, I lose control and come hard down her throat.

My breath comes in gasps as I float back to reality and feel the pounding water on my back again. One hand extends to support me against the shower wall, and I open my eyes to see that, of course, I'm alone in the shower. But the image of a naked Lynn on her knees with my cock in her mouth and her hand between her legs is compelling enough that I jerk off one more time before falling asleep, utterly exhausted.

LYNN

The drive takes less than four hours, so we arrive in Raleigh just before noon to stake out the Mintz Gallery. It's a brick-front building with large windows in a funky part of town with a bunch of cool shops and restaurants. We've been watching the building for the last half hour, but no one has ventured in or out, so it's time to step things up. My pulse jumps as I hop down from the passenger seat of Joey's truck and onto the sidewalk.

Despite his offer to let me drive, I'm not used to such a large vehicle, so I let him do his thing. He's started using his left hand now that he's gaining more strength and mobility. The few mentions he's made about his temporary replacement have tipped me off to his anxiety over getting off the injured list. So, it's good to see him using the wrist without any apparent pain.

"So, what's the plan here?" Joey asks once he reaches my side. "Are you going to tell them about Larry or not?"

I shake my head. "I'm just going to pretend I'm browsing for now."

"Got it." Joey nods and holds the door to the gallery for me to walk through.

The exhibit space is airy and bright, with several defined areas for different styles and media. We wander past the paintings in the front and continue to a central space holding metal sculptures.

"Good afternoon," a tall man in a suit and a trim mustache greets us. "Is there something I can help you with?"

"Just browsing," Joey answers for us, and I send the guy a polite smile before he retreats behind a small desk along the wall.

When I turn to one of the back spaces, I gasp and quickly cover my mouth, hoping Mustache didn't hear me. "There it is," I whisper-hiss to Joey. We close the space between us and a carving that is the spitting image of Larry. The hulking figure of Bigfoot lumbering across the forest floor is so familiar that my eyes begin to well with tears. I dash them away because, dammit, I need my full vision to assess if this is the real Larry or just a close cousin.

When I lean down to get within inches of his huge feet, I gasp again. "Right there!" I whisper, and Joey leans down so our faces are only inches apart. "You see that little groove in the foot?" When Joey nods, I explain, "That's where Miller tried to put flip-flops on him when he was little. Thankfully, Mama caught him in the act before he carved more than a scratch."

"So this is the real deal?"

I nod, biting my lip as we both straighten again. I hadn't let myself genuinely believe Larry would be here, so I have no concrete plan for proceeding from here. Didn't the gallery authenticate the sculpture before buying it, like Carter said? I don't actually know how any of this works, I remind myself.

Joey points to the plaque nearby. "This just says 'Morton Frye' and 'unknown date.' Not a lot of info to go on."

I push back my nerves and turn to seek out Mustache again, but I stop short when he magically appears in front of us. "Ah, the Morton Frye piece. Intriguing, isn't it?" He's all smiles, and I have trouble reading anything but pride and pleasure in his expression. This guy doesn't look like someone who regularly bashes in patio doors and steals family heirlooms.

"I'm a big fan," I manage. "Can you tell me about the piece?"

"Not a lot, I'm afraid." His lips even again. "This piece is on loan and not for sale. The owner is quite the collector, but he didn't have much information either. We know it's a Frye from signature analysis on the underside, but that's about it. There are many undiscovered Frye works out there, as he was a very prolific artist even early on."

We both nod, and I venture ahead. "So, who is this collector, if you don't mind me asking?"

"Not at all. Although I feel I should warn you, he doesn't part with his pieces easily."

Joey's arm goes around my shoulders, and he pulls me into his side before I can even begin to guess his intentions. "Well, my wife is used to getting what she wants. I'm sure she can sway him."

Mustache raises a brow and heads back to his desk. "I'll get you his contact information, then."

Ten minutes later, we're in the truck again, and my phone

is to my ear as I wait for a Mr. G. Taylor to pick up his phone. "Voicemail," I say to Joey as the greeting plays. When the beep comes, I say, "Hello, Mr. Taylor. My name is Lynn, and I got your information from the Mintz Gallery. I was hoping to speak with you about the Morton Frye piece you've so kindly lent to the gallery. Could you please call me back at your earliest convenience?" I leave my number and end the call before bringing the phone to my lap.

"What now?" Joey asks, one hand on the steering wheel and his handsome face turned my way.

"It would suck to come all this way just to go right back home without more information."

Joey stares at his hand for a few seconds before opening his door again. "Be right back," he says before jogging down the sidewalk and disappearing behind the gallery doors. What is he doing?

He's back less than a minute later and climbing into the driver's seat, his phone in his good hand. "I snapped a picture just in case we need it."

Why didn't I think of that? "Oh. Good thinking." If we do have to head home, at least I can prove to my brothers—and the cops—that it is indeed our Larry in that gallery. "Do you think we should try to find out where this Taylor guy works and maybe hunt him down there?"

That plan is dashed when we look up G. Taylor online and find over fifteen people living within the Raleigh-Durham area. Damn.

"We'll just have to wait, I guess."

I drum my fingers on the armrest and rack my brain for ideas.

"We should go have some fun," Joey says. His eyes suddenly widen, and he furiously types into his phone before turning to me again. "The Bulls have a game starting in thirty!."

"The Bulls? Aren't they a basketball team from Chicago?" I may not be a sports nut, but everyone knows Michael Jordan.

"The Durham Bulls. Minor League Baseball team? You have to have heard of them."

"Hmm. Isn't there some old movie about them?"

Joey looks at me like I just called his mom a skank. "You're screwing with me, right?" When my expression doesn't change, he bangs his head on the steering wheel. "*Bull Durham*. It's the first of Kevin Costner's three-part love letter to the game of baseball!" He lifts his head and adopts a pleading tone. "*Field of Dreams*? *For Love of the Game*?"

I brighten. "If you build it, he will come!"

"Oh, thank God."

His level of despair and subsequent relief have me laughing out loud. "I warned you."

He shakes his head, finally recovering from the torture I put him through. "So, how about it? A summer afternoon at the ballpark?"

I fight a nose wrinkle. "Maybe we should focus on our mission. Besides, we spend half our time at a ballpark as it is."

"That's not the same. I promise. The audience experience is a whole other ball game, pardon the pun."

"You and Sadie," I mutter, immediately wishing I hadn't.

"Who's Sadie?"

I wave him off. "Just a friend who loves to give me a hard time. Never mind."

When Joey looks at me like a dog in front of a store

window full of tennis balls, I relent. "Okay, Mr. Costner, let's go to the ballpark."

It might do me some good to get Larry off my mind. I can't fathom how he ended up in that gallery. If this Taylor guy stole him out of some sick desire to have this particular piece among his collection, why would he put it on display in public? There's got to be an explanation, and G. Taylor is the key. I'm not leaving Raleigh until I talk to him. So, I may as well do something that makes my friend happy while I wait.

Joey grins and starts the car, almost bouncing in his seat. It's easy saying yes to him, and I'm beginning to fear I can't resist any of this man's suggestions—which could spell real trouble for my future.

TWENTY-SIX

WHY DO HOTEL ROOMS HAVE BIBLES ANYWAY?

JOEY

"Come on, guys! Run faster!" Lynn shouts, both hands cupped around her mouth, as one Bulls player advances to second while the batter outruns the first baseman to safety on first. I don't even try suppressing my grin.

Turns out that Lynn has been watching baseball all wrong. And when I say that, I mean she's only seen it on TV.

When she catches me smiling at her, she smacks my good arm. "Stop laughing at me."

"I'm not laughing at you; I'm enjoying your company."

Heat rises to her cheeks, and it's not from the sunny afternoon. "Okay, you were right. Baseball is pretty fun."

"The beer doesn't hurt either," I say, reaching down to snag the plastic cup resting at my feet. We're sitting in the stands here at Durham Bulls Athletic Park. We scored good seats behind the visitors' dugout, and it's the ideal place to catch all the action. The Bulls aren't an Arrows' farm team, but I follow them more closely than most other minors teams since they're sort of local. They've got some good talent, and I imagine I'll end up playing against some of these guys at some point or another.

"No, it does not," Lynn agrees, taking a sip of her beer. "But don't tell my brothers I'm drinking mainstream light beer. Their pride will be wounded to the point where it will never recover."

"Consider it our secret."

"So, I've been watching the shortstop." Lynn props her sunglasses on top of her head and eyes me. "That does *not* look like an easy job at all."

"Nope. But I enjoy a challenge."

"No kidding, Ace." She rolls her eyes on a grin, and I wink at her. Her meaning didn't get past me.

"As much as I love earning a nickname from you, I feel it's my duty to tell you Ace is reserved for pitchers, not shortstops."

She turns back to me with narrowed eyes. "I've already got too many baseball rules filling up my brain for one day, so you're gonna have to let that one go."

I chuckle and give her a pass. "So, are you going to become an Arrows fan now?"

"Possibly. Although I work during all the home games, so…"

Time to test the waters and see if they're shark-infested or not. "Maybe I'll have to fly you out for an away game then."

Instead of scolding me for laying it on too thick, she shrugs and turns her eyes back to the field. "Maybe."

Fuck, yes! I'm thinking I can bid farewell to the friend zone pretty damn soon. Maybe even today.

When we hit the seventh inning stretch, Lynn belts out

"Take Me Out to the Ball Game" louder than anyone in our section, even throwing her arm around my waist and making me sway with her and the rest of the crowd. I could get used to this—afternoons at the ballpark with Lynn Brooks? That wouldn't suck.

"I'll be right back," Lynn says before taking off for the bathroom. While she's gone, I take a shot of the mascot running around on the field and text it to Gunner.

ME:

I might be able to live with this bum wrist after all.

GUNNER:

Is that the Bulls? You're an ass.

ME:

Hey, it's not my fault I can't play. Blame it on Niederman.

GUNNER:

Enjoy yourself while you can, buddy. There will be no time to rest when you're off the IL.

ME:

How's Colorado?

GUNNER:

Cold. Like your heart.

My lips curve as I shove my phone back into my pocket and the players retake the field.

Lynn is gone for a while but reappears at the top of the eighth with an armful of nachos and a Durham Bulls ball cap on her head. Fuck, why is that so hot? I'll need to get her an Arrows cap to amp up the look.

"You just couldn't stay away from the nacho cheese, could you?"

"Sauce, remember? There's no cheese in here. Only delicious chemicals." She smiles as she settles in next to me again and hands me a container of nachos. I dip a chip into the sauce, careful to catch a jalapeño slice before crunching it in my mouth. "I don't care what's in them. They taste *amazing*."

She giggles, and it hits me in the solar plexus. "I know, right?" When she shoves a stacked nacho in her mouth and snorts at the sauce dribbling down her chin, I'm pretty sure I fall in love.

At several points during the game, Lynn pulls her phone out to check for any sign of G. Taylor, but his number never appears. Not that it affects Lynn's enjoyment of the game. She watches each play like someone's life depends on it and cheers at the Bulls' every success. There are lots of times where I have to explain what's happening or tell her why someone is called out, but it only fuels her interest.

When the last out is called, the Bulls have won 9 to 4, and we both stand to clap for the team. I consider heading down to chat with some of the players, but I'd rather spend my time alone with Lynn.

"What next?" I ask when we're walking through the parking lot to my truck. Lynn's shoulders are sun-kissed in the snug tank top she's paired with her pink shorts and sneakers. She wore a more conservative skirt and short-sleeved sweater for our visit to the gallery but swapped it out in the stadium bathroom as soon as we arrived. I've noticed her preference for more casual attire, and it only makes me more confident in our compatibility.

I'm unsure what Lynn wants to do about Larry at this

point, so I throw an offer out. "If you want, we can head home, and you can keep trying this Taylor guy by phone. Or if you'd rather hold out for a face-to-face, we can always grab a hotel and hope to set something up tomorrow."

Lynn's teeth tug at her bottom lip as she thinks it over. Part of me was worried she might read into my hotel suggestion and tell me to back off. Not that I don't have plenty of ideas of how to entertain ourselves in a hotel room, but I've already vowed not to push it until I get the green light.

She glances down at her watch and asks, "Can we maybe grab dinner and play it by ear? I'm hoping he'll call, and I'd hate to miss my chance."

"You sure you can eat after those nachos?"

"Those, sir, were an appetizer at best," she declares, hands on her hips beside my truck. The fact that she doesn't hide her enjoyment of food is an absolute turn-on. It tells me she's not concealing her true self from me like so many women I've known. There's no façade, just Lynn, and that's hot as hell—as are the hips that curve out so nicely from her waist.

I open the passenger door for her. "By all means, then, take me to dinner, madam."

We end up at a burger place near the stadium, where we eat until our stomachs hurt. I stick to water since I'm driving, but Lynn orders a wheat beer, claiming she needs to redeem herself in the eyes of the craft-beer gods.

"Ow." Lynn sinks down into her chair, one hand resting on her stomach. "I'm afraid that was a horrible mistake. But it was so good." She groans and shifts her eyes around the pub. "Would it be rude of me to unbutton my shorts in the middle of a restaurant?"

I narrowly avoid choking on my water. "I'm always in favor of clothing removal, no matter the venue. Have at it."

"I walked right into that one, didn't I?" She grins on a sigh. "I'm thinking Mr. Taylor isn't going to be calling me back tonight."

"Why don't you try him one more time?"

"You don't think he'll find it a little stalkerish?"

"Nah. Go ahead."

As she's dialing, the waiter comes with our bill, and I hand him my credit card.

Lynn scowls silently with the phone pressed to her ear, mouthing, "I was going to get that."

"You paid for the nachos," I whisper back in exaggerated fashion, making her wave me off in a gesture I peg as half amused and half irritated. I just smile to myself.

She pulls the phone from her ear and jabs the end-call button. "Voicemail again. Damn."

Since she knows I'm up for staying the night, I don't say anything, instead waiting for her to suggest it. Which she finally does after some hemming and hawing.

"If you're sure you're okay with it, let's get a hotel and try hunting this guy down tomorrow. I don't feel right leaving town with Larry so close."

"Sounds like a plan," I agree, hoping whatever hotel we choose only has one room left. A guy can wish, right?

Twenty minutes later, I use a keycard to open the door of a room on the tenth floor of a downtown Hilton. If I thought winning a game against the Devils was a battle, I've been proven wrong by the war I just waged at the front desk with Lynn.

There's a convention in town that's jacked up all the hotel rates, so despite Lynn's insistence that she'd pay for a room of her own, she wasn't prepared for the price tag. Her face went a bit ashen, in fact. When I offered to pick up the tab for her room, she balked, as expected. We ended up arguing back and forth for a good five minutes in the lobby before she finally relented, satisfying herself that she could live with me paying for one room with two queen beds where we'd each take one bed. Good Christ. But it was all worth it because now we're sharing a room, just as I'd hoped.

Did my man, Justin Verlander, have to work this hard to win over Kate Upton?

The light automatically turns on when we enter the room, sans luggage but with a set of toothbrushes from the front desk. Since I normally sleep in just my boxers, I'm good. Lynn, on the other hand, I suspect will be sleeping fully clothed and maybe with a partition from maintenance erected between our beds.

"Thanks again," she says, setting her giant handbag on the closest bed and looking at her shoes. "We probably should have just gone home, huh?"

Hell no. "No." I shake my head. "I told you before, I get paid well—and I'm not saying that to brag; it's just a fact—so this is no skin off my nose. And I would have been happy to pay for a second room." When she tries to interrupt and start another battle, I put my hand up. "But I understand you don't want handouts, and I'm good with it."

She closes her mouth and nods before sitting on the edge of the bed and looking at her phone screen again. It remains blank. "Thanks for understanding."

The last thing I want is for her to feel guilty for standing up for herself. "No problem. I actually prefer sharing a room. Other people's snoring helps me sleep."

She bites back a laugh. "That might be the weirdest thing I've heard. But you're out of luck because I don't snore."

"Damn." I snap my fingers in an *aw shucks* gesture. "Well, in that case, let's ditch this place and head back to Asheville."

She smiles and watches me for a few seconds, her posture relaxing and her eyes going soft in a way I haven't seen before. "You're a really good guy, Joey Martel. Do you know that?"

Not sure what to say in return, I simply shrug and respond, "I try." Then, wanting to get us out of both her guilt spiral and the serious mood permeating the room, I draw in a breath and throw my arms out. "So! What should we do first? Raid the minibar or read the Bible?" I head for the overpriced minibar to examine its contents, but when I turn around to share our options, Lynn is standing right in front of me.

"Oh. Hey." I look down at her. "What'll it be? Smirnoff or Jack Daniels? I don't really see you as a whiskey kind of—" Lynn's lips cut off my words as she boosts herself up to her tiptoes and plants a kiss on my surprised mouth.

Hell. Yes.

TWENTY-SEVEN

IS THERE A CURE FOR THIS KIND OF FEVER?

LYNN

I can't allow myself to think about how stupid I might be for doing this right now. Kindness is apparently my kryptonite. I never saw myself getting all swoony over an athlete or someone as conventionally cool and masculine as Joey, but I was wrong. He's turned out to be everything I could ever want. And even though I'm not in a place where I'm ready for a relationship, there's nothing wrong with having a little fun with a nice guy who happens to be hot as sin and built like a Roman god—if Roman gods played baseball and had fantastic forearms and thighs like Joey's.

I knew he'd be surprised by my kiss, but it takes him no time to get on board with my new plan for passing the evening in this hotel room. His arms wrap around my middle, and he pulls me into him so our bodies come flush from knees to lips. His kisses are addictive, and his scent of sunscreen, copper, and sandalwood has my senses buzzing. Joey's hands slide from my waist to my butt, and I can feel his growing arousal against my belly. I want it. I want him.

And I don't want to think about anything else right now besides Joey and how it will feel to have him inside me.

Joey's thumbs catch the waistband of my shorts and start stroking the bare skin beneath, sending my belly swinging down and then up like I just flipped upside down on a roller coaster. The friction of his calluses against my skin has a bolt of desire shooting directly to my womb.

Since I have no desire to pretend or play games now that I know what I want, I slide my hands down his back to the hem of his T-shirt and pull up. He reads my intentions, releasing my lips for only the time it takes to yank his shirt over his head, giving my hands and fingers the treat of a lifetime.

This boy is *cut*. My fingers skate over his skin, exploring the topography of his stomach, chest, shoulders, and back. I can't get enough of the warm, smooth skin covering all that firm muscle. It's a literal party for my hands.

It doesn't take long for Joey to return the favor and rid me of my T-shirt as well. His fingers are crafty, and my bra is only a memory as our mouths remain engaged in wet, seeking kisses. My panties are so wet, I know he'll be able to feel how turned on I am even through my shorts. While the thought might embarrass me with anyone else, it emboldens me with Joey.

My fingers continue gliding across Joey's skin as he breaks our kiss to nuzzle down my neck, trailing his lips over my pulse point and making me shiver with desire. Goose bumps rise to the surface of my skin, and he pulls his mouth from my throat to ask, "Are you cold?"

"No!" I practically shout before delving my fingers into his hair and almost suffocating him by pulling his face back into my neck. I feel the vibration of his chuckle against my skin, and the sensation is dizzying.

Joey's hands slide lower until they settle on the backs of my thighs, and I let out a little yelp when he picks me up off the floor, our chests and mouths finally aligning without me having to be on my tiptoes or him having to give himself a crick in his neck.

"Your wrist!" I scold.

"Can't feel anything. Ignore it. I'm fine," he murmurs against my neck. Oh well, he should know if it hurts or not.

It's only fair that I help him, though, so I circle his waist with my legs and lock them behind his back. This brings a groan from his throat, and his hands immediately cup my ass again.

Next thing I know, my back hits the bed in a maneuver Joey somehow manages without re-injuring his wrist. My legs retain their boa constrictor hold on his body as he slides down a touch and covers one of my aroused nipples with his hot mouth. My back arches off the bed when he draws the peak in and swirls his tongue around it just right. I grasp his hair and let out a long moan that our neighbors can probably hear. But they'll just have to deal.

A wildfire spreads through my lower belly and down my thighs, causing them to tighten around him, placing my heels against his firm butt in our new position. I need my hands on that ass sometime very soon. When he bites down on my nipple, I make a sound I've never made before, causing him to let out a ragged growl before he moves to the other nipple.

But I need to feel the hardness of his arousal against me, skin to skin—to rub my aching center over him and feel his heat and thickness. I've had enough of these pesky clothes between us.

Before I become a complete panting mess without the ability of speech, I plead, "Joey, I need you." My voice is so breathy, I don't recognize it as my own. I sound wanton and needy, a candid reflection of my every feeling.

His mouth makes a popping sound as he releases my nipple, and his eyes come up to meet mine. If I thought those espresso depths were beautiful before, it's nothing compared to the wonder of visceral desire and emotion in them now. My pterodactyls have been scattered to the wind by the blazing fire sweeping through my lower region, leaving nothing but an ache and a void that only Joey can fill. I've never felt so desperate in my life, and it's both exhilarating and terrifying. I don't lose control, and right now I have zero power over my body or brain.

Which is why I don't protest when Joey unpeels my legs from around him and goes down on his knees at the side of the bed. His fingers work the button of my shorts loose before he yanks them and my panties down in one quick motion, leaving me completely naked on the bed.

That's when I decide I need to get my wits about me—and fast—if I'm ever going to have my way with this man. To that end, I knife up in bed.

"No, stay where you are," he instructs with a jaw so tight I'm afraid he might crack something.

When I go for the button of his jeans, I barely get it loose before he grabs both my wrists with a strength that surprises me. This boy is *keyed up*.

"We've got all night," he says in that deep rumble I love so much. "I want to taste you."

Mother mercy. I've never had someone speak so explicitly about their desires. Of course, I've only really been with boys, not men. I'm beginning to understand the difference, and it's an imperative distinction.

I pretty much collapse back onto the bed at Joey's statement, my limbs suddenly not feeling so eager to hold me up. His lips trace a path up my right leg and down my left as his calloused hands caress me, and then I feel the light stubble of his chin tickling my inner thighs. He hauls my thighs over his shoulders in one quick movement, and then his mouth is *right there*. Thank you, Jesus.

My back arches right off the bed, my heels digging into his shoulder blades now, as I moan into the quiet of the room. I think I hear him whispering as he licks and nuzzles my center, but I can't be sure. And there's no way I'm interrupting him to ask because right then his tongue delves inside me, and a shiver of ecstasy consumes my entire body.

"Fuck, you taste good," Joey rumbles when he comes up for air, never giving me a moment of reprieve as his fingers take over where his tongue left off. They twist and swirl, working me into a frenzy that has only one place to go.

When his tongue rejoins his talented fingers, it's only seconds until my cry of release bounces off the hotel room walls. And it's not a dainty little sigh; it's a full-blown damn-that's-fucking-hot pronouncement. Joey groans in satisfaction and licks my center like he's searching for the last drops of hot fudge at the bottom of a sundae bowl. It's only then I realize I've been yanking and pulling his sweat-dampened hair the entire time, possibly rendering him prematurely bald in spots.

Before I can do so much as apologize or regain my breath, he releases my legs and stands, shucking his jeans and boxers and releasing his hard cock for my eyes to feast.

He's thick and long, impossibly hard, and my mouth begins to water. I've never in my life had my mouth water at the sight or thought of a man's cock. It's like I've contracted some fever that makes me want to gobble a man up in one bite. Best sickness I've ever had, bar none.

I'm too busy admiring his penis to notice he's produced a condom from somewhere until he says my name. "Lynn." My eyes dart up to meet his, and I find two warm espresso pools gazing down at me with molten desire. "Are you good?" His rumble has a healthy dose of gravel now, and I feel it everywhere.

I know what he's asking and can't nod fast enough. I want him inside me like I've never wanted anything before. He doesn't waste time rolling the condom on his length and then climbing on the bed to settle his weight over me.

His elbows fall to either side of me, supporting his weight as his eyes roam my face and his thumbs brush my cheeks. For some strange reason, tears spring to my eyes, but I refuse to have anything cloud my view of his face so close to mine while our naked bodies align. My fingertips skate down the muscles and ridges of his broad shoulders and back until I slide one down to reach between us and take him in my hand. When my knees fall open, he takes over, notching himself at my center and nudging into me with care.

"You don't need to be gentle," I tell him, and he takes me at my word, pushing forward until he's half seated. We both groan at the sensation before he pulls out and thrusts back in, fully inside me now. My head falls back, my eyes closing, so I can focus only on my sense of touch for this brief moment.

I'm more full than I've ever been, but I need him to

move. I need friction and pressure along with this delicious fullness.

Joey reads my mind and pulls halfway out before thrusting all the way in again. Then he begins to establish a rhythm, one that works me up into a panting mess once more. The strokes that began carefully quickly increase in power and abandon, the sounds of our bodies connecting drawing in another of my senses. Joey's scent of clean sweat and spice engages my sense of smell next, so I open my eyes to watch the intensity in his gaze as he powers in and out of me. The only sense left is taste, so I lift my head and capture his mouth in a kiss that has me seeing stars.

He's captured all of my senses now, tying me up with his entire presence, his whole being, and as my second orgasm of the night begins to wash over me, I fear this man might be capturing something else I'm not ready to give—my heart.

JOEY

"Were you whispering to my vagina earlier?" Lynn asks as we're spooning in the hotel bed.

I choke out a laugh, and it takes me a minute to catch my breath. I'm just now recovering from the near heart attack I experienced from coming harder than I ever have before. Everything with Lynn feels like the first time, and I can't make heads or tails of it. But it doesn't have to make sense for me to want to hold onto it just the same.

"Well?" I can hear the smile in her voice.

"Yes, I was." I'm not ashamed to admit it.

Her responding laugh has her naked ass pushing back into my cock, making me stifle a groan. "Care to share?"

"Nope. It's between me and Little Lynn."

"You did not just call my privates *Little Lynn*."

"Hey, if you can break the rules and call me Ace—*and* name a car and a statue—I can give a nickname to my favorite spot on Earth."

She snorts, and I find it adorable. Hell, Lynn could probably burp the alphabet, and I'd find it cute. "Somebody's laying it on a little thick."

"Not at all." I slide the hand that's at her curved belly down to cup her pubis, a move that has her squirming. "I'm thinking about moving in."

"It's gonna be a little hard catching and throwing a baseball with one hand stuck in my pants the whole time."

I skim my hand back over her belly and up to cup her breast. She has got a spectacular set of boobs, and I can't wait to get in more playtime. "I'm committed to making it work."

"You're ridiculous."

"And you're beautiful," I murmur as I place a kiss behind her ear.

She squirms again and stifles a yawn. "I'm tired is what I am. I couldn't sleep last night thinking about Larry."

I don't tell her that I slept like a baby after jerking off while picturing her in my shower. Instead, I say, "Go to sleep," tightening my hold on her and settling into the pillow.

I'm awoken in the middle of the night with Lynn's lips around my cock, and it takes a good ten seconds to realize it's not a dream. Her ministrations blow my biggest fantasies out of the water, and I return the favor by fingering her to another orgasm before we both drift off again.

Sunlight filtering through the hotel curtains finally wakes me hours later. I open my eyes to find that Lynn has taken over most of the bed, sprawling herself in a big X and using my chest as a pillow. I try not to laugh, knowing the movement will disturb her. Instead, I let my eyes roam over her naked body, freed from the sheets by her thrashing during the night.

Long, shapely legs lead to a perfect heart-shaped ass that tapers into her narrowed waist. Her skin is luminescent and silky, touched by the sun almost everywhere but her ass and the strip of light skin across her back. I want to taste every inch of her. I want to worship her body and make her laugh and draw more of those playful scowls from her. I want to hear her orgasm and watch her ride me. I want to have her every way I can and then invent new, impossible ways. I want to hear her secrets and worries. I want to take care of her. Even if that's the last thing she wants.

Lynn stirs, nuzzling into my chest as she awakens. My cock perks up, thinking it's go time, but I ignore it the best I can.

"I can confirm you don't snore," I say once I'm sure she's awake. "You do, however, thrash."

She lifts her head, half-lidded eyes scanning my face and then the bed before she faceplants back into my chest. "I forgot to mention that." Her words are garbled against my skin.

"As long as you're naked when you're thrashing, I'm all good."

As if only now realizing how bare she is, she yelps and catapults off my body to drag the loose sheet around herself, completely exposing me in the process. This has her yelping again and throwing a pillow over my junk. By the time she stills, I'm laughing so hard I'm afraid I'm going to bust something.

"It's not that funny," she finally says, her cheeks a pretty pink and her eyes trying their best to battle against a roll. "Okay, fine," she finally concedes when I start laughing all over again. She's such a contradiction sometimes—steadfast in her independence and maturity, yet even a mention of being naked fills her cheeks with heat.

When she climbs off the bed, though, I stop laughing immediately. "Hey, come back here!"

"I'm going to the bathroom," she calls behind her as she strides away covered in an impromptu toga. "Not streaking in the lobby."

I can hear the water in the sink and figure she's brushing her teeth, something I could probably afford to do myself before I scare Lynn away with my dragon breath. By the time she emerges, I've donned boxers to keep her from possibly assaulting my cock with more pillows. On my way past, I stop at her side and drop a kiss on her bare shoulder, exposed by her sheet toga.

But I've barely stepped on the bathroom's tile floor when I hear Lynn's voice. "No!" I quickly retrace my steps to find her sitting on the edge of the bed, phone in hand. Her eyes flash to my face. "He called." She lets out a pained whimper before finishing, "Last night."

My chin jerks back. "We would have heard it. Did you have your ringer off?"

She bites her lip and fixes her eyes on a spot somewhere over my left shoulder. "Um, no. I think maybe we were just a little… unfocused."

Ah. Yeah, that tracks. "Shit. I'm sorry. Call him back."

"He left a voicemail." She thumbs her screen and presses the speaker button on her voicemail message.

A man's deep voice says, "Hello, this is Guy Taylor returning your call about the Morton Frye sculpture. Looks like I missed you. I'm at the airport headed overseas in a few minutes, but I'll be back on Tuesday and will try you again then. Cheers."

Well, shit. I glance at Lynn's face and see that it's fallen. "I'm sorry, Lynn. At least you know the statue is safe until he gets back, though."

Her expression brightens a bit at that. Part of me worried she might take the phenomenal night we just had and turn it upside down in her head into something negative. Thank God she hasn't.

"You're right. Larry isn't going anywhere. But we probably should." Her nose wrinkles like she's not too fond of the notion, which echoes my sentiments exactly. But when I look at my watch, I know she's right.

"Crap. It's almost checkout time. How did we sleep in so late?"

"I guess I tired you out, Ace." The renewed sparkle in her eyes has me wanting to tackle her to the bed and have my way with her again, but we've got all the time in the world now that the friend zone is in our rearview.

"ARE you sure this is a good idea?" Lynn asks for the fifth time since I told her I was dropping her off at her mom's house. "What if one of the He-Men has stopped by?"

"Then we deal. They're going to find out sooner or later." When I picked her up yesterday, nobody was home but her, so we were met with zero reaction or resistance. I didn't even get to meet the famous Mango the skunk.

I'm pleased when she doesn't argue with my intimation that we're now a couple that will be seen as such—outside of work, that is.

"It's your funeral," she mumbles under her breath. I reach out and squeeze her hand in reassurance.

"I got this. Just you wait."

I don't hear whatever she mutters into the passenger mirror in response, but that's okay. She's got nothing to worry about.

But when we round the bend to approach the set of three houses lined up at the end of the road, my confidence takes a little bit of a hit. One brother would be a breeze. Two would be a fun challenge. But all four? I wasn't prepared for that. Oh well, no prize worth winning was ever won easily. Bring it on, Brooks family.

"What in the world?" Lynn asks from beside me, her brow furrowed at the sight of four grown men crossing their arms, legs shoulder-width apart like identical sentries guarding a queen. Or, in this case, a little sister.

Lynn is out the door before I can even put the truck into park on the gravel drive.

"Are you serious with this shit?!" She's spitting mad, but not one of them appears the least bit ruffled by her fire.

"Quiet down!" Carter yells, making me move my ass from the driver's seat with increased urgency. No way is he going to talk to my girl like that.

"I can say whatever I damn well please, however loud I like, you asshat!"

Okay, so maybe she doesn't need me as much as I'd maybe hoped. Oh well.

"What are you going on about?" the only unfamiliar one in the foursome hisses. This must be Denny Brooks, the only brother who doesn't work at the brewery. "Be quiet. We don't want to clue them in."

Lynn's stomping halts, and she stops a few feet from her brothers. "Wait. What?"

I'm only a couple feet behind at that point, but none of the brothers are looking at me. Their gazes are either on Lynn or the house next to their mom's.

Miller throws a chin at the neighbor's house. "One of those developers is in Winston's house. She was here yesterday, asking for Mama."

Lynn's jaw drops, and she spins on her sneakers to face the house. A blue Lexus sits in the driveway, but there's no sign of anyone. "That's the same car I saw the other day in his driveway! I knew I recognized it from somewhere!"

Cash curses. "She's been in there since this morning. Miller called us." He turns to his brothers. "One of us has to go open the brewery."

"I'm not moving until I talk to this interloper," Carter declares. Interloper? Maybe he plays Scrabble too.

"And I'm not moving until Winston explains himself," Miller challenges, hands now on his hips.

"Don't look at me," Denny chimes in, palms out. "I don't know how to open."

Cash scowls at each one in turn before muttering, "Fine, I'll do it myself. But you'd better call me the minute you find anything out."

"You got it." Carter nods, and Cash storms toward a beat-up car that could give Lynn's ailing Priscilla a run for her money.

It isn't until he's a couple feet from the car that he spins around, a finger jabbing my way like he wishes he were close enough to remove one of my eyeballs with it. "And what did I tell you, Martel?!"

I can only shrug. "I've never been a particularly good listener, Brooks."

Another few curses under his breath, and Cash tears his gaze from mine before hopping in his car and speeding from the driveway. Gravel spews from beneath his tires, and I jump out of the way to avoid it. That could have gone worse. One down, three to go.

LYNN

I shake my head at Joey and then turn my attention to my remaining brothers. "You guys look ridiculous out here. Stop being so obvious, and at least go inside and watch from the kitchen window."

They meet each other's gazes and silently agree to follow my suggestion. Joey and I trail behind by a few feet.

"Next thing you know, they're going to pee on Mama's front door to mark their territory," I hiss as we approach the bright yellow front door decorated with a Bigfoot sign that says "Believe."

We all file down the hall and into the kitchen before Joey speaks up again. "So, uh, what's going on?"

Denny runs his fingers through his light brown waves as he looks Joey up and down. Here we go. "Anybody want to explain what Joey Martel is doing in Mama's kitchen?"

I step in front of Joey as a human shield. "I invited him."

For once, Carter sets his caveman tendencies aside and answers Joey's initial question. "Developers come sniffing around now and then wanting to buy up these three properties—either to build a mountain mansion or clear the forest and build a whole neighborhood of them, I don't know. Either way, it doesn't matter because we're not selling."

"They can do that?" Miller asks. "Clear the forest?"

Carter shrugs and heads for the refrigerator before pulling out a few bottled waters and offering them around. Joey and I each take one.

"They can do anything they damn well please if they get the properties." Carter opens a bottle and throws back half its contents in one go.

"But the Blue Ridge Parkway," Denny says, and I'm unsure of his exact meaning. "These properties all back up into the Blue Ridge Parkway National Park land."

"No. They can't touch the state lands or any of the national parklands. But anything private that butts up to it is fair game," Carter explains.

I try to imagine what it would look like to have Winston's entire property cleared of trees and filled with fancy houses. "Why would someone ever want to clear the forest? That's... crazy!" I exclaim.

I'm surprised when Joey is the one to answer. "For a picturesque view. For money. Because they can. You've got to be careful with these kinds of assholes with big budgets. They have their ways of getting you to sell, even if you don't want to. I'd watch your backs for sure."

Everyone falls silent for a few seconds until Miller thrusts his balled fist into the doorjamb. "Fuck! If Winston folds, I'm gonna punch him in his shriveled old balls."

My brother will have to get in line. Winston is a quiet but grumpy old neighbor who keeps to himself when he's not birdwatching in his underwear from his back porch. He's not the best neighbor, but I never thought he'd think of selling.

"Where's Mama?" I ask, glancing around in case I somehow missed her.

"At the senior center. They've got a resident art exhibit she's helping set up."

"Oh, god, tell me it's not more penis bouquet paintings." Denny winces from his spot in front of the kitchen window, where he's watching Winston's house for activity. When Joey looks like he's about to ask for some explanation, I wave him off in a gesture I hope communicates that he's better off not knowing. Mama told me about some of the art instructor's previous projects with the senior center residents, and it sounds like she enjoys letting them explore their creativity in lots of ways I don't need to witness.

"Well, we need to call her and tell her." I pull my phone from my pocket, but Cart swipes it from me before I can dial. I glare at him.

"No way. She doesn't need to worry about this until we know there's something to worry about."

My eyes flash Joey's way as if to say, *see what I'm dealing with here.* But his expression signals he agrees with my brothers, so I huff my indignance and decide to save my fight for the next battle.

"I say we all go over and knock on the door. See what they have to say for themselves," Denny suggests.

"Four burly dudes and a mad-as-hell woman pounding down his front door isn't the way to reason with Winston," I argue.

Denny cusses and then concedes, "Yeah, you probably have a point."

"Mama is the best one to talk to him. He likes her, and

she can sweet-talk him into confiding in her. You know it's true."

"Lynnie's right," Carter admits, and I fight the smile that's trying to take over my lips. Damn straight, I am. Mama can talk a bald man into buying a curling iron. She can certainly get the dirt from an old man.

"Just make sure Adrina isn't within a two-mile radius when she does," Denny adds, making all of us but Joey nod in agreement. On the occasions I've witnessed them together, Adrina and Winston butted heads on every topic. Best to keep her clear for sure.

We all stare out the window, drinking our water for a few silent minutes, and I'm sure my brothers' minds are racing just as fast as mine. A strange prickling sensation starts at the base of my spine and works its way up to the back of my neck, where it shocks me like mid-winter static. Now I understand what people mean when they say a ghost just walked over their grave.

"Joey?" He turns at the sound of my voice. "What did you mean when you said these people have ways of making you sell even if you don't want to?"

As my words hang in the air, Cart, Denny, and Miller turn their eyes to me one at a time. We share heavy glances before every single one of us simultaneously mutters, "Shit."

"I DON'T GET IT. How did we get from a real estate developer inquiring about a property to arson, burglary, and attempted murder?" Joey asks from his spot next to me on the sofa. He doesn't look so good. Maybe I should get him to lie down.

All my brothers but Denny have scattered, each taking off for work and likely racking their brains like we're doing. We collectively decided it wouldn't be smart to tip the developer lady off until we'd had more time to think. Denny summoned Luca up the mountain to compare notes with him as well. In addition to being neighbors, the two of them have been best friends since the womb, so it's no surprise Luca was brought into the circle. He can keep his mouth shut so his mom doesn't hear about it and parade over to Winston's with a pitchfork to demand the developer woman's head.

In the meantime, I've dug the woman's card out of the junk drawer in the kitchen, and we're all gathered around the coffee table in the den staring at it. Maude E. Christopher works for a company called The Diamond Group as a developmental specialist, whatever that means.

"Does Martel need to be here?" Denny asks instead of answering Joey's question.

"Yes." My voice is firm as I throw daggers at my brother.

"What's going on between you two?" His jaw tightens, and I fight another eye roll. This surgery is getting closer and closer, I swear.

Joey's "We're dating" and my "None of your business" leave our mouths at the exact same second.

At Joey's words, I cradle my forehead in my hand, bracing for what comes next.

What I don't expect is for Luca to speak first. "Cool." He reaches a hand across to Joey, and my sort-of, kind-of new boyfriend (EEK!) takes it. "Luca Carmichael. I guess we haven't officially met."

When I chance a peek at Denny, hoping maybe he's taken a cue from his best friend, I'm unsurprised to see his jaw ticcing under the scruff on his chin. I send him what I can only describe as a glare combined with an expectant jerk of my chin. A glare-jerk for my jerk of a brother.

But instead of being a grown adult like Luca, Denny averts his gaze and finally answers Joey's question. "It's obviously just conjecture at this point, but a lot of shit has been swirling around our family in the last year and a half, and not all of it can be explained. Like the fire that was set behind the house—it could have burned all three houses to the ground, and the cops never caught whoever set it. It would be a hell of a lot easier convincing three reluctant landowners to sell if their houses were no longer standing, right?"

We all nod before I take over. "Then the break-in at the brewery when Larry was stolen. He's the only thing of real value our family owns. If Mama were to get in real financial trouble—like, say, a fire that burned her house down— having Larry's value to fall back on might become crucial. Cash and Cart are barely in the black with the brewery, Miller can't be making much, and Mama's job at the senior center sure as hell isn't about making money."

"I bring home an okay paycheck, but not the kind that can save a house," Denny adds.

"So, you think the developers might have set the fire and stolen Larry?" Joey shoots me a concerned look. I know what he's thinking. I haven't told my brothers I found Larry yet.

Denny shrugs and collapses back in the armchair across from us, finally having loosened his tight jaw. "Hell if I know."

Thankfully, Joey lets the Larry thing go for now, asking

instead, "And the, um, attempted murder?" He looks decidedly uncomfortable.

"Okay, that one's a stretch." Denny rolls his eyes at me. "Lynn still has faith that our little brother can drive a car without crashing it."

I narrow my eyes at my brother. "Miller is a good driver when I'm in the car with him. It's not like him to run a red light and crash into a fence. He's got great reflexes from his dirt bike days." I'm pretty much the only one who ever comes to Miller's defense, although he's earned a lot more respect this past year, for sure. Still, old habits die hard.

"Yeah, he drives carefully with you because you're precious cargo." Well, shit. How am I supposed to glare at Denny when he puts it like that?

Joey nudges me with his knee, and when I glance over, he's not even trying to hide his grin. All these men will be the death of me.

Luca decides to shed more light on the situation for our newcomer. "Miller crashed Carter's car last year, breaking his arm and getting banged up real good. It could have been a hell of a lot worse. He kept saying the brakes weren't working, but we all pretty much decided he was full of shit. Now Lynnie is backtracking."

"Because we have new information!"

"So you think developers tried to kill Miller?" Joey's incredulous expression has me thinking twice.

"Well, when you say it like that, it sounds a little far-fetched." Chagrinned, I lean back into the sofa cushions before giving my last comment on the subject. "To be fair, it was Carter's car, and up until very recently, he was making bank working for that senator and on his way to becoming a big shot. The kind of big shot who could bail his entire family out if needed." I throw my hands out. "That's all I'm saying." Yeah, probably not.

"What about the guys who broke in here and trashed the place last spring? They tried getting into my parents' house too," Luca says.

"Nah," Denny waves him off. "That was Carter's crooked politicians, Clarence Cody and Grace Hopkins, looking for their blood money."

I glance at Joey to see his face has lost some color. Perhaps I should have eased him into this a little slower.

"Or not!" Luca gets to his knees from his spot on the rug. "It could have been somebody trying to make our parents feel unsafe. Maybe move in closer to town?"

Our gazes bounce from face to face for a few silent beats before Denny pulls his phone from his back pocket. "I'm calling Cart."

We all get on our phones, Denny to make his call, me looking up The Diamond Group, and Luca doing who knows what. The only one without thumbs racing over his phone screen is Joey.

He rests his elbows on his knees and looks my way with a weary expression. "FYI, your definition of a 'normal' family is *way* different from mine."

JOEY

I never thought I'd see the day when hand-feeding sunflower seeds to a pet skunk in someone's kitchen would be the most conventional activity on the docket. My mind is whirling after our midday chat in the Brooks family den.

By the time Denny and Luca left, the trio had added one more potential sabotage-slash-crime to the list, with Luca's suggestion that maybe his dad losing his job a couple years ago was all part of some scheme as well. He said his parents couldn't have made their mortgage payments without help from him and his sister.

I have no idea if any of their ideas hold water, but they're not ruling anything out in this absolutely insane clusterfuck. My parents' biggest drama in the last year has been trying to decide between taupe and beige paint for their bathroom walls. Lynn's family seems to live in some alternate universe where mobsters with Tommy guns lurk around corners and rogue real estate developers cut brake lines. I mean, my god.

I was afraid I'd get bored while on the IL, but this is more action than game seven at the World Series.

Add all of that to Lynn's story about Carter bringing down two famous senators, and I'm ready for a nap.

"Why is he doing that?" I ask Lynn while I watch Mango stomp his feet on the wood floor of the hallway.

"Because my mama spoils him and wants more treats. It's his way of telling you off." She grins, surprising me at how calm she can be after the drama of the last couple hours.

We just watched Maude E. Christopher strut to her Lexus in a designer business suit before driving away with a satisfied smile on her lips. That's likely bad news, but you'd never know it from the way Lynn is chatting easily about her family pet.

And since there's nothing we can really do at the moment, I have a couple ideas of how we could pass the time before her evening shift at Blue Bigfoot. *What? I'm a guy. This is what we do.* "Want to give me the grand tour?"

Being the intelligent woman she is, Lynn sees right through my request and leans into me to place a quick kiss on my lips. And being the wise man I am, I made sure to buy condoms at a gas station on the way back into town. "Are you trying to seduce me under my mama's roof?" she asks against my lips.

I cup her jaw and deepen the kiss, sliding my tongue into her mouth for a deeper taste before drawing back. "That depends. Is it working?"

She boldly grazes her fingers over the denim covering my thigh and cups my half-hard cock through the material. "Seems to be." Her lips curve, and I'm ready to take this conversation horizontal.

Lynn doesn't resist when I ease her back onto the sofa. In fact, she parts her knees to allow me to rest in my favorite spot between her thighs. But as much as I want to fuck her brains out, I need to check in with her state of mind first. "You okay?"

Her immediate response is to furrow her brow, but she quickly understands my meaning, and her entire face softens. "I'm okay. We're used to a little drama around here."

"You didn't tell them about Larry," I remind her, making her scrunch her nose.

"Yeah. I probably should have, but I want to see if there's any connection between Guy Taylor and The Diamond Group before I say anything."

"You know you need to be careful, right?" When her eyes begin to narrow, I add, "What I mean is if this company has done one-tenth of what you guys are suspecting, they're not going to bat an eye at aiming all their firepower at a college student from Asheville. And you know it."

Her expression settles on half-amused. "You're worried about me."

"Absolutely." My nod is vehement. "And now that we're dating, you'd better reconcile that independent brain of yours with the idea that I'm going to give a shit about your state of well-being."

"Okay. I think I can do that." Her half smile grows to a wider, more amused one. "So, we're dating, huh?"

"You're damn right, we are," I say. And, since I'm done with this conversation for now, I close the distance between us and capture her lips with mine. The kiss goes from tender to needy in the blink of an eye, and I've got my hand up her shirt and my fingers teasing her nipple through her bra in seconds.

Lynn's back arches, and she lets out a mewling sound that goes right to my balls. I pinch her nipple in response, and she nearly bucks me off the sofa with her hips as her greedy little pussy comes begging for attention.

I release her lips to let my tongue trail down her throat while my fingers get busy unbuttoning her shorts. Her zipper is next, and then my fingers find home, burying themselves in her hot, slick channel. "Fuck," I groan while Lynn's head falls back and her eyes close. She is so fucking gorgeous right now, I wish I could take a picture. But I've got more important things to do. Namely, eat Lynn's pretty pussy.

To that end, I straighten and grasp the hem of her shorts with both hands, intent on ridding her of these impeding clothes.

"Lynnie? Are you home?" an unfamiliar feminine voice calls from the hallway, and when my eyes flash to Lynn's face, it's abject horror I see reflected there. Lynn's mother is about to walk in on me trying to bang her daughter.

Not exactly the introduction I hoped for.

I've never seen a single ballplayer move faster than Lynn as she untangles her legs from mine and springs off the sofa to come to a stop on the other side of the den, leaving me on my knees on the couch. She sends me wild, panicked eyes as she buttons her shorts and straightens her clothes. Without the benefit of a mirror, however, she misses the small detail of the wild cloud of tangled dark waves surrounding her face. Well, at least my dick is still in my pants.

I've just managed to resume a seated position on the couch cushion when an animated woman who looks to be in her fifties enters the room. "There you are," she says, and I immediately notice a resemblance between the woman and her daughter. They share the same nose and chin, along with similar frames. While Lynn's hair is dark and wavy, though, her mother's is lighter and curly, its untamed wildness bearing a striking resemblance to Lynn's hair right now in its ruffled state.

Sensing my presence, Mrs. Brooks turns, her lips parting in an open, friendly smile. "Well, hello. Who do we have here?"

Before either of us can respond, Mango comes tearing into the den at a sprint, practically leaping into his mistress's arms as she bends to intercept him. "Hello, my darling," she coos at the animal.

"Hey, Mama. This is Joey. Joey, this is my mom, Ginny Brooks."

"It's a pleasure to meet you, Mrs. Brooks," I say, standing from the couch and moving toward her with an outstretched hand.

"It's Ginny." She waves off my hand and pulls me into a half hug, one made a bit awkward by the skunk in her arms, as can occasionally happen to anyone. Thank God my hard-on deflated in all the panic, or this hug might be even more strange.

"How was work?" Lynn asks, still maintaining the distance between us, and I get the impression she's not eager to entertain questions about our relationship and why I'm in her mom's den.

Ginny takes a step back from me, petting Mango as the skunk purrs like a cat in her arms. "Fabulous," she gushes. "Lizzie has worked wonders with all the residents on their self-portraits. You'll have to come to the exhibit tomorrow and see. Everyone is just tickled pink." Ginny turns to me. "The senior center residents are trying to raise money to repair and resurface the swimming pool, so we're holding several fundraising events this summer. The first is an art exhibit and sale. You should come too, Joey."

Lynn looks like she's about to intervene, but Ginny's mention of the name Lizzie and the swimming pool has me connecting some dots I never expected to find here. "Are you talking about Elizabeth Wright?"

Two sets of eyes widen at my question, but Ginny is the one to answer. "Yes. Lizzie is our art instructor. Do you know her?"

My mouth spreads in a grin. Elizabeth was talking about the fundraiser for her volunteer gig the last time I saw her. "Her boyfriend is one of my closest friends."

Ginny's free hand clutches her chest. "I adore Gunner. That boy puts the butt in buttered biscuits."

"Oh my god, Mama!" Lynn protests, but I'm already laughing.

"He's does fairly well with female fans, I gotta give it to him."

"Mama, Joey doesn't want to hear about his bestie's rear end."

"Okay, okay." Mango starts to squirm, so Ginny sets him on the rug and turns for the kitchen. "Can I get you two something to eat or drink?"

"No thanks," Lynn responds in a forced sunny tone before mouthing, "I'm sorry," to me. I can only shake my head and keep grinning. Ginny is harmless. Lynn doesn't need to get worked up on my account.

But I realize I may have spoken too soon when the next words out of Ginny Brooks's mouth are, "You're probably parched after whatever it is you were doing to make my daughter's hair look like that."

LYNN

The day after my dad's funeral seven years ago, Denny packed up his car and drove out of town. He didn't set foot back in Asheville for another four years. Cart and Miller were spitting mad at him, saying abandoning his family at such a difficult time was selfish. Cash was convinced he could make Denny come back if he tried hard enough. It didn't work. Miller eventually stopped caring, and Carter left Asheville again to continue pursuing his political aspirations in DC and Raleigh. Mama and I, on the other hand, were just sad. It was impossible to be angry with Denny because we knew he was doing whatever he needed to in order to deal with the pain of loss. We all do what we have to.

For Miller, it was getting in trouble any way he could find. Cash threw himself into replacing Dad and being the rock for everyone to lean on. Cart focused on making something out of himself and the Brooks name. Mama vowed to make the most out of each day the Lord gave her on this earth. And me? I tried my best to follow in Mama's footsteps. But there was one thing I refused to make the most of and embrace in this life, and that was letting anyone else in close enough that the loss of them could break me apart like it did our family when Dad died.

It broke us all, including our mama. Sure, she tried to hide it, but I knew. My bedroom is right above hers and Dad's, and I slept with a pillow over my head for a year after Dad's death so I wouldn't have to listen to her crying herself to sleep. Mama's acting job might have been impeccable, but even the best actor in the world has to break character at some point.

So, two days after my mama busted Joey and me making out in the den, I'm entirely unprepared for Joey asking out of the blue, "Have you ever had your heart broken?"

First, what guy asks you that when you've only been dating for like two days? And second, we're cuddling on his sofa at his condo right in the middle of watching *Field of Dreams*. I mean, come on! I don't want to talk about love right now—especially when I've been doing my damn best *not* to think about any feelings I might be catching for Joey.

But since I can't exactly pretend I didn't hear him or, say, fake an injury, I go with a classic evasive maneuver. "Have you?"

His answer is direct. Of course it is. "I maybe thought so at the time, but looking back, not really. She dumped me when I got traded to the Arrows, and I realized later that I never actually knew her." He shrugs, shifting his arm so his hand cups my belly over my shirt. I secretly love it when he does that. At first, I was a little self-conscious, like any woman I know would be, but after his declaration that bony women do nothing for him, I got over it real quick.

Joey's answer about heartbreak doesn't surprise me all that much, apart from the baffling concept that any woman would dump him. He's always been so upfront with his thoughts, I can tell he's never been burned by putting himself out there. Hell, I have to assume any previous relationship of his has garnered accolades and international awards for its levels of healthy communication.

"What about you?" he asks again.

Hmm. I've not received a single award for vulnerability, and that's probably not changing anytime soon. "Nope." I hurry to change the subject. "Do you think James Earl Jones's character is only pretending not to hear the voices?"

Joey ignores the second part of my response, pausing the movie and staring at me until I can't stand it any longer and have to look up at him. The skin around his eyes is crinkled with amusement. "I knew it. You're a stone-cold heartbreaker, for sure."

"No, I'm not," I scoff. "I've slightly bruised maybe one heart, and it healed itself as soon as the next girl came along."

"I doubt that."

"You don't even know who I'm talking about." Why can't I sit still?

"No, but I know you could break *my* heart. And I also know it would be worth it."

Who *is* this guy?

I snort and force a laugh to cover my discomfort. "Please. I've seen the way women look at you." It's true, too. I thought a woman on the sidewalk yesterday was going to concuss herself on a lamppost.

"But have you seen the way *I* look at *you*?"

I have seen the way he looks at me, and it's enough to poke holes in that bulletproof vest surrounding my heart.

Joey won't break eye contact, and I feel flames rising from my chest, lighting my skin and organs on fire as they cover me. I've never met anyone as open and unafraid to be vulnerable. Before I know it, the words tumble out, "Aren't you afraid of anything?"

All traces of amusement fade as Joey takes my hand and brings it to his chest. "I'm fucking terrified. But I'm a big believer in giving the important things in life everything I've got."

I realize then that I've been holding my breath. All the air in my lungs releases at once, and I draw in a deep lungful of oxygen. Joey dips his head to give me a light kiss on the lips before turning the movie back on and settling us back the way we were, this time with my hand still tightly clasped in his.

I pretend not to cry when Ray plays catch with his dad at the end, but my red eyes give me away, and Joey hands me a tissue. "I think it took about twenty viewings for me not to cry at the end too." At his words, I decide not to lie and say a rogue eyelash caused my tears.

My phone vibrates when the credits are rolling, and I bring it to my lap to see who's texting. I haven't parted with my phone for a minute in the last couple days, as we've all processed the new information about The Diamond Group and Winston. Everything is so up in the air, we're all waiting for something to happen. I've been unable to find a link between Guy Taylor and any real estate developers, so I've hit a dead end on that. There's nothing more I can do until Mr. Taylor returns from his overseas travel on Tuesday.

Mama played her part like freaking Dame Helen Mirren with a southern drawl, luring Winston out to his porch with the promise of homemade muffins and iced tea. We all almost simultaneously passed out when she shared that Maude E. Christopher is actually Winston's estranged daughter! She supposedly came to town wanting to reconcile, and Winston doesn't even know who she works for. Mama was cool, though, making it all sound like small talk so as not to raise any suspicions.

Denny thinks we should tell Winston his daughter is up to no good, but Mama insists on leaving it alone for the time being. No sense in breaking an old man's heart—if he has one, that is—by suggesting his daughter might have ulterior motives for mending fences. The bottom line is that we need some proof.

But it turns out not to be any of my siblings on my messaging app tonight, in fact. It's Jeremy. And it's just my luck that my phone is positioned in a way that makes it impossible for Joey not to see what he texted.

JEREMY:

Hey, beautiful.

I know the second Joey clocks the text because he lets out a very manly grunt. I chance a glance in his direction to see him scowling at my phone.

"Don't pay any attention to him," I say, but Joey doesn't respond. And knowing it will only make things worse if I try to hide my screen, I decide to take control of this situation by texting back within full view of my new boyfriend.

ME:

What's up, bro?

Yeah, Jeremy still texts me, even though he and Carter are tight again and nobody's balls have been threatened in the last year. Sometimes he reaches out for advice on women—the dude must have no other female friends if he's asking a college student about women in their mid-thirties. What do I know, though? Maybe he prefers women half his age, and I'm the target demographic.

If it's not about women, it's silly things like sharing a funny social media post or seeing if I know why Cart isn't answering his phone. And sometimes it's just to make sure the family is doing well. But the few times he's visited in the last year, he hasn't made any more awkward declarations about "caring," for which I'm thankful.

But, since he's incapable of not flirting, the "Hey, beautiful" greeting isn't unexpected.

JEREMY:

Bro? Ouch.

"Okay!" Joey declares. "You want to tell me who this guy is?"

I throw a hand out. "You met him last summer. Jeremy Rossi. Carter's friend? They used to work for one of the senators I told you about—Grace Hopkins—although she's no longer a senator, so I don't know who Jeremy is working for these days. I just know he's in Raleigh." When I realize I've gone off on a tangent, I add, "He's flirty with every single female on Earth—my mama included. It's just the way he is. Besides, he's almost old enough to be my father."

"Wait, that guy you were meeting the night I ran into you at Blue Bigfoot?" When I nod, the tension in his shoulders relaxes. "Oh. He's not your type at all." His expression is the same one he probably wears when he tastes something rotten, and I can't help my laugh because Joey isn't my usual type either. Yet here I am.

"See. Now, can I get back to finding out what he needs?"

Joey has the grace to look the tiniest bit chagrined as he nods and flips channels, probably looking for sports.

ME:

> You always say you want to be part of the Brooks family.

JEREMY:

> True.

JEREMY:

> Anyway, I need your help convincing Carter and Sunny to come to Raleigh for a visit. He claims he can't leave the brewhouse, but I know that's bullshit.

I imagine it has more to do with Carter spending every minute of his free time banging Sunny than anything else— well, I take that back. Sunny doesn't like leaving her grand-father, Duke, alone for too long. But we can always bring him to Mama's like we've done before.

In fact, that gives me an idea, and I make a mental note to see if I can arrange an introduction between Duke and Winston. They're both cranky SOBs, so they'll likely either kill each other or get on like a house on fire, no pun intended. Maybe Duke can get some more dirt for us. That old man loves a good caper.

I tell Jeremy I'll do my best, and then, behaving entirely on impulse, I add something else.

ME:

> Gotta run. Watching TV with my boyfriend.

There. I said it out loud. Well, sort of.

Before he can reply, I shove my phone under a throw pillow and nestle back into the crook of Joey's arm. I'm really getting this whole girlfriend thing down pat.

JOEY

It's been three weeks since my injury, and my wrist is feeling stronger every day. But when I try batting, that's when it bitch-slaps me and tells me to slow the fuck down. I hate waiting. Just like I hate not knowing what the coaching staff might be thinking. I tried getting a sit-down with Coach Gibbs, but he has yet to name a time, which makes me all the more nervous.

"Doc and I are both pleased with your progress," Nora says when I work through my exercises and stretches under her watchful eye Tuesday morning.

"Any guesses as to when I'll be off the IL?" I'm not even trying to disguise the hope in my voice.

"Don't rush it, big shot. You'll only set yourself back and prolong our visits, not that I don't enjoy your sparkling personality." She hooks up a blue band for increased resistance, and I loop my arm through it as she instructs.

"Patience isn't really one of my strong suits."

She almost chokes on her laughter. "Show me an athlete

who excels in patience, and I'll give you the keys to my beach house in Bora Bora."

"You have a beach house in Bora Bora?" I ask, impressed.

"Nope." She grins at me before turning her head with a raised voice. "Hey, Lynn. Can you bring a fresh towel over?"

Of course, I've been watching Lynn in my peripheral vision the entire time I've been in the treatment room. But, as promised, I'm not engaging in any behavior that will give away our relationship or demonstrate even the tiniest degree of familiarity between us.

When she walks over in her black scrubs, however, it's hard not to kiss her or at least touch her. We've spent the last four days attached at the hip when she's not working and I'm not in therapy, working out, or at team meetings. I even hang out at Blue Bigfoot for a little while when she's on shift. Her brothers are so worked up over this developer business, they haven't even given me a hard time, apart from a few well-placed sneers.

Everyone is on pins and needles as they search for a link between The Diamond Group and any other homeowners who they may have victimized. So far, they've had no luck, but Lynn says they've put a guy named Duke on the case. The only thing I know about this guy is that he's Carter's girlfriend's grandfather, and he's a little nuts. I have to assume he has some connections nobody wants to talk about because they all appear confident he'll dig something up. In the meantime, Lynn is keeping her spirits high, probably because she knows Guy Taylor is finally back home today.

Gunner is the only one in my orbit who knows Lynn and I are dating, and I intend to keep it that way until Lynn's internship is over. Unfortunately, that means we don't get to watch any home games together and share disgustingly good nachos in the stands while she cheers for my team.

We went to the art exhibit at the senior center, and I finally introduced Lynn to Gunner and Elizabeth, although Elizabeth was busy trying to sell paintings. I bought one to support the cause and was surprised to learn it was a painting by the very same Duke who's helping the Brooks family investigate. He didn't strike me as someone who's got his finger on the pulse of much of anything, but what do I know?

As for the painting, there's no way I'll be hanging it anywhere in my condo. It was supposed to be a self-portrait, but it looks more like a schizophrenic rendering of an open wound than anything. Various shades of red, black, and blue cover the canvas, resembling dripping blood. When Lizzie pulled Duke over to Lynn and me, explaining that the painting was more of an expressionist take, I asked Duke what his inspiration was. His response? "How the hell am I supposed to know? Are you a moron?" At that point, Lynn dragged me away to grab a glass of champagne.

I take the towel from Lynn and use it to wipe the sweat from my face. Rehab isn't as easy as it looks.

"Which color band is next in resistance level?" Nora quizzes Lynn, who immediately answers, "Black, then gray." Nora nods her approval. My girl knows her shit.

"And what exercise is Joey doing now?"

"Resisted wrist flexion" is Lynn's response. I have no idea if she's right, but Nora's repeated nod tells me she nailed it.

Nora winks at me but speaks to Lynn. "He'll be ready to ice down after this."

Lynn nods and goes to retrieve the familiar ice pack and

towels. When Nora declares me finished, she goes to her desk, leaving Lynn and me alone on the opposite side of the room.

"Let me guess. You were always the teacher's pet," I tease.

Lynn frowns down at me before taking Nora's vacated seat. "Not always."

"Ha! I knew it."

"Come on," she responds. "*You* are such a people pleaser, I'll bet you sat in the front row with an entire pack of sharpened pencils." She places the icepack over a towel and molds it to my wrist with practiced movements.

"I am not a people pleaser," I argue. Am I?

Clearly forgetting her rule about familiarity in the workplace, Lynn laughs. "You so are. When that waitress brought you chicken instead of fish, you straight out lied and said everything looked great."

"I like chicken."

"But you wanted fish."

"I think you're forgetting I'm a guy. We just like to eat. We don't actually care what it is as long as it's not still moving."

She raises her eyebrows and lowers her voice. "You told my mama you like romance books."

Yeah, I did that. But Ginny had to know I was joking, right? "That's different. I'm trying to get in her daughter's pants, so I need her to like me." I waggle my brows.

Appearing to remember where we are, Lynn glances back at Nora, but she's paying us zero attention. "Don't come crying to me when she gives you a box of soft-core porn, expecting a book report on each title."

My grin falls. "She wouldn't do that."

"Ha! Just you wait. She and her friend Regina devour those books, and Regina owns an escort business."

"Now you're just making shit up." At least I'm pretty sure she is.

Lynn raises her right hand. "Hand to God, Ace."

My chest warms for some reason. Maybe it's because I just like being around Lynn, no matter where we are. "I like it when you call me Ace."

Her responding smile has the warmth moving from my chest downward. But Amy chooses that moment to walk through the clinic door, sending Lynn back to her feet. "We need to watch our backs. I'm going to wait over there," she whispers.

"Hey, wait." I stop her just as she starts to turn. "It's Tuesday."

Lynn nods, an amused yet quizzical expression taking over. "And some people say athletes aren't smart."

"Shut it, you," I whisper, glancing to see if we've captured anyone's interest. Luckily, we haven't. "Guy Taylor is back in Raleigh."

"I know. I'm calling him right after work." Lynn's eyes go wide like she's suddenly gone giddy with anticipation.

She turns her back on me and starts walking away, but I manage to whisper-hiss, "Wait for me. I want to be there with you."

She does a little spin on her heel, mouthing, "Okay. I'll meet you at your place... Ace," before skipping off toward Nora and Amy.

Damn, I'm in deep with this girl. I just hope like hell I'm not alone.

THIRTY-THREE

JODI FOSTER IS USUALLY RIGHT

LYNN

"Any fan of Morton Frye is a friend of mine," Guy Taylor pronounces over the phone speaker. "Are you a collector of his work as well?"

"You could say that," I respond, sending Joey a tense smile. I hope I can get through this call without losing my shit.

"So, what is it you'd like to know about the piece at the Mintz?"

"Well, the gallery had such limited information about its origins…" I trail off, hoping Guy, as he insisted I call him, will take it from there. I can't exactly accuse him of stealing it, now can I?

"Yes." He sighs. "As I'm sure you know, so many of his early works have limited provenance. Its previous owner received it as a gift from Frye himself—or, at least, his family did. I was surprised he was willing to part with it, but since it worked to my benefit, I didn't work too hard to convince him otherwise." He chuckles good-heartedly, clearly having no idea that I'm seething on the other end of the line.

"Oh. My. God!" I mouth to Joey as we sit side-by-side at his dining table. His condo is kick-ass, with an open-concept main living space and clean, unfussy decor. He said Liv and her best friend helped him pick out stuff that was simple but not minimalist enough to make it look like a serial killer lived here.

Joey rolls his hand in the air, indicating I need to keep this convo going, so I gather my wits and dive back in. "Hm. Do you, um, happen to have the seller's contact information?" At least now I know to stop investigating Guy Taylor. But I need the name of my new target.

"Oh dear. I'm afraid he doesn't own any more Fryes. Believe me, I asked." He chuckles again. It's not his fault I kind of want to strangle him right now.

Shit. What now?

Time to become a bullshit artist.

I clear my throat and squeeze my eyes shut, hoping to God this works. "It's just that my family has a Frye that's so close in resemblance, they could be twins. I'm certain they were carved around the same time. It was my father's. He was friends with Frye, and I thought it would be nice to connect with this family that apparently ran in the same circles as my father and Frye back in the day." Am I really going to do this? *Forgive me, Dad!* "It's been difficult since we lost him." I feel like absolute crap using my dad, but I remind myself this kind of bullshit would have him laughing his ass off if he were still here. Nothing about my dad was straight *or* narrow.

"I'm so sorry for your loss. Of course! Would you like me to text the information?"

I stifle a victorious shout and manage a subdued, "That would be wonderful. Thank you."

We say our goodbyes, and I hang up, immediately leaping from my chair and beginning to pace Joey's kitchen.

"He's going to be pissed when he finds out he bought a stolen sculpture," Joey says from his chair.

"Yeah." I bite my lip and continue my loop across the tile. "But I'll have to worry about that later. We need to catch this developer first!"

My phone pings, and Joey and I both leap on it like it's the last brownie of the apocalypse.

"Does the name ring any bells?" Joey asks, looking over at me.

The name Eddie Dante stares up at us, followed by a phone number with a Raleigh area code.

"Not even a little."

We both begin searching the internet on our phones looking for one Eddie Dante, but all we come up with is an author, a mechanic, and several social media profiles of random men of all ages, none of whom even live in North Carolina.

"Well, we know we can't call this guy." Joey leans back in his seat with a sigh.

I straighten, ideas swirling in my mind. "Or can we?"

"No way." Joey's headshake is emphatic. "Do not put yourself on this guy's radar, Lynn."

He's jumped into protective mode. "He wouldn't even know who I am. I can block my number." It'll be a breeze. I can say I'm a friend of Guy's and strike up a conversation. I'm bound to find out something useful.

But Joey is clearly of a different mind, if his subsequent freakout is any indication. "And tip him off!" Now he's the one pacing. "If your family's theories are correct, this guy knows who you are already. You don't think he'll be able to put two and two together? And even if you guys are wrong, this man *knew* where to find Larry and how much he's worth. That, to me, says he already knows too much about your family to risk it." When I try to interject, Joey steamrolls me. "He obviously didn't expect Guy Taylor to parade the sculpture around Raleigh, and you calling about it may be the first he's heard of it. That's going to make him panic, and panicked people do rash things." He makes an X with his arms before throwing his hands out. "No way. You're not calling him!"

He did not just say that! I jump to my feet and square off with him. "Did you just *forbid me* from making a phone call?"

"You're damn right I did." Smug bastard.

I need to keep my calm about me. Yelling will only make this worse. I take a breath and moderate my tone. "Joey, you're jumping to worst-case scenarios."

Joey apparently didn't get the memo about calm because he jabs his index finger at me. "You need to give this information to the police and let them handle it."

Fuck calm. "I can't do that yet! Not while we have this Diamond Group thing still so up in the air. If this guy gets busted, they'll go to ground and cover their tracks. Then we'll never be able to prove anything!"

"Good! Then maybe they'll back off and stop trying to buy the properties. It will scare them off, and you win."

He doesn't get it. He doesn't know how much shit my family has been through since the day my dad died. We can't just… give up. "But they can't be allowed to get away with everything they've done!" I can't help the tears springing to my eyes.

To my surprise, my watery eyes act as a bucket of cold water on Joey's temper. He exhales and takes a beat before inching closer and taking one of my hands. "Lynn, you don't even know they did any of that." Well, he has a point. "Maybe Miller is just a shitty driver. Maybe kids were playing with fireworks in the woods. Maybe your family got targeted and robbed by a regular old criminal like tons of other people." He shrugs, and I let out a sigh before he continues, "If you follow Occam's razor, that's the most likely scenario."

I've lost my fight, and my lips quirk without my permission. "Are you going all intellectual on me?"

He pulls out the lopsided grin. "You don't think I can? You forget I beat you last week with *quixotic* in Words with Friends. I'm no idiot."

"I know you're not. Sorry." I squeeze his hand. "I just wasn't expecting classic philosophical theory when we're dealing with Bigfoot."

He shrugs again. "To be fair, I only know about Occam's razor from that Jodi Foster movie."

"Oh! *Contact*. I *love* that movie." My eyes widen.

"Me too."

"So, are we done arguing?" I ask. I don't like being at odds with Joey. But anytime someone tries bossing me around, I just can't help myself.

His tone turns serious again, but he's lost his anger. "That depends. Are you going to call Eddie Dante?"

I need to be truthful with him, so I answer, "Not tonight. That's the best I can give you for now."

He sighs and pulls me into his chest. "I guess I'll have to take that, then. For now."

We don't talk any more about Guy Taylor or my family drama, instead pushing it to the side to salvage something of our evening together. But it will still be there tomorrow, and I need to decide what I want to do about it.

Joey seems to have forgotten that the hero of *Contact*, Jodi Foster's character, wasn't the one invoking Occam's razor—the idea that all things being equal, the simplest explanation is usually the correct one. No, she knew her crazy-sounding story was true, even if nobody else believed her or backed her up. Good old Jodi and I might have something in common. I just need to figure out my next move.

CHAPTER
THIRTY-FOUR

BETWEEN A ROCK AND A HARD-HEADED WOMAN

JOEY

"It's enormous!" Lynn exclaims.

"I know, right? Care to take it for a spin?"

"Now?"

"Sure, why not?" I shrug from my spot in the doorway of my master bathroom. "Those jets at the end of a long day are just what the doctor ordered."

"I feel like I might need a life vest," Lynn comments.

I wrap my arms around her from behind and press my front to her back. "Don't worry. I'll keep you afloat."

It's Wednesday evening, and we're back at my condo. While I like Lynn's mom just fine, I prefer the privacy that hanging out at my place provides. Although my presence has been requested at dinner tomorrow night, where the entire family is expected to gather. Lynn's brothers are even leaving the brewery in the hands of other staff, so I have to assume this dinner will be a meeting to compare notes on The Diamond Group. The fact that Ginny wants me there must say good things, right? I sure as hell hope so.

"This sounds like a ploy to get me naked," Lynn says knowingly.

"One hundred percent."

When she turns in my arms and puts her hands up in the air, I don't hesitate to pull off her sundress before skimming my eyes down her body. She is utter perfection, with her perky breasts captured in a lace bra and her hips curving out from her waist and leading down to those fantastic long legs. Even the healthy roundness of her belly turns me on, and it pleases me to no end that she doesn't try to hide it by sucking it in. I don't want to see a woman's ribs when she's naked. I much prefer some softness I can sink my fingers into and enjoy.

"You are so fucking beautiful," I tell her, my voice coming out a little hoarse.

She blushes like I knew she would, and I reach out to brush my knuckles along the skin of her collarbone.

"Your turn," she urges, a touch of impatience in her voice.

"Give me a minute. I just want to look at you."

The heat in her cheeks heightens, and she starts shifting on her feet.

"You don't need to be shy, Lynn. There's nothing I'm seeing that I don't find perfect."

Her eyes shift to the side, but she doesn't cover herself, thank God. "It's just... nobody has ever been this... vocal before."

"You don't like it?" I ask, knowing that she does.

"I do. I just... need to get used to it." Her eyes finally come back to meet mine.

"Yeah. You do. Because I'm not about to stop telling you how I feel or what you do to me."

"Well, you're not going to like what I do to you if you don't strip, Ace."

I grin and acquiesce, pulling my shirt over my head and discarding my jeans and boxers in one swift movement. As I straighten, standing fully naked and half-hard in front of Lynn, she squares her shoulders and looks me right in the eye. She holds my gaze as she removes her bra and slides her panties down. Thatta girl.

My grin grows into a full-blown smile. "What are your thoughts on bubble baths?"

She laughs. "You own bubble bath? How evolved of you."

I shrug. "Well, Liv left it here last time she took over my bathroom to go swimming." I turn and take the bottle from a cabinet shelf, handing it over to Lynn.

"Lavender. Remind me to thank Liv next time I see her."

When she looks up at me again, I take her hips in my hands and drop my head to kiss her.

We almost don't make it into the bath since we make out the entire time it takes to fill the giant tub, and by the time we get in, I'm hard enough to pound concrete, and Lynn has already had one orgasm from me fingering her.

"I'm never leaving this tub," she groans as she lounges in the hot water, jets pulsing against our bodies and bubbles piled high on top of us. She's using me as her lounge chair, a role I'm more than willing to play as my hands run over her skin and my cock nestles against her lush ass.

When I pinch her nipple, she gasps and arches, so her ass shifts and my cock gets dangerously close to its favorite place. "Condom," I mutter through gritted teeth.

"I'm on the pill, but—"

I cut her off. "I got a clean bill of health three months ago, and I haven't been with anyone but you since." The truth is, I haven't been with anyone since I tried to fuck the memory of Lynn away this past winter. It didn't work.

"I've never not used a condom."

The words are barely out of Lynn's mouth before I nudge her entrance, and she arches her back so I can enter her from behind. Fuck, that feels fantastic.

"Oh, god," Lynn moans as I thrust up and fully seat my cock inside her. Holy shit. I might not last long. It's been years since I had bareback sex, but I don't remember it ever feeling like this. "Joey," she pleads, and I bring both my hands up to caress her tits while she meets another of my upward thrusts.

It's not long before she pulls her torso upright for better leverage, and then she's riding me like my dirtiest fantasy come true. Water sloshes over the side of the tub, and bubbles launch into the air while she bounces on my cock, taking me to my balls with each downward motion.

I can feel her inner walls start to quiver, so I leave one hand on her hip and stretch the other over her to reach her clit with my middle finger. I swirl and rub that little bundle of nerves while Lynn rides me faster.

"You almost there?" I ask because I feel the familiar tingling at the base of my spine that says we don't have long.

"Yes," she pants, flexing her hips as she continues her frantic pace.

Fuck. Here it comes. I just manage to hold back until her spasms massage my cock, and she comes with a series of moans and whimpers. I thrust up into her with abandon as my orgasm leaves me and her pussy milks me dry.

She collapses back into me, both of us pulling in ragged breaths, and we come down from our high. My cock is still cradled inside her slick heat, and I have no plans to move anytime soon.

Reading my mind, Lynn asks, "Do you think Grubhub will deliver breakfast to a bathroom?" My responding laugh almost has me slipping out of her, but she holds onto me.

Despite our determination to settle into the tub for the long haul, the water eventually grows too cold and our fingers turn into prunes, so we get out. I wrap Lynn up in a fluffy towel and haul her into my bedroom before depositing her on my king-sized bed and telling her to stay there.

Surprisingly, she does as I say, her eyes unabashedly trained on my ass while I go to fetch cold water from the kitchen.

"I finally get what all the hype is about," she says when I return. At my questioning look, she continues, "The whole baseball player butt thing."

I choke on my first sip of water. "The *what*?"

"How all the female fans talk about players' butts in their uniforms," she says before face-palming. "Even my mama, apparently."

I climb onto the bed and draw the sheet over my lap before pulling Lynn to my side. "Yeah, well, we run and work out a lot, so the booty is hard-earned. It's nice to know our work is appreciated."

Lynn shakes her head at me. "No wonder y'all are so cocky."

She's not wrong, so I can only shrug. I switch to a topic I've been meaning to bring up. "So, anything I need to know before this dinner tomorrow night?" I'm hoping not to be blindsided by anything other than the expected glares and conspiracy theories.

"Nope. Just the usual, so you may want to wear that cup."

"Noted," I say. "Any news from that Duke guy yet?"

"Carter and Sunny are bringing him, so I expect we'll be updated over dinner."

"And what about Larry?" We haven't talked about the whole Eddie Dante thing since last night, but we've been together almost all day, so I'm confident she hasn't tried calling him. She'd tell me if she had, right? Fuck, I hope so. "You're going to come clean, right?"

When Lynn bites her lip before answering, I brace. "About that…"

"Lynn." I straighten, causing the sheet to slip, but Lynn isn't paying attention to anything but my face now.

"Don't *Lynn* me, Joey." She sets her water on the bedside table. "I have some news." When I nod to prod her along, she says, "I found an Edward Dante living in Raleigh while I was researching over lunch today."

"And?" I ask, trying like hell to keep my tone from giving away my fears.

She pulls the sheet up to cover her breasts and arranges herself so she's sitting and facing me. "And I want to go stake out the address. See if I can maybe get a picture or something. Then, when I tell my family, I'll have something concrete. Maybe one of them will recognize him as a developer representative from a past visit to the house."

I pause to maintain my composure. "Setting aside for a moment that you're not, in fact, a private investigator and that this guy could be dangerous, why can't you tell your family tomorrow, and then maybe it could be a group activity? Safety in numbers and all that."

"Are you kidding? My brothers will never let me go if I

tell them first. They'll handcuff me to my bedpost and throw away the key while they traipse off and play hero. Trust me."

"Just tell them you're coming along. You're an adult."

She throws a bare arm out. "Have you not heard anything I've told you about my brothers? When I was seventeen, Cash actually had my car towed from my work parking lot because he found out I was driving a friend and myself to a concert in Charlotte that night."

I take another sip of water before responding, "You were a teenager. Surely he wouldn't do that today. I mean, they don't show up at your college campus to boss you around during the school year, do they?" I think she's underestimating her brothers. They're probably more bluster than action.

"Because I don't tell them what I'm up to." Her expression tells me she's had enough.

"Okay." I sigh, trying to think of a solution. "Then *I'll* go with you. We can go on Saturday." I have a mandatory team outing on Friday for a charity gig. And we've got dinner tomorrow, so those two days are out.

"I'm going Friday. It's my only day off. I have to work tomorrow and through the whole weekend, and I'm not waiting another week. The Diamond Group could have Winston's deed by then, for all we know."

"All the more reason to tell your family," I argue.

"Joey, please. I'm not going to be in danger. I'll drive over, take a few pictures, maybe talk to a neighbor or two. That's it."

"Are you hearing yourself? Do not get on this guy's radar, Lynn!" Why can't she understand why I'm worried?

"I promise I'll be careful. You'll see. It'll be a breeze. Then I'll tell my family. I promise. We can add whatever I find to

Duke's notes and decide if we want to go to the police from there."

"Lynn."

"Joey." She reaches out and grabs my hand, giving it a squeeze.

I know I'm going to regret this, but I exhale loudly and then nod my head. What the hell am I doing? I just pray Duke has found enough to make Lynn's little field trip unnecessary.

LYNN

It's clear I'm way more nervous than Joey is as we wind our way up the mountain to Mama's house the following evening in his truck. The fact that I've been staying at his place means there's no doubt everyone in my family and beyond knows we're sleeping together. Which probably spells trouble for both of us tonight. No way will those yahoos let this slide without at least commenting, no matter that it's none of their beeswax.

"You've had jimmy leg for the last ten minutes," Joey says, pulling a hand from the steering wheel and reaching over to lace his fingers with mine.

"Your wrist." I gesture to the only hand steering us up the mountain, even though I know his wrist is fine. I'm coming to terms with my feelings for Joey in the innermost secret section of my heart, but my avoidance instincts haven't gotten the memo and refuse to quit.

"I'm fine. You've seen the progress I'm making."

Since we both know it's true, I move on. "It isn't too late to back out, you know." Half of me wishes he would, and the other half wants to strut into the house carrying a banner declaring him my hot-ass boyfriend.

"I'm not backing out," he declares, lifting our joined hands and kissing the back of mine. Damn, he is just too good to be true sometimes. When he drops our hands to the center console again, he smiles at me, holding my gaze a little too long for someone whose eyes should be trained on the steep, winding roads ahead. "Did I tell you I did a deep dive into the Counting Crows last summer?"

I raise my brows at him. He knows good and well he never told me that. "Oh yeah? They're one of my favorites."

"I know."

"You texted me that Adam Duritz is a poet, but I never texted you back to say I agree."

His lips quirk. "I already knew from the way you listened to 'Round Here' the first time I kissed you."

Warmth suffuses my chest. "You remember that?"

"Of course I do. I remember everything when it comes to you."

He's trying to melt my heart like an ice cream sundae on a hot Carolina sidewalk. And it's working a little too well. "Joey…" I begin before trailing off. I don't know what to say. I'm not used to this kind of openness, and it scares the shit out of me. Letting him in this far wasn't part of my plan.

He lets me off the hook by focusing his gaze on the road and asking, "Do you have 'A Long December' in one of your millions of playlists?"

"Duh." I roll my eyes in mock disgust and plug my phone into his truck's USB port, happy to sweep my emotions aside. Seconds later, the familiar piano intro fills the air.

Then Joey Martel rocks my world. "I used to listen to this all the time and think of you," he says.

Oh, god. So much for an escape from my emotions! Joey's eyes remain trained on the road, but try as I might, I can't help riveting mine to his handsome profile as Adam Duritz's vocals begin.

From the way Joey occasionally snags my gaze while the song plays, I can tell those are some of the lines that made him think of me.

"Maybe this year will be better than the last."

"If you think that I could be forgiven, I wish you would."

"All at once you look across a crowded room to see the way that light attaches to a girl."

Each time, the intensity in his eyes has my heart threatening to claw its way from my chest. Holy shit. That bulletproof vest around my heart is being torn to shreds right here in this truck cab.

I'm falling in love with this man.

But since my voice is stuck in my throat, I do the only thing I'm capable of at the moment. I squeeze his hand and smile.

"NOTHING?" Cash asks, his tone incredulous.

"You got cotton in your ears, young man?" Duke responds, his bushy white eyebrows drawing together.

Cash turns his gaze from Duke, who's seated across from him at the joined picnic tables, to Carter and Sunny at their spot down the way. "I thought you said he could find anything."

"He can." Sunny defends her grandpa.

I've introduced Joey to enough people tonight to challenge Jumbo's memory skills, but there's no way he could forget Sunny's name. The woman is the physical embodiment of sunshine, with fiery red hair and a yellow sundress with bright red trim and shoes to match. I adore her.

There were too many people to fit in Mama's kitchen, so we're all packed onto two picnic tables in the backyard as we feast on the best chicken and waffles for a hundred miles. Joey must agree because he's already on seconds beside me.

"Maybe… there's nothing to find," Carter chimes in, but it's met with scoffs from Miller and Denny.

"Maybe Winston's daughter just wants to reconnect for real? Is that so hard to believe?" Rosie adds.

"Yes," most of the Brooks family replies in unison. I hold my tongue because now that we know Duke didn't find anything, I'm in a quandary over the whole Larry situation.

"Oh, come on. Winston is perfectly nice. He's just a little crusty around the edges," Mama says, standing to grab the serving platter. "Now, y'all better wrap up this conversation because Adrina and Wes will be here soon." She turns to stride into the house. "I'm gonna top up the chicken."

"Hey, Duke," I say, catching the older man's attention. "I think you should introduce yourself to Winston, maybe have a sit-down."

"And why would I want to do that?" He frowns at me with a drumstick poised in front of his mouth.

"You could pump him for information."

"That's not a bad idea," Maisy says. "A little guy talk could reveal things he might not say to Ginny."

"I've got enough friends. I need another one like I need a flippin' top hat and a tuxedo. Besides, I don't trust people I don't know," Duke responds before chomping into his drumstick.

Sunny sends us a subtle gesture, communicating that she'll work on him.

"So, we've got no leads. Just conjecture." Cash sums up the situation, tossing his napkin onto the table. Hollis, his girlfriend, puts an arm around his shoulders.

I look at Joey to see him watching my brothers. When I catch his eye, he raises his brows and jerks his chin in their direction. I know what he wants me to do.

Luca sighs next to me. "Some kids started a fire, Miller crashed a car, the brewery had a break-in, Larry was stolen, Clarence Cody's goons trashed Ginny's house and tried to shut down Blue Bigfoot, and my dad got laid off. Bad shit happens. Apparently, it just happens more often around here. Is that what we're thinking now?"

Glances are exchanged across both tables before Carter finally speaks up. "I guess so. Damn, I wish I'd had the brake lines checked before they towed my car to the junkyard."

"I'm not saying anything." Miller throws his arms up, and Cart elbows him in his unprotected gut. Miller groans and cradles his stomach.

Everyone looks so dejected and lost. I mean, having proof that a giant, rich real estate conglomerate has it in for you wouldn't exactly be welcome news, but it would at least give us all a united enemy and purpose.

In lieu of that, I feel a duty to open my mouth. "I found Larry." A dozen sets of eyes swing my way, and I audibly swallow. Joey gives my knee an encouraging squeeze, and I force myself to continue. "I followed that lead Miller gave me about the customer who thought he saw Larry at a gallery in Raleigh."

"You didn't tell *me* about that." Maisy turns to Miller while Hollis, Rosie, and Sunny all swing narrowed eyes at their respective Brooks boyfriends. *See?* They all keep things from the women in their lives.

"Joey and I went to the gallery. It's definitely Larry," I say. "I could tell by Miller's flip-flop marks on his foot."

Several sets of eyes turn to Miller, who shrugs. "I was eight. What do you want from me?"

I continue, knowing I can't exactly stop now. "The gallery didn't buy Larry, nor is he for sale. He's on loan from a collector who bought him from who I assume is the thief."

"You know who these people are?" Denny asks, rising to his feet like he's about to run off chasing the burglar.

"Yes." I nod. "I spoke with the collector, and he gave me contact info for the person he bought it from. Whoever it is lied and said Larry has been in his family for years. The guy who bought him is a Morton Frye expert, so he knew it was the real deal the minute he saw it."

"Then let's go get this asshole!" Cash stands as well, followed by Miller, Denny, and Luca.

"I'm not done eating!" Duke shouts, waving another drumstick in the air. My brothers ignore him.

"Wait!" Hollis yells. "You need to let the police handle this."

"No way," Cash responds. "This guy broke into our business and stole our dad's prized possession. This is personal."

"If you go stomping off to Raleigh to go head-to-head with this unknown criminal, I'm calling the cops myself!" Rosie declares.

All conversation devolves from there into individual couples bickering and pointing, and I can't get a word in edgewise. Even Hollis and Cash's dogs get in on it, barking and howling as they run circles around the tables. I look at Joey and sigh. This is gonna be a long night.

JOEY

Everyone is glaring and practicing the silent treatment by the time the neighbors, Adrina and Wes, arrive. This family is ten times the size of mine, and they've all argued so much that I've lost track of who's on which side. Luckily, Adrina is too busy chatting about Rosie and Denny's wedding to notice the frigid vibes in the air. Lynn and Ginny keep the conversation going with Adrina while Wes focuses on the plate before him and nothing else. I'm tempted to join him on that end of the table.

When Lynn excuses herself to use the restroom, I notice Cash following her inside. This can't be good. I'm proven right a minute later when Lynn stomps back to the table, leaving her brother inside.

"If he thinks I'm giving him that contact information, he's nuts," she mutters more to herself than to me. "He's gonna take off to Raleigh, and Hollis will be on the phone with the cops in two seconds flat."

Since she's still whispering in my direction, I figure I can join the conversation. Adrina is talking loud enough that nobody is even paying us any attention. "Why is that so bad? Since now you know there's no connection with The Diamond Group."

Lynn's eyes widen. "We don't know that for sure. Just because Duke didn't find other homeowners who were victimized doesn't mean these asshole developers aren't behind all of this."

"Lynn." There's a warning in my voice that I know will ruffle her feathers, but the bottom line is she can't go do this on her own. I'd never forgive myself if something happened to her, and I could have stopped it.

"Joey." Her eyes narrow as her lips thin. "I just had a run-in with Cash, and I'm sure every one of my brothers will pull me aside before the night is through. I really need at least one person on my side in this."

Fuck. Why does she insist on doing everything herself? We're going to have a long sit-down soon so I can get to the bottom of this. I can't keep giving in just to keep the peace when she could get herself in real trouble with her one-woman heroine act.

"Lynnie," Carter calls down the table, and we both turn his way. "Can I have a word?" He gestures to the house.

Lynn pastes on a smile. "No thanks. I'm enjoying hearing about Denny and Rosie's wedding plans."

I'm pretty sure I hear Carter growl in response. When I glance around the table, I notice every one of her brothers—plus Luca—are now watching their sister as she absently picks at the food on her plate. It's her against all these men; all she wants is her boyfriend to have her back.

So, I set my doubts aside again and grab the hand resting in her lap, lacing my fingers with hers and squeezing it. "I got you," I whisper, knowing she heard me when she squeezes my hand back.

AN HOUR LATER, I'm at the kitchen sink, washing dishes. My mom didn't raise an idiot.

"You think anyone would believe me if I told them I've got a professional baseball star washing my dinner dishes?" Ginny asks her neighbor Adrina. They're both covering food and putting it in the fridge, handing me the dirty dishes as they go. Lynn volunteered for cleanup too, not wanting to give her brothers an opportunity to pin her down.

But Adrina's got other plans for my girlfriend. "Lynnie, *cara*, could you please fetch my good Tupperware so I can pack some leftovers for Wes's lunch?"

"Sure thing," Lynn responds before heading down the hall.

Just about everyone else is still in the backyard, either playing with the dogs or arguing. As the new guy, I'm glad I'm inside.

"This is the last one, darlin'." Ginny hands me a large platter with a sunflower pattern. "I'll get one of the other boys to haul the trash," she says before walking through the den toward the back door.

"Don't forget! You were going to show me those flowers!" Adrina calls after her, hustling to catch up with her neighbor.

I wash and dry the platter and am just about to head out back to locate Lynn when I find myself surrounded by four frowning Brooks brothers. It's like a bad western, except nobody's packing heat. At least, I hope not.

Seeing what's coming, I beat them all to the punch. "Let me guess. You're here to ask me what my intentions are with your sister. No offense, but unless you've got at least two goats and a carriage load of grain, I'm out," I quip.

Denny and Miller shift their feet and break eye contact, making me want to laugh. But I don't. Like I said, my mom didn't raise an idiot.

"Don't act like you don't know why we're worried," Carter says, holding my eyes. "You know damn well ballplayers have a reputation for a reason." He's not wrong, so I can only nod.

Denny is next. "We don't have a problem with you sowing your wild oats, just so long as our baby sister doesn't get run over by your tractor in the process."

"Really? Farming analogies?" Miller asks, shaking his head at his brother. Denny only shrugs.

"Look, guys." I put my palms out. "I know all about your family history and your protectiveness of Lynn. I get it. But you don't have to worry about me. I'm not gonna hurt her."

After a beat of silence, Cash is the one to speak up. "Listen, just because she acts all evolved and independent and like her generation is the first one to run free with their sexuality and shit—"

Denny cuts him off. "Damn, bro, where'd you learn all that lingo?"

Cash flips him off without a glance in his direction as he continues, "Doesn't mean her heart can't be broken. Lynnie feels things deep, even if she pretends not to."

"Look, guys." I settle in, butt against the counter. I'm not leaving until I get through to them. "I actually *appreciate* you looking out for her. Believe me, you're giving me peace of mind, whether you know it or not. But you've got nothing to worry about from me."

Carter narrows his eyes. "What does that mean?"

"Which part?"

"All of it."

I run a hand through my hair, letting out a breath. "Just that I've run into her independent streak a time or two and learned that your sister is as stubborn as a mule."

One or more of them let out a satisfied chuckle, which I suppose is a good sign.

"So, she doesn't listen to you either?" Denny asks.

"No. And that's okay—well, most of the time." I feel my lips quirk as I picture Lynn facing off with me. "It's actually one of the things I love the most about her."

"*Love?*" Miller's voice cracks like an adolescent whose balls are about to drop.

"Yeah." I look Miller in the eye. "Love. I love her, guys." My gaze runs across each of their faces to make sure they heard me.

"You don't even know her." Cash scoffs.

"Yes, I do."

"Does she love you?" Denny asks, his voice having lost its challenging edge.

"I have no fuckin' clue." I let out a mirthless laugh as I drop my head back and look to the ceiling for answers. "See what I mean about you not having anything to worry about from me?"

One of them—I'm not sure which—laughs. "So, our little sister has you wrapped around her finger, huh?"

I straighten my head to respond. "That about sums it up."

But Cash is still watching me with narrowed eyes.

"Which means you're not about to let her do anything stupid, right?"

Shit. When I don't answer, he steps forward to study my face before turning to his brothers. "She's under his skin so far, no way he's giving away her secrets. Let's go corner Lynnie," he instructs his brothers, and they all turn to leave.

"Guys! Wait." When their eyes hit me again, I sigh. "She just wants to be treated like an adult, not like the teenage girl she once was."

Carter clears his throat. "No offense, man, but our family has been through enough for us to let our sister go it alone on anything. You think we could live with ourselves if something happened to her on our watch?"

"No. We've lost enough," Denny adds, his voice tight. I remember Lynn telling me how Denny was so racked with grief after their dad's passing that he left for four years, figuring if he did the leaving, nothing could hurt him again. It took his now-fiancée, Rosie, to bring him back.

"She's not going to tell you," I mutter.

"We'll see about that," Carter finishes before they file into the den toward the backyard.

Fuck! They clearly have been through enough. And they're right. None of them could go on if something happened to Lynn, and neither could I. My choices are down to skipping the team charity gig and further endangering my spot on the team or telling Lynn's brothers about her plan and making her pissed as hell. With neither one sounding that great, I make a split-second decision.

"But *I* will," I call after them.

And with those three words, I might be kissing the best thing that's ever happened to me goodbye. But at least she'll be safe.

THIRTY-SEVEN
NANCY DREW, AT YOUR SERVICE

LYNN

My phone alarm goes off at six thirty the next morning, and I immediately silence it, cursing myself for not leaving it on vibrate. I can't afford for anyone to question what I'm doing up so early. Especially since Cash, for some unknown reason, decided to stick around and spend the night in his room last night. He must be mowing Mama's lawn this morning or something.

This is the first night since the weekend that I've spent without Joey, and I have to admit I missed waking up in his arms. I've truly become addicted to that man. The thought has me smiling as I head for the hall bathroom to quietly shower and get ready.

Today is the day I'm heading back to Raleigh to track down Edward Dante. Despite my brothers' best efforts, I remained mum about any names and specifics last night. They'll get the dirt when I have something concrete to share. If this Dante guy is a serial criminal, surely we can find out more when we get a picture of him. Or it could be a dead end, for all I know. It might not be the same Eddie Dante who stole Larry, in which case I'll have to switch to plan B and call the number Guy gave me. Whatever happens, I'll figure it out.

I do wish Joey didn't have that charity thing today so he could come with. Playing private investigator with him was fun last time, and then he wouldn't have to waste all his time worrying about me. The way he kissed me goodbye by his truck last night told me he's going to spend today worrying himself sick. I'll have to be sure to check in as often as I can to ease his mind.

I dress in black shorts and a black tank to stay on theme, and I sweep my hair up into a high ponytail as I quietly descend the staircase. But when I get to the key rack in the kitchen, I notice my keys aren't there. I backtrack up the stairs and check my shorts pockets from yesterday. Still no key. Which is odd considering I've been hanging my keys on that rack every day I've been home since I was sixteen.

"Looking for these?" Cash asks, scaring the ever-loving shit out of me when I reenter the kitchen.

"Jesus, Mary, and Jolene!" I smack my chest, checking to make sure my heart didn't splat against my ribcage. "You know I can't handle jump scares!"

Instead of him reveling in my pain with a laugh, however, my brother's face is a study in sobriety as he watches me from his spot at the kitchen table. My car keys dangle from his index finger like he's some Hollywood supervillain who's just caught his archnemesis in the act.

When I approach and swipe at his hand to grab them, he catches the keys in his palm, and they disappear into his pocket.

"What are you doing?" I ask, beginning to get irritated.

"Funny. That's exactly what I was going to ask you."

I glare at him, my annoyance clocking in at a high seven now. "Going to work. Give me my keys."

"No." He stands then, using his height to his advantage by peering down at me with flinty eyes. What the hell is going on here?

"You're really starting to annoy me, Cash."

I expect him to break character and laugh before handing my keys over and maybe ruffling my hair like I'm still five. But his next words have all the blood draining from my face and settling in my Chucks.

"You really think we were going to let you go to Raleigh by yourself to chase down that asshole?"

Dammit! How did they guess I was going today? I made sure to tell Mama last night that I had work today—I even said it loud enough to make sure every damn person there heard me.

"What are you talking about?" I try lying, even though I know my face already gave me away. Why, oh why didn't I join drama club in high school?

"Nice try. I know all about Eddie Dante and Guy Taylor, and there is no way you're going into the lion's den. One of us is gonna figure out a way to go without our women calling the cops."

My hands hit my hips at his words. "Yeah, and that one of us is *me!*" I lunge for his pocket, not even caring if I accidentally punch him in the nuts in the process. But Cash easily captures both my wrists in one of his giant fists. Why couldn't my brothers be a bunch of wimps instead of these overly-fit brutes?

"Not a chance."

"Cash Brooks, you do not own me! I can do as I damn well please!"

Mama stumbles into the kitchen, her hair a wild mass of curls around her head and her eyes heavy with sleep. "What in tarnation is goin' on here?"

"Nothing," Cash insists, letting go of my wrists but maintaining his glare.

I hold his eyes too, determined not to be the first to break contact. "Just the usual, Mama. Cash treating me like I'm five and telling me what I can and can't do."

"Cash!" Mama scolds, but it bounces right off my brother.

"Lynn wants to drive halfway across the state to chase down a criminal all by herself." His jaw is tense enough to crack nuts.

"What?" Mama gasps.

Why is he telling her this? I specifically waited until Mama was out of earshot to share about Larry last night at dinner. And now he's spilling the beans?

"It's nothing, Mama. Cash doesn't even know what he's talking about." How in the hell did he get those names, though? Did he track down that customer like I did?

"Yes, I do. Lynn knows where Larry is, and she's heading to Raleigh to stake out the house of the guy who stole him."

It's my turn to gasp. How does he know about the stakeout? It takes my brain less than ten seconds to put two and two together and get... Ace.

LYNN

When the elevator dings, I look that way to see Joey step through the metal doors. He's wearing a dark suit with a gray button-down, and I realize I've never seen him this dressed up. He looks good.

His face brightens the second he spots me leaning against the wall by his condo door. "Hey!" He smiles as he closes the distance between us.

"One of your neighbors buzzed me in. You might want to talk to the building manager about security." I don't know why I'm making small talk when I'm only here to say one thing.

When Joey bends to kiss me hello, I pretend to have an itch on my knee and duck his gesture. I can't kiss him. Not when I'm so fucking angry with him.

He unlocks his door and holds it open for me, and I quickly walk through. The sooner I get this over with, the sooner I can leave for my shift at Blue Bigfoot. Since I have no car and no freedom, I may as well earn some money while I seethe and plot murder. I'm thinking Cash will be first in line.

Only when Joey removes his jacket and turns to face me do I notice the awkwardness in his movements. He's nervous. He should be.

"Why did you do it?" I ask.

At least he doesn't try to deny it. I can always say one thing for Joey: he's an open book. But I'm not expecting the answer I get.

He exhales slowly, propping his hand on his hips, before meeting my gaze with those espresso beauties I want so desperately to despise. "Because I love you."

My head goes light and spots start dancing in front of my eyes, so I blindly reach for the nearest solid surface. I brace myself on the entry table until I'm able to blink the spots away. But my heartbeat thumps loudly in my ears while I stand there and try wrapping my mind around his answer.

When the silence stretches for what feels like an eternity, he finally breaks it. "Did you hear me?"

Oh, I heard him all right. I just have no idea what to do with that information. Half my body wants to melt into a puddle of goo and run into his arms, but the other half is way too rational for that—and way too mad. I decide to go with what's most familiar.

"You don't love me," I declare, shaking my head.

"I think I know my own feelings, Lynn." His voice is soft, even with the familiar rumble, and there's that lopsided grin. He's trying to kill me.

But I'm stronger than that, so I straighten my shoulders and press on. "If you loved me, you'd respect me and treat me like an equal."

"I do treat you like an equal." He throws one arm out. "Hell, I hold you up on a damn pedestal, if anything."

My chin snaps back. "That's exactly what I'm saying!"

"Holding you in high esteem means I don't think you're equal to me?"

"I'm not some treasure, Joey." I bring a fist to my chest, still not wanting to release the table that might be holding me up. "I'm a woman. A thinking, breathing, capable woman. All I want is to be treated like one."

Joey mirrors my gesture with both his hands. "I do treat you like one!"

"No, you don't. If you did, you wouldn't have tattled to my brothers like we're all children on a playground." I can't be with someone who promises something in one moment and breaks that promise the next.

"I did it because I fucking love you, Lynn, and it would gut me to my core if anything happened to you. Can't you understand that?"

"Nothing is going to happen to me," I insist.

"Did you think anything would happen to your dad when he went in for that surgery, never to come out again?"

I gasp at his words, leaning on the table for support now. "I can't believe you said that."

He takes a step closer, his hand extended like he wants to pull me to him. When I halt him by thrusting my palm out, he stops. "I'm sorry. The last thing I want to do is hurt you." He runs frustrated fingers through his hair, leaving it looking like he just woke up. It's normally my favorite look on him, but not today. "I was just trying to make a point. Everyone cares about you and wants you safe. Putting yourself in the path of a criminal is the definition of unsafe. You won't even let anyone go with you."

"I would have welcomed you. But since you couldn't, I had no choice but to go alone."

His eyebrows spike. "So, you went?"

"No."

He lets out a heavy exhale. "But you're going to." Before I can respond, he continues, "Please, just take one of your brothers, at least, if you can't wait for me."

I bark out a humorless laugh at that, my sarcastic inner bitch taking over. "Wow. Great idea, *Ace*."

Joey's face falls, and I fight against the regret clawing at my heart. "Don't say that name when you're angry. Please, Lynn."

"Fine. What I was going to say is that I'd love to take one of my brothers with me, but none of them can leave town, and I've been forbidden from driving my own fucking car."

"What?" He appears genuinely surprised.

"What did you think they'd do, Joey? I told you what they were like, and you kept saying you thought it was *sweet* and *nice*. They literally stole my car keys—and Mama's! And I can't even ask any of the girls to drive me because they all want to call the cops. So, now we're stuck, and Winston will probably sign his house over to his evil daughter, and these developers will find a new way to force Mama and Adrina out!"

"You don't know that will happen." He shakes his head, but I have a ready response.

"You don't know it won't."

Joey drops his eyes to his shoes, but I watch him, still simmering with anger and frustration. "There are other ways to end this. Ginny can be honest with Winston. You all can set up a meeting with The Diamond Group. You can call the cops about Larry and get him returned. Would that be so bad?"

Tears start welling, and I honestly don't know if I want to laugh or cry. "You don't get it."

"No, I guess I don't." His face swims in my vision, every handsome feature distorted. "Explain it to me. Why is this so important?"

The tears win, spilling down my cheeks. "Because I want my dad back, and I can't have him."

Even through my tears, I can see the pain etched on Joey's face. "I don't understand."

I genuinely want him to understand. I need *someone* to understand. So I try piecing the words together, unsure if they'll make any sense but pushing forward nonetheless. "I play the tough girl—always. But inside, my heart is *broken*. When Denny left after the funeral, I had to make a choice: crumble apart and die or toughen up. So I toughened up." My voice cracks, but I keep going. "But my heart stayed broken, and I never learned how to fix it. So, yeah, I'm defensive and independent and determined, and I refuse to apologize for it. Because life breaks your heart, and that's a fact. It's up to you to protect yourself." I press a balled fist to my chest again, desperately trying to hold the tears back.

"When all this bad shit started happening, my brothers kept it from me, thinking they were doing right by me in protecting me from hurt or worry. But what they don't understand—what they've *never* understood—is that standing on my own two feet and fighting back with my own fists is the only way to get back my power—to keep that awful helplessness at bay. I couldn't control what happened with my dad, but I can damn sure control other things. And with each battle I win, I'm not only carrying on, I'm doing it in a way that would make my dad proud."

"Fuck, Lynn." Joey moves closer, but again, I stop him. "I don't know what to say." He stands in front of me, hands limp at his sides.

"I think you've said enough already. I have to go." I swipe the tears from my cheeks and suck in a cleansing breath.

"Let me at least drive you. We can talk more on the way."

"No." I shake my head and turn for the door. "Miller's waiting for me downstairs." I had to get a ride from my brother to break up with my boyfriend. Am I the only one who sees how ridiculous this is?

"Precious cargo," Joey whispers from behind me, and I can't tell if he meant for me to hear or not.

Either way, as I close the door behind me, I say, "Yeah, watch out, or I might break."

JOEY

I'm not sure I could have fucked things up any harder if I tried. At least I gave it my all. Go big or go home, right?

The first thing I do after Lynn walks out of my door is chug a beer. Then I remember I'm not an idiot frat boy who thinks alcohol is the answer to every problem, and I turn on a ball game instead. It only takes one inning for me to break down and text Lynn.

ME:

I know you're angry. Thank you for explaining things.

ME:

I'm truly sorry I hurt you. I'm begging you to give me another chance.

I drop my phone on the couch and try to focus on the game. It doesn't work, so I pick up the phone again. No reply.

ME:

I'll give you space tonight, but can we
please talk tomorrow?

Another inning and no response. At this point, I'm rethinking the whole alcohol solution—until I remember the only thing worse than waking up heartbroken is waking up heartbroken with a hangover. That's when I do something I'd typically advise myself against and call Liv.

"I fucked up" is the first thing I say.

Instead of a response from my cousin, I hear her muffled voice shouting, "Brett! Put your therapist cap on and get in here, STAT!"

Terrific.

I talk the entire thing out with Liv and Brett, refusing their bizarre offer of help from their friendly neighborhood hacker named Ollie. Honestly, this situation has had enough people thrown into it as it is. I do, however, take their advice on a few things, and we devise a plan that I'm hoping might work.

I finally fall asleep at two in the morning in the most pathetic manner possible—listening to the Counting Crows and hugging a pillow. Good fucking god.

First thing the next morning, I call the Mintz Gallery and get Guy Taylor's number, reminding the associate of my recent visit and pretending I misplaced the information. After phoning Guy, I call Blue Bigfoot Brewery, where Carter answers the phone. I communicate my plan and give him an earful he likely won't forget anytime soon.

Then I'm off to Raleigh for the day.

Lynn still hasn't texted me back, which isn't surprising since she's at work at Ardent Park today. I considered stopping by and kidnapping her to take her with me, but I know this internship is important to her. She not only would hate me for making her miss a day, but she'd have my hide for exposing our intimate connection. So, I decide it's best for her to stay where she is. She'll have her chance to kick ass once I'm back.

When Guy texts me the name of a café midway through my drive, I start believing I might actually pull this off.

I park in front of the café a half hour early, having left with plenty of time to figure in possible traffic. The hostess seats me at a table for two on the outdoor patio flanking the sidewalk, and I sip my water while anxiously awaiting Guy's arrival. Every instinct I have about this man tells me he's a reasonable human being who simply loves collecting art. Which is why I'm trusting he'll agree to my plan to help Lynn bust this Eddie Dante, whoever the hell he is.

I rehearse my prepared speech in my head, knowing I've only got one shot at this. Mr. Taylor thinks he's meeting me for a friendly chat about art, so I need to tread carefully if I don't want him running to the cops.

As I'm sipping my water and running through my lines, I sense a presence to my right on the sidewalk. When I glance over, I see the vaguely familiar face of a man in his mid-thir-ties wearing a suit. He's smiling at me and pointing.

"You're Joey Martel," he says.

I relax, realizing it's a fan, not some person from my past. I reach my hand out to shake his. "Yeah. Nice to meet you."

He tilts his head. "Actually, we've met before. Jeremy Rossi. I'm a friend of Lynn Brooks. Well, the whole family, in fact. I can't believe I didn't recognize you then." His face finally registers, and I stand to make up for my lapse in memory.

"Of course. Sorry. I'm a little distracted. Good to see you again."

"No problem," Jeremy says with a good-natured shrug. "What brings you to Raleigh?"

"Just meeting somebody for lunch. Business." Part of me is still suspicious of his intentions toward Lynn, but he appears genuinely pleased to run into me, so I force myself to make conversation even though all I want to do is focus on what I'm going to say to Guy. "You?"

He hooks a thumb behind him. "I work around the corner. State legislature."

"Ah. Got it. Sounds...swanky." I have no clue what the fuck I'm saying at this point, but I'm relieved to no end when Jeremy gives me a nod.

"I'll leave you to your lunch. Gotta grab a bite of my own before my full afternoon." He walks away, and I sink back into my chair to resume rehearsals in my head—which is why I don't notice a nicely dressed older man approach my table.

"Mr. Martel?" the man inquires.

I stand again, forcing a casual manner to hide my nerves. "Mr. Taylor. Thank you for meeting me."

"My pleasure." His smile is warm. I can do this. No sweat. But before I can go with my rehearsed opening line, he says something that has me wondering if I should get my hearing checked.

"I see you've already made Mr. Dante's acquaintance."

My brow furrows. "I'm sorry. What?"

He points to the sidewalk, but when I look over, no one is there. Shit. Is he... having a senior moment?

But, no. I'm definitely mistaken. I know this when his

next words are, "The gentleman you were just talking to. Mr. Eddie Dante."

My ears start ringing as I look behind me to see Jeremy's back as he strides confidently down the sidewalk.

Holy. Shit.

"LYNN, I need to talk to you. Right now," I practically shout as I leave her a voicemail while tearing out of my parking spot. "This isn't about you and me. It's about Eddie Dante. Call me back as soon as you hear this. I'll try again in a few minutes."

I click the end-call button as I speed through a yellow light on my way to the highway. I need to get my ass back to Asheville, traffic rules be damned.

Fucking Jeremy! A fox in the Brooks family henhouse. I slam my palm on the steering wheel before reminding myself I'll do nobody any good if I die on the way there.

My plan had been a good one. At least Liv and Brett thought so. I was going to lay the situation out for Guy Taylor and lean on his sympathies for a family trying to right wrongs and honor their dad. Once I got his cooperation, I planned to organize some kind of sting operation where Lynn could confront Eddie in a controlled environment with me, Guy, and the gallery dude all present. The gallery has a metal detector, so Guy would ask Dante to meet us there on the pretense that he had some gift for him. Then Lynn could enter and press him for any connection to The Diamond Group. With the threat of police involvement, hopefully he'd spill anything he had. And there would be no chance of him having a weapon with the metal detector, so she'd be as safe as I could make her. I've already told Carter as much, except for leaving out some details and thus precluding him from taking over my plan.

Obviously, the second Guy connected the dots for me between Larry's theft and Jeremy, I abandoned my plan, not even spilling one word about Larry or the theft to Guy. There were bigger things to take care of first.

I make it to Asheville in three hours flat, having called Lynn several more times with no answer. So, I drive straight to Ardent Park and come to a screeching halt in the players' parking lot before racing inside to the medical hall. That's when I force myself to stop and take a breath.

Lynn won't thank me one bit if I blow our connection wide open, no matter how urgent the situation is, so I simmer my ass down and count to ten. On eleven, I calmly open the door and force my feet to take slow, even steps.

"Hey, Joey! I thought you weren't coming in today?" Nora greets me from her desk.

"I wasn't, but I was hoping to have a word with Lynn. I need to ask a favor."

Nora looks to the other side of the room, where Lynn emerges from a side door to face me. Her stance is neutral, but her eyes are on fire.

I paste on a smile for Nora. "It'll just take a sec. Lynn, can I have a quick word?"

"Sure." Her response comes out a little too sharp to be convincing, but Nora doesn't appear to notice as she drops her eyes back down to her laptop. "What's up?" Lynn asks, stabbing me with daggers from her gold-flecked irises.

However, as soon as we're out in the hallway with the door closed behind us, she loses all casual pretenses. "What are you doing here?"

"You didn't get my voicemails," I state the obvious.

"I'm at work," is, understandably, her response.

I glance around the hall, and despite not seeing anyone, I pull her into an alcove away from any possible prying eyes. "I just got back from Raleigh, and I had to find you immediately. Eddie Dante is your family's friend, Jeremy Rossi."

"Joey, I don't have time for jokes." She tries turning to walk away, but I grab her shoulders, desperate for her to listen.

"Lynn, I'm being one hundred percent serious. Guy Taylor identified him. It's Jeremy."

She tilts her head but continues not to hear what I'm saying. "You went to Raleigh *and* met Guy? Without me?" If the situation weren't so urgent, I might feel guilty for the injured expression on her face.

"You're not hearing me," I say through gritted teeth as I release her shoulders. "Jeremy is Eddie Dante. Guy pointed him out to me."

"What are you talking about? You only met Jeremy once, and that was a year ago. You probably don't even remember what he looks like. Wait. Did you talk to Eddie too?"

How is she not hearing me? "I was waiting to meet Guy, and Jeremy walked by. He reintroduced himself to me before Guy showed up. When Guy sat down a minute later, he pointed Jeremy out to me. I promise I'm not making this up. Jeremy is Eddie."

Her skeptical expression begins to fall, replaced by confusion. "Are you being serious?"

Finally! If I weren't so in love with this woman, I'd probably strangle her. "I've never been more serious in my life. Jeremy broke in and stole Larry from you. And who knows what else he's done." I had the entire drive home to think about it, and I can't make heads or tails of anything anymore. I only know that Jeremy has been up to no good taking advantage of his relationship with the Brookses.

"But why?" Lynn's confusion is now mixed with pain, and I want to take it away. I want to pull her into my arms and sweep away anything that could hurt her. But that's not my job.

My job as someone who loves her is to give her the facts and then support her in any way I can. So I shake my head, about to tell her I haven't the slightest clue. But her mouth drops open before I can.

"Oh my god! He lost his job because Carter busted their boss. Do you think…?" She trails off before gasping again. "The timeline fits for both the fire and Larry. Not Miller's car crash, but I suppose that was just Miller being Miller, like everybody said. This isn't about The Diamond Group at all."

"What do you want to do? I'm here to support you, no matter what you decide. If you let me, that is."

She's staring at the wall behind me, her mind probably running a hundred miles an hour, so I'm not sure she heard me.

But I'm shocked when her only response is, "I need to get back to work."

"What?"

She shakes her head as if to clear it before meeting my eyes again. "I need to think, and I'll do that best if I keep my hands busy."

"Okay." I nod. "Will you call me when you're done for the day?" I don't realize I'm holding my breath until she nods, and it comes rushing from my lungs.

"I gotta run," she says, turning to go. But before she gets

more than five steps, she turns again. "Jeremy doesn't know you busted him, right?"

I shake my head. "He has no idea. And Guy doesn't know Larry was stolen either."

She nods and starts to turn back to the clinic again but pauses at the last second. "Thanks, Joey." And then she's gone, the door closing behind her.

That could have gone a lot worse, all things considered. But I still can't help wishing she'd called me Ace.

YOU'D NEVER KNOW ENGLISH IS
MY FIRST LANGUAGE

LYNN

J eremy.
Fucking Jeremy.
Mother fucking freaking Jeremy!

I knew he was slick, but I never imagined he could be so *slimy*. Who does something like that? Stealing from a friend —and almost burning down their mom's house? All while pretending to be so concerned about our family. What a complete and utter asswipe! Maybe he's a sociopath—that could explain a lot.

"Lynn, can you track down Doc and remind him about that script for José?" Nora asks, forcing me to snap back to the job at hand.

"Oh, sure." I abandon the inventory list that—let's face it —I wasn't doing a great job with anyway and head to the next room and then the hall in search of Dr. Bhatia. But my head continues to swirl with Joey's revelation. And with the fact that, instead of chasing Jeremy down or calling the cops, Joey came to tell *me*.

I've had to completely set aside any feelings I might have about Joey going ahead to Raleigh and interfering like he obviously did. The importance of his discovery outweighs both his reasons and any potential feelings I have.

There's so much to plan and consider now that I know about Jeremy's betrayal. But one thing keeps nagging me, and I'm afraid of what it means.

Somehow, I thought it would feel a whole lot better finally being the one in the know, the one leading the charge. But this doesn't feel good in the least. Instead of wanting to come in to save the day and show everyone I can kick ass too, all I can think about is how this news is going to break hearts and cause more pain. And there's nothing to celebrate or feel proud of about that.

Dad, what am I doing? Did I get it all wrong?

"Lynn? Hey!"

I look up at the sound of my name to find Gunner Nix, the Arrows' left fielder and Joey's friend, entering the hallway from a door up ahead. Despite my distraction, I muster a smile since he's not responsible for any of this mess.

"Hi, Gunner."

He hooks his thumb over his shoulder toward the door he just exited. "Any idea why our boy is acting like somebody peed in his Cheerios this morning?"

Crap. "Uhhh..." What am I supposed to say?

Gunner's eyes widen. "Oh. Damn." He's obviously added two and two together.

"No! It's not...I'm just... he's..." I finally cough out a frustrated laugh and drop my chin, eyes to my shoes. "I'm still not fluent in English, apparently."

Gunner kindly chuckles at my very lame joke. "I should

probably just mind my own business." God, he's almost as nice as Joey.

Freaking Joey.

"No." I exhale, absently taking in Gunner's appearance. He's an incredibly handsome guy, built like a movie star, and friendly too. And he has absolutely *nothing* on Joey freaking Martel. "Have you ever gotten what you wished for and then wondered why it sounded so damn important in the first place?"

"Oh." His nose wrinkles as his hand goes to the back of his neck. "Elizabeth is better at the existential life questions. But I absolutely kill at sports trivia and history."

I can't help but smile at him. "It's okay. I'm just thinking out loud."

Gunner gives me a half grin. "Try to take it easy on our boy, yeah? He's a little lovesick."

I roll my lips between my teeth at his words, unsure how to respond. In the end, I simply nod and say, "I gotta run."

He lets me go, and I continue my search for Doc, but my mind keeps racing for the rest of my shift—and the Uber ride to Blue Bigfoot after.

"IF YOU'RE HERE to chew me out, get in line. Sunny started inventing new words because the English language doesn't seem to contain terms to adequately capture my degree of stubbornness for not calling the cops on your Dante guy." This is Carter's greeting when I close the brewhouse door behind me to give us some privacy.

"Oh, believe me, I'm still pissed about the car key stunt, but I have some news that takes precedence." Oh, how I'm dreading this. But I've concluded a few things from my afternoon of nail-biting. And the first one is that Carter deserves to hear about Jeremy first.

Cart keeps looking back and forth between the kettle thermometer and his notebook, his dark eyebrows scrunched together all the while. I take a step closer, preparing my words, but he beats me to it. "Well, in that case, if it's about your boyfriend going to Raleigh to talk Guy Taylor into helping you confront Eddie Dante without your brothers or the cops there to back you up, I already got an earful about that this morning."

I stop in my tracks. "What?" What is he talking about?

He finally looks my way, and I swear there's a hint of a smile behind all that scruff on his face. "Martel. He made it clear when he called me this morning that we're a bunch of overbearing idiots, especially if we think he's going to help us steamroll our sister. He also suggested we grow up and enter the twenty-first century. Oh, and—I almost forgot this part—that you've got more smarts in your little finger than the rest of our heads combined, so we should trust you not to unnecessarily endanger yourself when all you want to do is stand up for your family and do everyone proud. I'm *pretty* sure I got all that right."

I try swallowing, but my throat is too dry. I finally manage to croak out, "He said that?"

My brother nods and drops his notebook to the work table beside him before perching his hands on his hips and studying me. "Did Cash give your keys back?"

I shake my head, and Cart rolls his eyes. "I'll go grab them from the office."

When he moves to leave, I step in his path. "Wait!" We got sidetracked, and I need to tell him about Jeremy.

Once again, he beats me to it. "I know we get carried away. We owe you an apology."

"No!" Crap! "I mean, yes, and thank you, but no! Not right now, Carter." I grab his forearms, and he lets me lead him back to the table. "I have some upsetting news."

Something in my tone gets through because his expression changes to wary alertness.

"Joey came to see me," I begin. "He went to Raleigh today to meet with Guy Taylor like you said. He ran into Jeremy on the street, and when Guy arrived a minute later, he identified *Jeremy* as Eddie Dante. Jeremy, Carter. Jeremy is the one who stole Larry. And maybe even started the fire."

I can't read my brother's expression now, and when I open my mouth to continue my explanation, he cuts me off.

"That's not possible."

"That's what I said too at first, but Joey is positive."

"No way." He shakes his head. "Did they both talk to Jeremy?"

"Well, no. I don't think so." I shake my head now, remembering Joey's story. "No. Just Joey. If the three of them had talked together, the whole thing would already be out in the open. Jeremy doesn't know he's been busted."

Carter chuckles and pulls from my grip, causing my pulse to pound in my ears for the second time today. "Lynn, this is a misunderstanding. Jeremy probably looks like Dante from a certain angle. This Taylor guy caught a glimpse of him in passing and made a mistake."

I consider that, but then I remember the look on Joey's face—the panic in his eyes. And the fact that he came racing back to Asheville to tell me what he found.

"Carter, Joey is sure."

But Carter isn't listening. He throws his arm around my

shoulders and laughs. "Look, let's get your keys, and then I'll tell the boys we're going to let you and Joey take point on this whole Dante thing with Taylor. Martel's plan sounded fairly safe, all things considered."

"Carter, I swear to God, if you don't listen to what I'm saying, I'm going to nut punch you."

That, thankfully, makes him pause and face me again. "Lynnie, I know Jeremy. He's always had my back, even when I don't ask him to. When I tell you he's not involved, he's not involved."

And since *I* know my *brother*, I know it's no use talking myself blue in the face about this right now. What I need is to get my keys and then get some proof.

And I know just the man for the job.

LYNN

"Respond, dammit!" I growl at my phone as I shift restlessly on a kitchen chair two hours later.

"What did that phone do to earn such a talking to?" Mama sends me a grin as she enters the kitchen with a giant tote bag on her arm. "Or is it Joey who did something to draw your ire?"

"What?" I shake my head. "Sorry. I'm just waiting for somebody to text me." Since I don't want to involve Mama in this drama, I change the subject. "How'd you get your keys?" The boys stole hers as well as mine, knowing I'd just take Mama's car to Raleigh.

"Darlin', that's what the spare set is for." Her tone implies I should have known to do the same. Too bad Priscilla only has one key, poor girl.

Mama sets her tote on the table with a loud clunk.

"What's in the bag?" I ask.

"Well, I figured it might be good to have some hooch

when I talk to Winston again about what might be going on."

Crap. Mama now thinks this Larry thing is tied to Winston's daughter somehow. I knew Cash should have kept his mouth shut.

"I think we should hold off on that, Mama," I say.

She pats my hand that doesn't have a death grip on the phone. "I know you wanted to go confront that man about Larry, but y'all know you'll have to call the police eventually, right?"

"I'm afraid it's not as simple as that." I'm hoping that answer will suffice and she won't press me for details. Predictably, it doesn't work.

Mama parks her butt in the chair next to me and gives me *that* look. The one every mom uses when she's got something to say that you're not gonna like. "Did I ever tell you about the time your dad took me to get a fresh chicken?"

Huh? "No?" It's supposed to be an answer, not a question, but I'm scared of where this conversation is going. With Mama, you never know.

"It was when we were still dating as teenagers. Your dad started bragging about how he was teaching himself to cook, so I told him I wanted him to make me a chicken dinner."

"Dad couldn't cook," I remind Mama. The man could grill a mean burger, but anything involving an oven was just asking for trouble.

"Don't I know it," Mama says, smiling like she always does when she talks about my dad. "But he was determined, and I thought it was sweet. Since he didn't have two pennies to rub together, though, he decided we should visit the farm down the way and barter for a bird. After he and the farmer worked out a deal, we all went back to the pen where they kept the chickens. I don't know what my naive brain was expecting, but it sure wasn't to see the farmer grab a chicken by its neck, throw it on a propped-up sheet of plywood, and hack its head off with a giant cleaver like it was nothing."

I slap my hand over my mouth. "Oh my god, Mama! That's disgusting!" The universe keeps sending me evidence that I should become a vegetarian, so I don't know why I'm still walking around eating bacon and burgers and... chicken. Maybe I'm not so bright after all.

"Well, it was shocking, I agree." She laughs at my expression. "But not nearly as much as what happened next."

"I am so afraid to ask."

"I swear on Adrina's bolognese recipe, that chicken jumped right off the plywood and started running straight for the barn—with no head! The damn thing disappeared through the barn doors before we could blink. I'll never forget your dad and the farmer running after it, shouting like it could hear them. 'That's my girl's dinner!' Dad was yelling." She wipes tears of laughter from the corners of her eyes while I stare at her in horror.

"Mama, what in the world does this have to do with calling the police about Larry?"

Still giggling, she manages to say, "Well, if you'd let me finish..." I put my hands out to indicate she has the floor, although I'm sure I'll regret it. "It took them nearly a half hour to find that chicken. Of course, it had keeled over by that time, as I'm sure you've guessed. And when we finally got back to my parents' house, wouldn't you know there was a police cruiser in our driveway waiting to bring your dad down to the station."

"Why? What did he do?"

She bats her hand in the air at my question. "Oh, probably nothing. I don't remember. He was always on the local cops' list of boys to talk to when trouble cropped up in town. I ended up having to pluck and cook that darn bird in the end, although it was probably for the best since nobody got food poisoning that way."

I shake my head at her. "I can't believe you never told us that story." We have a tradition of telling all sorts of stories about my dad, especially on his birthday. Yet I've never heard that one, not that I really care to again—at least not in such detail. "So… what does it have to do with Larry?"

Mama shrugs and starts unpacking the booze from her tote bag. "Not much. I just thought you'd like to hear a story about your dad. I know he's been on your mind, darlin'. Just like I know he'd be damn proud of his girl."

As usual, Mama is ten steps ahead. "Mama." It's all I can say since tears are suddenly clogging my throat.

"I know you and the boys are probably hatching a plan, and you don't need to tell me about it if you don't want to. I trust you all to do what's right and use your heads."

And that's when I realize we've all been treating Mama the same way *I've* been complaining about how everybody treats *me*. Even *I've* been shielding Mama from things out of worry for her—things she has a right to know more than anybody. Hell, I was determined to leave this conversation without telling her about Jeremy or any of the new suspicions I might have. Not because I don't think she can handle it or has no right to know, but because I love her. And I don't want to see her hurt or worried if I can do something to fix it.

Just like Joey has been doing.

And just like my brothers always want to do for me. And for each other. They've *all* kept shit from not only me but each other these last months, always with the hope that they could leave their siblings breathing easy after all we've been through.

But that shit's about to end. Right now.

Because, just like when Dad was alive, we Brooks are stronger together than we ever could be apart.

Right on cue, my text notification dings, and when I tap the screen, my text chat with Guy Taylor appears, complete with the photo of Jeremy I texted an hour ago asking Guy to identify him as Eddie Dante.

> GUY:
>
> Yes, that's the same Eddie. Good luck with your conversation. I hope you find some connection to your father.

I push back my anger at Jeremy long enough to look Mama in the eye. "We've got a *lot* to talk about. You may as well crack open the hooch because this is gonna take a minute."

TWO HOURS LATER, Mama and I have formulated a plan and called in a few reinforcements to execute Operation Nail Jeremy to the Wall. Eh, we're still working on the name, but at least we're confident in both the plan's success and Jeremy's predictability.

I've got to say, Mama's got quite the elaborate revenge fantasy going on for someone who was a huge Jeremy fan before today. Jeremy won't know what hit him.

"Plotting a sting operation is tiring," Mama says over a yawn as she takes her glass to the sink.

"I don't know. I feel restless more than anything," I respond, propping my chin on my hand and spinning my empty glass on the table. Maybe I should call Sadie.

"That's because you're thinking about Joey Martel."

"I am not," I lie. I'm absolutely thinking about Joey—and how unfair I might have been.

"Just because you change the subject every time I bring up his name doesn't mean I can't see right through you." Mama doesn't even try to hide her smug grin. "You wouldn't even know about Jeremy if it wasn't for him, that's all I'm saying." She wants to use Joey in our plan, but I pushed for Hollis instead. That girl can throw down.

I drop my hand and straighten in my chair. "Mama, I can make my own choices. I've been doing it for a long time."

"True. You've always been just as headstrong as your brothers—sometimes more so. I suppose you can thank both me and your father for that."

And I don't know why I choose this moment to tell Mama what I've been keeping to myself for years, but it just spills out. "I used to hear you cry yourself to sleep." Oh, who am I kidding? I know precisely why it's been on my mind. Joey. Specifically, me being scared shitless that he told me he loves me. And then he went and stood up for me in a way I can't possibly ignore.

All signs of smugness fade from Mama's face, so I know I don't need to explain further. But to my surprise, her smile remains, only it's softer now. "I still miss him. But I'm thankful for all the time we had."

"I know you miss him. Just like I know the way you walk around every day like life couldn't be better is you hiding your broken heart. And I know it because I'm walking around with the same heart." My voice cracks on the last words.

"Oh, sweetheart." She closes the space between us and bends to wrap her arms around me. "My heart heals a little more each day. It's not broken. I'm so sorry yours isn't doing the same."

"But how?" I ask into her wild curls. "Dad was everything to you."

She releases me to crouch at my side and cup my face in her hands. "Not everything. I have you. And your brothers. And Adrina and Wes and a new daughter-in-law soon. I have a full life, and the best way to honor your dad is to wring every bit of joy out of it that I can." She brushes away the tear that escapes my eye. "And he wants the same for you, I promise. He wants you to live big, love big, and fill your life up till your cup overflows."

"I'm trying, Mama," I croak.

"Darlin', I don't mean to call you a liar, but I see a woman who's holding on tight with both hands to keep in control of damn near everything. You're the oldest twenty-one-year-old I've ever met."

I try rolling my eyes, but it doesn't take. All I can think of is how Joey told me the exact same thing not so long ago.

"What's wrong with securing my future and staying focused?"

"Is that what you're doing? Or are you hiding behind it? Maybe pushing away the chance at happy by holding those reins so tight?" She tilts her head, her eyes warm on me.

"I know what you're implying, Mama, but I don't need a *man* to make me happy."

"You're right about that. Absolutely."

I give her a quick nod, and she releases my face. "Glad we got that straight."

My words make her smile, which is not exactly what I was going for. "But when's the last time you stuck your neck out there without knowing how things would turn out or without planning for every eventuality? Even in your wild teenage days, you never put yourself in any situation without a plan B and C. Don't think I didn't notice you only broke curfew or ran around with boys to try to convince me you were doing fine like any other teenager. There was no way you were ever going to run off with the likes of Ben Weller. Let's be real."

Dammit. Busted.

I sigh. "I sure did give Cash a run for his money, though, didn't I?" I can't help the curve of my lips at the mental image of Cash pulling his hair out over me messing with boys in high school.

"I'm surprised he's not gray yet, to be honest," Mama responds, patting my knee.

We smile at each other for a few beats of silence before Mama says, "Do something for me, darlin', would you?" When I nod, she continues, "Let go with both hands and throw your arms in the air. Enjoy that rollercoaster to its fullest. Your family will be the safety harness, and provided a hurricane doesn't take us all out, we'll keep you safe just like you'll keep us. It's time to go chase happy and leave safe behind."

She picks up my phone and holds it out to me.

I blink down at it before meeting her eyes again. "I thought we agreed happy doesn't need to be about a guy."

"It doesn't. But does Joey make you happy?"

I immediately open my mouth to rebut, but she cuts me

off with a finger in the air. "And don't lie to me, girl. I've known you since you were a tiny bald eagle chick screaming your naked head off."

So, I do the smart thing and take the phone from Mama, keeping my mouth shut as I do.

JOEY

"Did that hurt?" Nora asks, bringing my attention back to her.

"What?" I blink a few times before I notice her watching my face instead of my wrist.

Lynn's not here yet, and I'm unsure if I should take that as a good or bad sign. She did text me last night, but all it said was, *We'll talk tomorrow.*

"She's running an errand for the clinic," Nora says as if I asked a different question. I notice her biting back a smile. Great.

It's oddly fortuitous that I'm freaking out about Lynn today. Otherwise, I'd be stressing out of my mind about the meeting Coach finally scheduled with me following this afternoon's home game. I've been too worried about losing Lynn for good to think much about the potential demise of my baseball career.

"Oh. No, it doesn't hurt. The only time it hurts at all anymore is when I overdo it." Nora has me doing exercises twice a day now, one set at home and the other here on the days I come in.

"Gotta make sure you're at full strength and range of motion before we get you back out there." She pulls out her elastic bands and starts hooking me up. "You catch any balls with it yet?" When she sees my guilty expression, she laughs. "It's not like you're my first athlete, Martel. Y'all can't help yourselves."

"Yeah," I admit. Gunner and I have been playing a little catch to test things out. "Nothing too powerful—I mean, it was Nix throwing." She snickers before I continue. "But it feels pretty good."

"Excellent. Talk to me before you bat, though. You hear me?"

"Got it, boss." Oops.

Nora leaves me to do this set of exercises on my own, but I'm focused more on the door than my wrist, even though no one but Amy has entered it since I've been here. I'm halfway decided on ditching therapy and hunting Lynn down by the time the door finally opens and she sweeps through it. Damn, she looks good. Her hair is gathered to one side, and she's wearing her shiny lip gloss and black scrubs, same as always.

I can't tell anything from her expression, but the fact that she won't meet my eye speaks volumes. I let the black band fall to my lap, and my fingers squeeze the bridge of my nose as reality settles in. I crossed too many lines with Lynn. It's my own damn fault.

The sound of Lynn's voice has my eyes snapping to the other side of the room. "Nora, can I have a word with Joey out in the hall?"

Nora glances my way, but Lynn's eyes remain on her

boss. I don't miss Amy's curious gaze bouncing between all of us. What is Lynn doing?

"Have at it," Nora says, causing Amy's eyes to widen.

Lynn finally faces me, one corner of her mouth lifting as she asks, "Joey, can I have a minute?"

I'm out of the chair so fast I almost crack my nuts on the corner of the treatment table. I go through the door and hold it open for Lynn as she passes through behind me. The second it latches, I open my mouth to ask her what she's doing, but I'm cut off by her lips connecting with mine so hard I might have a fat lip later. Totally worth it.

Being a relatively smart guy, I don't question Lynn's attack, instead, going all in on that kiss.

"I'm sorry," Lynn says a few seconds later, breathing heavily against my lips.

"No, I'm sorry." I kiss her again, so it's another minute before the conversation continues.

She tastes like mint and sunshine, and I don't think I'll ever get enough.

"There's so much to talk about, but I have to get back to work. I'm free after, though." There's a touch of doubt in her eyes that I need to nip in the bud.

"Come find me when you're done. I'm staying for the afternoon game, and then Coach wants a word. Should be done just after you."

We make plans to meet outside the clubhouse and then get distracted by kissing again before I shove her through the door. I take a minute to talk my boner down before I go in after her.

When I enter, though, I notice Amy whispering something at Lynn, who shakes her head a couple times before shrugging and walking away. Shit. Is she getting in trouble?

I keep my eye on Amy as I continue my exercises with Nora's occasional input. When it's time to ice, Amy snatches the pack from Lynn's hand and marches my way, lips in a thin line. This can't be good. But when I catch Lynn's eye from across the room, the woman winks at me. How I keep forgetting my girl has it all covered is beyond me.

Since I can only make so many excuses for hanging out in the therapy room, I eventually head up to watch the game with José, who's sitting out two games for an ugly-ass contusion Doc wanted to keep an eye on.

"How's the easy life treating you?" he asks. "Is it all beers and babes, or are you drowning your sorrows alone in your condo?"

We holler when Gunner hits a double and then settle back into our seats. "Mostly sorrows. A few beers. Lots of leg days. I can't wait to get off the IL, man." My mind is obviously on Lynn, but I'm not about to go there.

"I hear you." José takes a swig from his water bottle, and I decide to ask him a question I might regret.

"I'm meeting with Coach after the game. You think I have any reason to be nervous?"

José knows what I'm asking because he takes his eyes off the field to give me his full attention. "You asking if I've heard anything?"

I nod, trying my best to keep my heart from jumping out of my chest. Dickson, the kid they brought up from Triple A to fill in for me, is starting to hit his groove. At first, I wasn't as concerned, but now? It's why my ass is parked in this seat next to José to keep an eye out. Hell, I wasn't even on the IL when I got traded from Baltimore.

José watches me for another couple seconds before surprising the shit out of me by busting out laughing. When

I just stare, he finally gathers himself enough to explain, "Dude, I'm telling you, when you showed up for training camp and hardly said a word that first month, I thought you were a colossal fuckwad. That you weren't talking because you thought your shit didn't stink and you weren't about to lower yourself to make chit chat with a bunch of palookas like us."

I'm so shocked I can't find the words to respond.

But José's not done. "By the end of training camp, it was clear to me and everybody else that you're just one humble-as-hell five-tool player who saves his words for when he's got something to say. Damn, if we don't wish we had a team full of guys like you. You don't talk the talk, but you sure as hell walk the walk. Unlike some people. I mean, it's been a minute since Paulie last got his lights knocked out, so we've got that to look forward to, I suppose."

I have no idea what to say, so I simply go with what I'm feeling. "Thanks, man. I appreciate it." I shrug. "I guess I'm more into observing than all the chatter."

"You're not the only one. And when I say that, I mean the entire coaching staff and everyone up to Bronte Hughes himself has got eyes in their heads. You ain't goin' anywhere, Martel."

I cough out a laugh. "Thanks, Riviera."

"Just get off the IL, would you? That bush league short-stop is driving me fuckin' nuts."

"On it."

Our attention goes back to the game, and my thoughts return to Lynn now that José's words have me feeling better about this meeting with Coach.

The Arrows end up losing, which sucks, but we've got a new series starting tomorrow. José and I head for the clubhouse, with him to shoot the shit with the guys and me to catch up with Coach Gibbs. I feel like an ass when it turns out he just wanted to feel me out about doing a little mentoring with Dickson to up his game. I quickly agree, anxious to do anything that'll get me back on the field and make me feel useful to the team again.

Our chat is short, so most of the boys are still in the clubhouse when I pass through on my way to hunt Lynn down. I shoot Gunner a chin lift and push through the door to access the hallway—where I literally run into Lynn.

"Shit!" I reach out to nab her around the waist before she bites it on the concrete.

Apparently, my exclamation grabs the attention of some of my teammates because several of them gather in the doorway. I send panicked eyes to Lynn but find her grinning up at me instead of shooting me the daggers I was anticipating. This is not the way to keep our relationship on the down-low.

She takes a step back out of my arms, and I'm about to tell the guys to move the hell along when I notice her shirt. Or jersey, I should say. Lynn's lips spread in a full-on, gorgeous smile as she throws her arms to the sides, showing off the Arrows jersey she's put on over her scrubs. The number eight emblazoned on the front has my inner caveman grunting in satisfaction. When she spins to show the name Martel across her back, all the assholes behind me start whistling and shouting like a bunch of idiots.

I turn back only for the millisecond it takes to yell, "Fuck off!" before I pull Lynn into my arms and lift her off her feet so I can kiss her properly. She laughs against my lips when we hear José say, "Sorrows and beers, my ass! Martel has been working his ass off on the IL."

But since none of these guys need to witness me grabbing my girlfriend's luscious backside, I stride down the hall away from the clubhouse, Lynn's legs dangling in front of mine until she thinks better of it and wraps them around my waist.

Life can be so fucking sweet sometimes.

LYNN

"I hate to say it, but if you don't get your hands off me and onto the steering wheel, we'll never get out of here," I scold Joey ten minutes later as his hand slides between my thighs and his lips travel up the column of my throat.

He doesn't move, instead murmuring against my skin, "You're the one pulling my hair out and making all those noises that have me hard enough to pound nails."

I giggle and release my grip on his hair. Oopsie. He pulls his head back just long enough for me to see the heat in his eyes before he drops one last kiss on my lips and says, "I missed you."

Something goes all gooey in my chest. "Me too." Which is ridiculous since it's been like two days, but it's true nonetheless.

Joey finally straightens and situates himself in the driver's seat so he can pull his truck from his parking spot. "I'm afraid to ask, but did you get in trouble at work?"

I grin to myself, remembering Amy's lecture from earlier. "Not really. Amy said she was 'disappointed' in me, but Nora didn't seem to think anything of it, so I refuse to worry about it." After my talk with Mama last night and a few hours of tossing and turning, I decided that I would make it plain to Joey that he matters. Just like he's been bending himself backward to show me. If that meant I got fired from a job I wasn't even being paid to do, so be it. I'm still young, and I've got time to get the right experience.

The jersey was just my way of making sure Joey got the message, which, by the way he was just kissing me, I'd say he received loud and clear.

I lace my fingers in his as he pulls out from the lot with his left hand on the wheel.

"That's a bit of a turnaround," Joey comments. "I've got to say, I'm happy as hell I can show you off now." He winks at me, and I know my smile is downright stupid.

"Wait until you hear the rest."

I go on to tell Joey about Carter not believing us about Jeremy. He's less surprised than I was, saying that it's got to be hard believing that kind of thing about a trusted friend. Then I share the part about Guy confirming Jeremy's identity.

"What did Carter say about that?"

"I haven't told him yet."

Joey's gaze flashes to me, but he stays quiet, probably wanting to avoid the appearance that he's telling me what to do. But we don't need to continue this same routine anymore. It's time I laid *everything* out for Joey.

"You know when we were watching *Field of Dreams* and you asked if I'd ever had my heart broken?"

Joey's eyebrows lift. He clearly wasn't expecting this little tangent. "Yeah."

I take a breath. "Well, I didn't tell you the whole truth."

"Your dad," Joey confirms, referencing our painful conversation from two days ago.

I nod because he's right, but it's not the full story. "It pretty much destroyed us. And even though we're stubborn as mules and refuse to let anything keep us down, I never intended to let anyone in close enough to break my heart again." We stop at a red light, and Joey watches me while he squeezes my hand. I shore up all my nerves to continue. "So, yeah, I've had my heart broken by the loss of my dad, but never a guy. Not once. Because I've never given my heart to anyone for them to break." Here goes nothing. "Until now."

Joey's eyes widen, and the car behind us honks because the light has turned green. Of course the first time I confess to someone that I love them, I choose to do it at a traffic light! Jesus, Mary, and Jolene. The tires squeal as Joey guns the accelerator. I bite back a laugh when he immediately signals and pulls into a drugstore parking lot to the right.

I've been so caught up in my boundaries and protecting myself that I haven't been paying enough attention to what's right in front of my face. Joey has been the one to put it all out there—not afraid of exposing himself while at the same time respecting my fears and moving around all the obstacles I've thrown up. It's time I set it all aside and took a leap. The look on his face right now makes it all worth it, and more.

Joey slams the truck in park and hauls me halfway over the console to lay another hot kiss on me. Once I catch my breath, I whisper, "I love you."

He breaks every speed limit in North Carolina after that

before hefting me over his shoulder in a fireman's hold and carrying me all the way from his condo parking garage to his front door. Only then does he let me down.

We leave a trail of discarded clothing from the front door to his bed like breadcrumbs for any creepy Peeping Tom who might happen to stop by. Joey's hard and gloriously naked body covers mine as he takes us down to the mattress, his lips already seeking out my peaked nipples.

"God, I love your body." His tongue swirls over one tip before he draws it into his mouth and sends my back arching off the bed. I could come from his above-the-waist skills alone. The boy knows how to worship every one of my erogenous zones, which I've only recently learned include both my earlobe and the hinge of my jaw.

But he's much more thorough than that. When I circle his torso with my arms and feel him up, he slides down my body, escaping my grip and leaving me with only his hair to hold onto as he spreads my thighs and dives right in with his fingers and tongue. I'm a panting mess in no time, squirming under him while he works me, the delicious tension building in my pelvis and racing toward release.

I pant his name as I come undone, pulsing and quaking around his fingers while he licks circles over my aching clit. Before I've even come down, his lips are back on mine, and I can taste myself in our heated kisses.

Finally able to have their fill, my hands go on an exploratory journey, concluding their field trip wrapped around his impossibly hard cock. My sex hums like it's calling out to be filled by him, so I'm not about to deny her. One jerk of my thighs has Joey rolling to his back, his hands skimming my body until they land on my ass as I kneel over him.

I keep his gaze as I lower myself, leading his cock to my entrance and pushing down with excruciating slowness. We both groan as he fills me up, my inner walls stretching to accommodate him.

"Joey." I breathe his name, and his hands shift to my hips while his eyes stay on mine. I can see everything I've been scared to ever want in their warm depths. He loves me. And I'm finally ready to let go with both hands.

Neither of us speaks as I flex my hips and begin moving over him, taking his cock deep and creating a rhythm that has every muscle in his gorgeous body strung tight. I'm so wet that when I put my hand between us, I can feel my juices all over his skin. His fingers dig into my hips as he thrusts upward to meet my every movement and bury himself to the hilt.

We pick up speed, both of us panting and grunting like— let's face it—the rutting beasts we are right now. I feel the familiar quiver begin, and there's no stopping it as I moan and ride Joey's cock like my life depends on it. My orgasm is so overwhelming, I barely hear him shout his release moments after my own.

I collapse onto his heaving chest, keeping him inside me and dropping tired kisses on his damp pecs as I lay there motionless. We both fight to catch our breaths before his firm arms wrap around me and he finally speaks.

"Damn, do I love you."

CHAPTER
FORTY-FOUR

"I LOVE IT WHEN A PLAN COMES
TOGETHER" – HANNIBAL, THE A-
TEAM

JOEY

"I guess I got a little distracted there for a bit," I say, letting my thumb trace circles on the bare skin of Lynn's hip.

"Hmm?" Her voice is lazy, which I take full credit for.

"We started talking about Jeremy and your brother, and then we sort of... got off track." I can't help the grin that accompanies my words.

"Oh yeah." Lynn laughs, covering her face with her hand. "Right." She rolls over so she can catch my eyes, but it puts her hip out of reach, so I bring her hand to my bare chest instead. "Before I tell you the rest, I need you to know that I value your opinion and your thoughts on all of this. From now on, I want us to be a team, and part of that is looking out for each other. As much as I made an issue of what I saw as you crossing my boundaries, I didn't take enough time to look at it from your perspective. But that's all done now, okay?"

"So, are you saying you're *not* going to face off with Rossi alone?"

She shakes her head. "Nope. I'm doing it with you. And Mama. And probably Hollis. And maybe a few more people."

I tilt my head at her answer, which just makes her grin. "And your brothers?" I ask.

"Subtlety is not their strong suit, and as soon as they get proof it was Jeremy, they'll lose their shit. Mama and I assigned them Act 2 in the operation."

"This is all sounding very cryptic. Care to explain?"

"What's the one thing a conceited, superior asshole like Jeremy loves the most?"

"Uh… hair product?"

Lynn snorts. "Besides that." When I only shrug, she answers her own question. "Proving he's better than everyone else. Well, that and the sound of his own voice."

"Okay." She definitely has a point. "So, what's the plan?"

"That kind of depends on you. How do you feel about playing bad cop?"

"Oh, I'm liking the sounds of this."

"HE'S HERE," Sunny hisses as she drops her pilfered brewery keys into Lynn's hand on her way to the back door of Blue Bigfoot.

It's nine thirty in the morning, so nobody is here except us while Ginny and Hollis hunker down next door at Hollis's dog grooming salon. I was told Rosie and Maisy, Miller's girlfriend, have been assigned to corral Lynn's brothers for what they're all calling Act 2. After this morning's preparations, I'd happily hire any one of these women to plan my next sting operation, should I ever have one.

Lynn turns to me, her eyes wild with both excitement and a little dash of worry.

"We got this," I tell her before taking her hand and leading her to the bar sitting along the wall of the cavernous taproom. I've never been here when it wasn't packed with people, and the sheer amount of Bigfoot kitsch on the walls is kind of staggering.

Lynn lets go of my hand and continues to the door, where I can make out Jeremy Rossi's form on the other side. I tell the part of me that wants to put myself between my girl and this asshole to back the hell down. Lynn's got this.

"Hey!" Lynn says after unlocking the door and swinging it open. "Thanks for coming so early."

"No problem," Jeremy says, casual as can be, before pulling Lynn into a hug. It takes effort not to slam my fist into the bar—or his face. He looks exactly like he did the first time I met him: expensive, meticulously groomed, and dressed in a designer collared shirt and pressed slacks. I'll bet he waxes his chest hair.

"I didn't know what else to do besides call you. Cart is gonna wring my neck for dragging you into this, but I'm afraid of what he might do. Ever since he figured out those developers were behind the break-in and the fire, he's been out of his mind." She wrings her hands with a shake of her head. "I didn't want a repeat of the past, you know?"

Even from my position a few yards away, I can make out the tic in Jeremy's jaw at the mention of what Lynn explained as Carter choosing not to confide in his friend when shit was going down with Senators Cody and Hopkins. Jeremy felt slighted—possibly another reason he has it in for Carter.

"You did the right thing," Jeremy says in what can only be described as a condescending tone before finally spotting me and raising a hand. "Martel." He looks surprised at my presence. "Good to see you again."

I play my part like we planned and don't say anything in return. I always secretly wanted to play bad cop, so I wasn't about to give up this opportunity. Jeremy, however, doesn't appear too concerned about my rudeness.

"Sorry," Lynn says to Jeremy with a roll of her eyes. "Some people thought we should keep things in the family."

That has Rossi sending me a hard look right before he puts a reassuring hand on Lynn's back. This fucker is going down. "You did good, Lynnie," he says. "I can help Carter."

So far, so good, as painful as it is.

Lynn settles them at a table, and now it's my turn. "Lynn, it's none of his business. If your brother doesn't want him here, why are you acting like he's part of the family or something?"

Jeremy whirls in his chair, right on cue. "What are you doing here anyway?"

I relax back against the bar, crossing one ankle over the other. "I'm Lynn's boyfriend."

Jeremy looks me up and down before turning back to Lynn. "*This* is the guy you're dating?"

"Well, yeah." She bites her lip, playing the part of damsel in distress to a T.

I add fuel to the fire by announcing, "I say we should send him packing."

The guy doesn't even spare me a glance this time. "Lynn, you can do so much better. You don't need him." He reaches across the table to grab her hand, and my fingernails dig into my palms. "I would kill to be your boyfriend."

"Really?" If Lynn ever decides to give up on her therapist dream, there's a spot in Hollywood waiting for her after this performance.

"Hey, asshole." I step toward the table. "Get your hands off my girlfriend!"

Rossi stands at my approach. "Back off!" His glare drops when he turns to face Lynn again, a carefully calculated *aw shucks* expression replacing it. "You know I've always had a thing for you, Lynnie." When she appears to melt at his words, he can't help himself from flashing me a smug-ass grin that must have Lynn grinding her back teeth.

And now for my big moment. I cross my arms and pin Jeremy's profile with a challenging stare. "Even after you broke into her brothers' bar and stole the family heirloom?"

Lynn feigns shock at my words and all but cowers behind Jeremy. It almost makes me want to laugh.

Jeremy's grin falters for the barest of seconds, but he catches it just in time as he looks back and forth between Lynn and me. "What are you talking about?" I've got to give it to him, he's an excellent liar. If it hadn't been for the initial flinch, I might have almost believed him.

"The jig is up, Jeremy," I say, offering no other details. We decided it was best just to hand him the rope and let him hang himself.

"You're not seriously listening to this guy, are you?" Jeremy turns his full attention to Lynn, who's sitting perfectly still with her hand over her mouth and her caramel eyes wide. Jeremy pushes on. "Why would I break in and steal a statue? That's ridiculous. Lynn, I'm practically a part of the family. Why would I hurt my own family?"

I step closer, getting in Jeremy's face now. Despite his innocent act, his jaw has gone tight. "Maybe because your best friend didn't trust you and he cut you out?" I offer with a casual shrug. "Or maybe because his actions made you lose your job?"

Jeremy's eyes dart to Lynn as he sputters, "This is preposterous." He's in such a panic now that he's not even questioning how I might know any of these details about Carter and him.

Lynn returns to the hand-wringing as I draw Jeremy's attention again and ask, "Is it? I don't know. Maybe you did it because Carter has everything you've ever wanted but can't get."

And just as Lynn knew they would, my words send Jeremy tumbling right over the edge. He rounds on me, completely forgetting about Lynn now. "That's bullshit! You think I want Carter's pathetic little life in a nowhere town serving beer to a bunch of losers?" His mouth twists in a sneer. "His hillbilly family and that freaky little librarian girlfriend with her psycho goat fetish?" I back up as he comes closer, an angry finger pointed in my face and spittle flying from his mouth. "You are insane if you think Carter Brooks could ever be better than *me*!"

Instead of arguing or reacting, I simply back up, cross my arms over my chest, and smile, finally giving Lynn the floor.

"Nice to know how you really feel, Jeremy." Lynn is on her feet now, her stance a mirror of mine, but I'm the only one who gets to see the realization dawn in Jeremy's eyes before he schools his expression and spins on his heel to face her again.

"Lynnie. I didn't mean that."

She sniffs, looking at him like he's nothing more than dog shit stuck to the bottom of her Chucks. "Too late, Rossi. You gave yourself away. Not that we didn't already have you dead to rights. We know it *all*. And you're going down."

With no further need for pretenses, Jeremy drops his lovesick act and thins his lips. "You don't know shit," he snarls before striding toward the front door. But when he tries opening it, it doesn't budge.

Lynn turns to me in fake confusion. "Did somebody bar the doors?"

I put a finger to my chin. "I don't know. Maybe?" Sunny and Hollis have been busy while we chatted.

Jeremy's laugh is caustic. "You all think you're so smart, just like Carter. But you're a bunch of *nobodies* who will never amount to *anything*."

In an obvious attempt to further rile the asshole into digging his own grave, Lynn looks to me. "I don't know. I think a professional baseball player is kind of a somebody, right? Not that I wouldn't still love you if you were a porta-potty salesman, Ace."

I shrug in return. "And Carter does make a *damn* good lager."

Our exchange sends Jeremy lurching toward us. "That idiot could have had it all if he'd just left well enough alone. But he *had* to be a fucking hero!"

Lynn's fake smile wavers and I'm at a bit of a loss. I don't have the first clue what Jeremy is talking about now. But I do my best to keep playing my part, hoping things clear themselves up before Act 2—which, if all the women did as planned, is about to begin in less than five minutes.

The idea had been to get Jeremy to admit to stealing Larry and starting the fire before Lynn's brothers arrived, but to do that, Lynn needs to tell him we know about Guy Taylor.

However, Lynn's not opening her mouth. I need to trust her on this, so I stay silent as well.

Jeremy, on the other hand, loves the sound of his own voice, just like Lynn predicted.

"Clarence Cody was going to set us up right. He was ten times the senator Grace Hopkins was! He was going to usher Carter and me into the good life—a huge future in politics. Power, money, women, all of it. And all we had to do was play ball. But your fucking brother had to be a Boy Scout." Jeremy shakes his balled fists and paces to the patio doors. When they don't budge either, he hits the glass so hard with his palm, I finally step between Lynn and him. Thankfully, she doesn't fight me on it.

I knew all about the mighty Clarence Cody going down, but I didn't know about Carter's involvement until Lynn told me about it. But now it's sounding like Jeremy was in bed with Cody the whole time.

Jeremy continues to ignore us as he paces in front of the doors, his voice adopting an almost hysterical pitch. "I mean, what kind of idiot gets a gun pointed in his face and a bag full of money thrown at him and still won't keep his nose out?" Shit! "That fucker had me running back and forth from DC so many times trying to clean up the mess he made going after Cody and Hopkins. It's like he has nine lives! He couldn't even die like a normal person in a shitty car with no brakes! How can he get that lucky?!"

What the actual fuck? Did he just admit to cutting the brake line? Lynn glances at me in horror—and in confirmation. With this new bit of info, I usher her behind the bar and block the entrance. Maybe we should have done this another way, but how were we supposed to know Jeremy would confess to completely different crimes than the ones we were here to bust him on?

It looks like I was just in time, too, because Rossi appears to suddenly remember our presence as he starts toward the bar, angry eyes focused on us again. "And now Cody is gone, and we're all stuck without a pot to piss in. And Carter? He doesn't even give a good goddamn. He's happy as a pig in shit with his nose in a fermenter and his pathetic life as a complete nobody." He throws his arms out on another acidic laugh, this one touched with mania. "It makes no sense!"

"Hey, man," I begin, trying to draw his attention to me instead of Lynn, but it doesn't work as he aims another glare at her.

"Your brother took it all away from me, and he deserves to pay one way or another. But I swear you *all* have the dumbest luck I've ever seen, just like you all think you're too good for everyone. You, you little bitch," Jeremy spits, pointing his finger at Lynn in a way that's going to get him a black eye in about zero point two seconds. "You always thought you were too good for me. Do you have any idea who I am? I would have killed to see the look on Carter's face after I fucked over his precious little sister—hell, I might even have knocked you up just for fun."

Jeremy's only saving grace is the sound of bootsteps on the hard floor telling me that Act 2 has begun. And, sure enough, all four Brooks brothers come striding into the taproom from the back hallway, each wearing an identical frown.

At the sight of Jeremy in a fighting stance, face red and eyes wild, Carter steps forward. "What the hell is going on here?"

Jeremy turns at the sound of his voice. We all watch as he tries to wrest control of himself. A grotesque smile forms on his lips as he forces a casual tone that comes out too strained to be subtle. "Hey, Cart."

Carter looks from Jeremy to me and then to his sister behind the bar. Something in Lynn's expression has Carter's jaw locking as he faces Jeremy again. *"You motherfucker."* I wouldn't be the least bit surprised if Jeremy shits his pants at the fury in Carter's voice.

Then everything happens at once. All four brothers start going for Jeremy while simultaneously clawing at each other, trying to hold their brothers back. Not wanting to get my head knocked sideways, I stay right where I am and watch on, but that means my attention is pulled from Lynn. Which is why I'm too late to stop her when she decides to climb over the bar and get her own piece of Jeremy.

By the time we all realize her intentions, it's too late. She closes the distance, pulling her arm back as she scrambles Rossi's way, so that when she gets within a couple feet of him, her fist is primed to make fortified contact with his nose. A sickening *crunch* precedes a spray of blood and more pandemonium.

It takes both Denny and me to pull Lynn back, the remaining brothers descending on Jeremy, who's howling in pain. The front and patio doors burst open, allowing a stream of pissed-off women and at least a half dozen cops to enter the melee while I search Lynn's expression, hoping to God she's okay.

When she lifts her eyes to meet mine, I'm met with a pained smile before she raises a red, already-swelling hand between us and says, "Ow."

FORTY-FIVE
WHAT DOESN'T KILL US

LYNN

"And, for your information, I don't have a goat fetish!" Sunny shouts after Jeremy as he's being led off in handcuffs. "If anything, I have a *gnome* fetish, but even then, it's only a casual interest, not a sexual preoccupation!"

"You tell him!" Hollis encourages her, barely hiding her smile.

We're all watching Jeremy Rossi's walk of shame after having spent the last hour talking to the cops and piecing together everything that's happened over the previous eighteen months.

"Don't forget to book him for attempted murder!" Miller shouts, his jocular tone belying the seriousness of the situation. But I suppose that's the Brooks way. What doesn't kill us makes us… laugh inappropriately.

Thanks to the security cameras the boys installed after Larry's disappearance, every word of Jeremy's deranged confession was being witnessed by Mama and the cops over at Hollis's dog salon next door. Since Mama knows everyone in town and is equally good at talking their ears off, she was the obvious choice to rope the cops into our plan without overtly calling them in through normal means. She just happened to be sitting in front of the taproom's live feed when an officer stopped by the salon to pick up the donation Mama had for his wife's charity.

As for my brothers, there was no trickery there. I meant it when I said we're all stronger together, so I knew as soon as Maisy and Rosie alerted them that I was at the brewery with the guy who stole Larry, they'd all come running.

Jeremy played the victim when the cops first arrived, but after I mentioned Guy Taylor and Mama shared how truly screwed he was in a way only Mama could, he lost all his defiance and crumbled. Knowing him—and all the evidence stacked against him—he's counting on striking some kind of deal. But that's hard to do when you're flat broke and can't even afford a lawyer.

The other thing that's hard to do when you're broke, it turns out, is engage in an effective revenge plot. Since Jeremy hadn't been counting on losing his job—or his sugar daddy—when Cody and Hopkins were taken down, he got a little desperate. The fire was a cheap attempt at hitting Carter where it hurt—namely Mama—but Jeremy turned out to be a terrible arsonist. He really should have stuck to politics.

Stealing Larry, on the other hand, was not only a middle finger to us Brookses but a way for Jeremy to eke out a living while he resurrected a low-level job in the state legislature. The year of peace we enjoyed was merely the result of Jeremy being broke as he moved on to devising cheaper ways to get back at Carter now that Cody wasn't around to bankroll his efforts.

"Hey, bruiser, how's your hand?" Cash yells over to me, where I stand in front of the building with Joey.

I don't miss the smiles each one of my brothers tries to hide. "Better than Jeremy's face," I respond, earning several hoots and hollers.

"Who taught you how to swing like that, sis?" Denny asks, looking down at the towel full of dripping ice I'm clutching.

"The same person who taught all of you," Mama answers for me before sending me a wink. Yeah, Dad taught me how to throw a punch too. He said every girl should know how to defend herself if she needed to. Lucky for me, I've never had use for the skill before today. Well, I suppose I didn't *need* to punch Jeremy, but I can't say I'll ever regret it.

Joey leans down to whisper in my ear. "Remind me never to make you mad."

"Does Martel need to be standing so close?" I hear Carter ask, but when I whirl around to give him a piece of my mind, he's wearing a shit-eating grin, his beefy arms crossed over his chest.

"Ha ha," I deadpan.

Miller opens his mouth to add his two cents, but Maisy beats him to it. "You'll never experience 'close' again if you open your mouth right now, Miller Brooks."

Joey almost pees himself laughing at Miller's chagrined expression in response.

"I think Lynnie has proven her point," Cash finally says after a few more jabs are exchanged. He walks over to Joey and me. "What can I say? It's hard letting go. I'm sorry it's taken me so long."

Since I'll never be able to stop loving those big lug brothers of mine, no matter what they do, I throw myself into Cash's arms and hug him just as hard as I'd hug our dad if he were standing in his place. "Love you, big brother," I say into his shirt.

"Love you more," he responds, squeezing me one more time before he lets me go. "Joey." He holds his hand out, and the two men shake. "Thanks for your help, man."

"Anytime," my boyfriend says.

"Well, now you're all just trying to make me cry!" Mama accuses, causing all of us to crowd her for a big group hug as she dabs her eyes.

When we all let go a minute later, Cart reminds us, "A few of us need to get down to the station. Who's staying here to open?"

"I can," I volunteer.

Joey's brow furrows. "You need to get that hand looked at."

"It's fine."

"It could be broken," he argues in that rumble that usually gets me.

"But it's not."

"How do you know? Did you have it x-rayed while I was grabbing that ice for it?"

I prop my good hand on my hip. "I just know."

Miller claps a hand on Joey's shoulder, saying, "Good luck, man," before he turns back to our brothers and declares, "I'm driving! And none of you assholes are allowed to argue now that my reputation has been restored!"

"One lousy brake-line redemption and he thinks he's Mario Andretti," Denny grumbles to Cart as he tosses him the keys instead. But Mama snatches them from the air before Cart can catch them. She throws them in a perfect arc to Rosie's waiting hands.

"Come on, boys, pile in," Rosie instructs.

With no other choice, they file in behind her and head for Denny's ride.

I turn to Joey and sigh. "Okay, fine. I'll get an X-ray." He starts to smile one of those lopsided grins that makes me want to do dirty things to him, but I manage to resist as I turn to the front door, adding, "After my shift," over my shoulder.

EPILOGUE

JOEY

"This one goes out to Joey from Lynn," the lead singer, Grady, says into the microphone as he strums the opening chords of a song I don't recognize. A few people clap and turn our way.

I lift an eyebrow at Lynn, who's looking too gorgeous for words in her blue bridesmaid dress. "Shall we?" She takes my hand when I hold it out to her and allows me to lead her to the makeshift dance floor in Adrina and Wes's backyard.

It turns out both Rosie and Denny finally lost patience with Adrina when she took things over the top by insisting on them each riding a white horse down the aisle. They threatened elopement if Adrina didn't stop spending money nobody had until she eventually gave in and agreed to a low-key backyard wedding. She still got her doves, though —but one of them pooped on Wes, so she's promised to tone everything down if Luca ever gets married. The way he's flirting with every single girl at this party, though, tells me she's got a long time to wait.

I fold Lynn into my arms while several other couples dance nearby, and she looks up at me with a smile. Just then, I realize what song it is. "Goodnight Elisabeth" by Counting Crows.

I smile down at Lynn. "Oh, I know this one." But my smile drops a second later. "Wait, isn't this about a girl who died? Why would you dedicate this song to me?"

She laughs and drops her head into my chest. "I couldn't decide whether to request 'Round Here' or 'A Long December,' so I just told them to pick one. They obviously misunderstood." I dip my chin to the top of her head and chuckle before she pulls back again, her long hair falling over her bare shoulders. "But I think it's about someone he used to date, and he misses her."

"Okay, I guess that's better." We sway for a few more seconds before I choke out another laugh. "Did he just say he was going to light himself on fire?"

Lynn snorts and wraps her arms around my shoulders. "Let's just ignore the lyrics and dance, okay?"

"I think I can do that." I skim my hands down the sides of her silky dress to rest on her hips.

It's a stroke of luck that the Arrows don't have a game today, or I wouldn't have been able to be Lynn's date. I'm back at a hundred percent after my eight weeks on the IL. It took longer than I wanted to recover, but everyone appears happy I'm back. My stellar batting average since returning probably hasn't hurt.

Lynn is now an insatiable baseball fan, which pleases me to no end. Her brothers all say I performed a miracle. Lynn says it's my butt's fault. I'll let my ass take the credit if she insists.

She's headed back to school next week, something I'm

not looking forward to, but once the season is over, I'll have four months to distract her from her studies before spring training starts. I've been warned she takes her studies seriously, though, so I'm sure she'll be setting up some boundaries. I'll figure out a way to deal, as long as she keeps her promise to continue our phone calls and Words with Friends matches like we do when I'm busy traveling during the season. It's not ideal, but we make the time we have together count, so that's the important thing. One day, when I'm too old to play ball and she's a busy therapist, I'll follow her around so much she'll get sick of the sight of me. For now, though, I'm just enjoying holding her on this dance floor.

"Did you see Ethan's finger last night?" Lynn asks into my shoulder, her tone more excited than a normal person might expect.

"Yeah, he's pissed." Ethan Finch—Finch to everyone but his mom and my girlfriend—broke his finger during last night's game. And since he's our best relief pitcher, nobody is thrilled except, apparently, Lynn. "Don't let him hear you talking about it like you just woke up and it's Christmas morning."

"It was absolutely gnarly," she says with the glee of a pitcher who's just thrown a no-hitter. "I'm just bummed I won't be around for his rehab. Did I tell you I'm thinking of setting him up with Sadie?"

Oh god. Sadie is Lynn's friend from college, the only one I've met. She's attractive, and Finch could do a whole lot worse, but I don't need my girlfriend to start matchmaking with my coworkers. "Why don't you focus on school and let Finch find himself a woman?"

She pulls back and frowns up at me. With her heels, we're much closer in height, and those things make her already long legs look a mile long. I'm suddenly getting some great ideas for later tonight.

"I'm a multi-talented woman, Joey Martel. I can do two things at once."

"Trouble in paradise already?" Carter asks, checking out the frown on Lynn's face as he and Sunny pause nearby. The height difference between those two can't possibly be helped, even if Sunny donned six-inch stilettos.

"Your sister was just bragging about her multi-tasking skills," I explain.

"Credit where credit is due, man," he responds, making Lynn grin. Her brothers have all been taking it easier on her since the whole Jeremy situation. "She used to ride a tricycle, pick her nose, and sing 'Who Let the Dogs Out' all at the same time."

"Wow." I look at Lynn, whose jaw is now hanging open. "Have you *always* been a nineties music fan?" She ignores me in favor of shoving Carter away from us.

"I'll take care of him for you," Sunny says over her shoulder as she pulls Carter away.

"In my defense," Lynn says. "I was three at the time. Carter was in high school, and he was in the Future Politicians of America club, so I'll let you decide which is more embarrassing."

"I was on the miniature golf team, so I can't really talk."

"You had a putt-putt team at your school? That actually sounds like fun." She nestles back into my arms as the band switches to another slow song, her encounter with Carter forgotten.

Personally, I enjoy watching all the Brooks siblings tease and torment each other. Being an only child, I didn't have that, so it never gets old for me. Sometimes, though, I'm surprised at the shit they can joke about—like Jeremy. Lynn says it's just the Brooks way. They love hard, live hard, and laugh just as hard.

As for Jeremy, he's currently hanging out in prison while the police and FBI sort through his multiple misdeeds. Carter told me a little more about their past over beers one night last month. Jeremy came from next to nothing, so it sounds like the lure of power and riches was a little too much for him to resist.

As for the relentless revenge stuff, everybody is still having trouble completely wrapping their heads around that. We all did have a good laugh, though, when Carter realized Jeremy's choice of alter ego, Eddie Dante, was a reference to the famous vengeful character, Edmond Dantes, from *The Count of Monte Cristo*. Talk about egos, Jeremy's can go down in the record books.

When they're not making jokes at Jeremy's expense, though, it's clear they're all thrilled to have everything over and done with and to have Larry back in his place of honor on the bar at Blue Bigfoot. It doesn't pass my notice that Lynn pats the sasquatch's foot each time she walks by him, and I know she's thinking of her dad.

Even their neighbor, Winston, has put the past in the past, having reconciled with his estranged daughter, Maude. Turns out she didn't even know he lived there until her company sent her on a scouting mission to his address. She took it as a sign and decided it was time to let bygones be bygones. She's also promised to strike the three lots at the end of this road from the company's list of prospective properties. Ginny, no doubt, can take care of anyone else who comes sniffing around looking to buy them out.

"Hey, mind if I cut in?" A voice comes from nearby, and I

look over and then down to see Maisy's brother, Bear, holding his hand out for my girlfriend.

Lynn rolls her lips between her teeth to keep from laughing as she looks at Bear and then me. The kid is dressed in black-on-black, complete with a silk tie and slicked-back hair.

I take a step back and release Lynn. "It's up to her."

"I'd be honored," Lynn says, placing her hands on the boy's shoulders.

I walk back to our table and have a seat, watching the two of them sway back and forth. Bear says something I can't hear that makes Lynn drop her head back on a laugh. Damn, she's gorgeous.

"Wade would have liked you," Ginny says, dropping into the empty seat beside me. "Lynn's dad," she clarifies, but I already guessed.

"Yeah?" I glance over for only a second, not wanting to take my eyes off Lynn. "From what I hear, I would have liked him too."

She pats my hand. "Take care of our girl." Ginny stands again and turns to rejoin the partying crowd, pausing to add, "And let her take care of you too."

I smile in response and bring my eyes back to Lynn on the dance floor, where the music has switched to a faster number, and she's now watching Bear show off his dance moves. As if sensing my gaze, she looks over and sends me a dazzling smile that hits me right in the center of my chest.

Lynn doesn't care if I'm the most famous ballplayer in the world or a bum on the street. She'll love me either way and any way in between. All she asks in return is for me to appreciate her for the smart, beautiful, determined person she is. And there's nothing I look forward to more in this life than doing just that.

So I rise from my seat and walk back onto the dance floor to take her into my arms again.

We hope you enjoyed *Stout of My League*. Not ready to say goodbye? **Get bonus scenes from ALL of the Brooks siblings** in my **VIP report** (http://bit.ly/stoutbonusnl). You'll also get Denny and Rosie's entire story **free** in *Full-On Clinger* for a limited time. Don't miss out!

Curious about Liv and Brett? Hop on over to the *Carolina Connections* series for **The Way You Are**. Read on for an excerpt.

Read Gunner and Elizabeth's story in **Nuts About You**. Excerpt next.

Want some side character tea? Check out the *Asheville Collection* (Standalone Stories from the *Love on Tap* World).

Listen to the **Stout of My League** playlist on Spotify! Just search for Sylvie Stewart Author.

EXCERPT FROM THE WAY YOU ARE

CAROLINA CONNECTIONS BOOK 5

"They say nice guys always finish last. I say the only place that should apply is in the bedroom—it's just good manners, after all." – Brett MacKinnon, *nice guy and frequent resident of the friend zone*

LIV: There are really only three things I need in life: sex, baseball, and winning. My hot boyfriend and season tickets take care of the first two, while I always do my best to cover the last. So developing an unexpected crush on a new friend is more than a little inconvenient. I don't have anything but friendship to offer Brett, but with the way he looks at me, he has me wishing I did.

BRETT: I've been put in the friend zone so often, they've got a sandwich named after me. You'd think I'd be used to it by now. But when it comes to the delectable Liv, I'm determined to ditch the friend zone and show her I'm boyfriend material. Too bad the position's already been filled by a ball-playing caveman who could flatten me with his pinky.

What will it take to show Liv that nice guys can be more than just friends, and that love is the one game truly worth winning?

CHAPTER ONE
COJONES ARE MY LIFE

BRETT

"Hey, Blue! Get off your knees—you're blowin' the game!"

My head snapped to the right at the unexpected taunt. Not that fans heckling the ump were anything unusual, but this comment came with a loud, feminine voice attached to it. I shifted in my seat to get a better look at the next section over, but a large man wielding his concessions stash of hot dogs and beer blocked my view.

The insult wasn't a bad one, I had to admit. I was never one to heckle the ump myself—especially this guy, Gleeson. The players, on the other hand, were fair game all day long. I just never wanted to get booted from the stadium and miss any of the game. And pissing the umpire off was just the way to find your ass watching the game from behind the gates.

"Come on, Franks! You got this!" I cupped my hands around my mouth, not that the Guardians pitcher could hear me anyway. My voice couldn't carry nearly as far as the chick over in section 104. I groaned as the batter caught a piece of Franks' curveball and hauled ass all the way to second. Turned out Gavin and Emerson weren't missing much. My best friend and his girl had joined me for the first game of this double-header with the Charleston Kings, but they'd begged off before the second game started—no doubt to go fuck each other's brains out. At least I wouldn't be home to hear it through the walls in case they decided to head back to Gavin's and my place.

At the rate those two were going, though, I was guessing it would be just my place before too long. I could see the writing on the wall. Everyone I knew was pairing up and it was starting to make me a bit paranoid. But I was being smart. Careful. The next time I got involved, it would be with the right girl for the right reasons. I was done letting a nice pair of tits turn me into a walking hard-on with the word "doormat" tattooed on it.

Shit. That was a horrible mental image. I looked down at my crotch and silently apologized to my dick.

The Kings' next batter hit a line drive to left field and got himself on first, but the inning turned over when he got cocky and drew the final out trying to steal second. He was gonna find himself back with the rookies if he didn't check his judgment.

"That's the way, Horner! Keep it up and you'll be scoring bigtime later tonight!" There came the shouting again, this time directed at the Guardians' new second baseman—some big dude named Troy Horner. He turned to the stands with a flash of white teeth while our shortstop, Joey Martel, looked in the same direction and scowled.

Interesting. Looked like someone woke up on the wrong side of the bed this morning.

This time, when I searched for the source of the comments, I spotted her. Though she wasn't yelling anymore, it could only have been her. The girl looked about twenty and was decked out in a green and gold Guardians jersey that swamped her small frame. Long black hair cascaded down her back from beneath the bright green ball-cap, and huge sunglasses sat on her small face. I felt my lips curve up at the sight. For someone so tiny, she sure could make a racket.

Looking around the stands, I noticed the crowd had begun to thin out—not unusual for a double header this early in the season. But where had this chick been for the first game? I knew I would have noticed her. Looked like I'd have more entertainment than anticipated this evening.

To me, there's nothing better than a Saturday at the ball park. Baseball is in my blood, thanks to my Pop and Grandpop. As a kid, it was my dream to make it to the majors, but I learned early on that you had to possess coordination and actual skill at playing the game to make it anywhere. In a word, I suck. But that never stopped me from being the biggest fan out there. Ask me anything about the game and I can tell you. Some of us, like Gavin, were meant to play. Others were meant to revere, obsess, and bask in the simple perfection of the game. That's me, all the way.

I took a sip of my beer and watched my team—well, one of my teams—prepare to bat. The Greensboro Guardians are a double A minors team, but the fact that their stadium is a fifteen-minute drive from my place makes them the team I watch most often. Then there's the Knights and the Bulls, coming from Charlotte and Durham respectively. Those guys are triple A and are only a couple hours away—best $25 a guy can spend to see some big names throwing the ball in a local stadium. But, hell, give me any game and I'll be there. In fact, Emerson's brother plays for North High School and I watch him at least once a week. That kid has a future, I'll tell you that.

Our first player came up to bat, and I found myself holding my breath, waiting to see if the little heckler would speak up. A glance in her direction showed her attention riveted to the field. Damn, that was my kind of girl. The Kings' pitcher threw a fastball, catching our batter off guard. I sighed, and sure enough, there came the shouting.

"Come on, ump! That was low! This is baseball, not bowling!"

I smiled to myself and shook my head. This girl was asking for it.

The next batter connected right in the sweet spot and hauled ass until he slid safely into second.

"It's okay, pitcher! At least your mom still loves you!"

Several snickers sounded from around me, including a couple Kings fans. It seemed nobody was immune to her taunts.

Without thinking, I grabbed my beer and rose from my seat. Then I shuffled my way up the aisle to the concourse level before making my way over to section 104. Nobody was checking tickets, as there was no point this late in the day. She was about fifteen rows down and all I could see was the back of her head covered in that green hat and dark, shiny hair. I forced my attention to the field again. The Guardians just had the one player on second, and that new guy, Horner, was up at bat—the same guy she'd promised some post-game action to. Before I even knew what I was doing, I found myself shouting in my loudest voice.

"This guy hasn't driven anybody home since junior prom!"

A few chuckles sounded around me, and then she

turned. She halted when she singled me out and I stared at her until she lowered her giant sunglasses and glared daggers my way. I couldn't stop myself. I burst out laughing and didn't miss the tiny twitch of her lips before she swung her head back around to the action on the field.

Another out and a couple more vigorous insults thrown at the ump from the glaring heckler, and I spotted two security guards taking the stairs down in her direction. Shit. Not that I didn't see this coming, but I knew how I'd feel if I got kicked out.

I found myself trailing the guards down the aisle and slipping into the row behind the girl as they shuffled their way into the row in front of her.

"Ma'am, I'm afraid we're going to have to ask you to gather your belonging and follow us."

"What do you mean? Why?"

"Ma'am, you've been heckling the umpire all evening."

She shrugged her small shoulders in that huge jersey and made no move to get up. "I call 'em as I see 'em. You can't fault me for that."

"Actually, we can. Listen," said the other guard. "Cheering is encouraged, but when you start using profanity and insulting the official's mother, we've got a problem."

I raised my hand to catch the guard's attention. "Sir." Three sets of eyes settled on me, one now stripped of the ridiculous sunglasses. "I believe the lady was referring to Gleeson's mother's china cabinet." They all looked at me as if I'd hit the beer concessions a bit too hard. I just shook my head and pressed on. "It's a common mistake. I imagine the cabinet, in fact, does have very large *drawers*—cajones." I mimed opening a drawer, still not sure why in the hell I was interfering. "It means drawers … you know, in Spanish." I eyed the girl, silently urging her to play along. I couldn't do all the work here.

She finally nodded and turned back to the guards with the fakest damn laugh I've ever heard. "Oh, you thought I was telling the ump his mom had bigger ..." she pointed covertly to one of the guards' crotches. "... than he does?" Her head switched to a shake. "Oh, no. I'm a lady. I don't—"

I cut her off before she could add any more layers of bullshit. "Like I said, common mistake. The one you're thinking of is spelled with two Os." I smiled innocently and gave my beard a scratch.

The girl turned her head to face me again, biting her lips to keep from laughing. Once she schooled her features, she turned back to the guards. "Yes. I'm a furniture dealer. Mrs., uh, Gleeson is one of my best customers. What can I say? Cajones are my life." She put her hands out in a *what are ya gonna do* gesture. "Sorry for the confusion."

The guards' eyes passed back and forth between me and the troublemaker before settling firmly on her again. The closest one pointed a finger at her. "I don't want to hear another peep out of you unless it's singing someone's damn praises, you hear me?"

She put her hand up in what looked more like a Vulcan salute than any kind of gesture of Scout promise. "Yes, sir."

The second guard narrowed his eyes at both of us before the two uniformed men beat it back up the steps.

"Well, thanks for that." She turned again to me. I moved a seat over so she didn't have to strain her neck. Her normal speaking voice was silky and low, making me want to lean in to make sure I caught every word. "Nice save with the bullshit Spanish lesson."

I shook my head. "All true. I swear. I knew those years

spent with Señora Berkovich would eventually pay off." I mimicked her ridiculous salute and she freaking giggled. The sound was like low-toned bells and my jeans were suddenly uncomfortably tight.

"I'm not sure if I believe you or not, but you saved me from missing my boyfriend's game so I'm giving you the benefit of the doubt."

Aaaaaand down went my semi.

"So, wait. How in the hell did both your cousin and your boyfriend end up on the same team? That's statistically impossible." I tried not to let the word boyfriend come out with a snarl. Not that I should have been surprised that a girl this cool was taken.

After turning around for the tenth time to make comments to me once the guards left, Liv Sun—short for Olivia because her mom had some weird preoccupation with the movie *Grease*—invited me to sit next to her for the rest of the game. We sipped our beers and talked baseball. She grew up with her cousin, the scowling shortstop from earlier, and had been indoctrinated into the sport from an early age. She confessed she generally cheered for whatever team her cousin was on at any given time, but her heart otherwise stayed with the Carolina teams. This pleased me beyond the point that could be deemed appropriate. I feared I was a bit screwed.

"Dumb luck, I guess. Troy and Joey were on their first minors team together and then each played for other farm teams for a couple years. They just happened to both end up in my neck of the woods this year, which works out well since I already have the jersey." She pulled at her shirt and I had to force my eyes from falling on her tits. "Although either one would jump at the chance to move up, obviously."

I nodded my understanding. These guys got shifted around a lot, and it wasn't unheard of for a few to get plucked right from the double As for a spot in the majors mid-season.

Liv's eyes went back to the field where the pitcher was warming up. "I've known Troy since they first played together, but we didn't start dating until the end of last season. He and Joey got an off-season gig laying floors here in town, so they've both been around."

I nodded, as it was really the only polite thing to do. Troy Horner seemed like a decent player, if you liked second basemen, that is. *What? Everybody knows second base is where the biggest assholes gravitate.*

"So why were you heckling him earlier, by the way? He's on your team!" She gave me a dirty look.

I just laughed. "Maybe I felt bad for the Kings. None of their fans can heckle for shit."

She scrunched her nose and I noticed freckles dotting the golden skin of her nose and cheeks. "You're weird." Then she offered me some popcorn and smirked. "No wonder you're here alone."

"Hey," I protested. "It's not my fault my friends left." I gestured vaguely toward the concourse. "My buddy and his girl were here for the first game but they had to—" I stopped abruptly before I let the rest of that sentence escape.

Liv's brows creased. "Had to what?"

I looked to the field and tried to change the subject. "So, your cousin's having a good game."

"Not so fast!" She grabbed my wrist and a zing of electricity ran up toward my shoulder. Then she laughed. "Oh my God. They left to go screw! Ha!"

I broke out of my daze at her touch and saw her lips curve up into the widest and most beautiful smile I may have ever seen. Her laughter washed over me, and my heart thumped heavily in my chest. I forced a casual shrug and a grin back.

"Oh, I like your friends, Brett. And I like you. I can tell we're gonna be friends." She sat back in her seat and shoved a handful of popcorn in her mouth.

Fabulous. Just what I wanted. Another hot girl calling me her friend.

Grab your copy of **The Way You Are** and read on for more fun!

Read FREE in Kindle Unlimited. Also available in paperback and audiobook.

EXCERPT FROM NUTS ABOUT YOU

AN ASHEVILLE STORY

Gunner Nix is God's gift to baseball, which naturally turns me into Satan's gift to awkwardness.
My feet tend to spend way too much time in my mouth, so my only Christmas wish this year is to get through this charity gig without running into my longtime crush and favorite ball player.
Too bad the fates—and my bestie—have other plans.
A valuable auction prize has gone missing, and now it's up to me and the father of my fantasy babies to save the day.
But it'll take a Christmas miracle to find the prize without my big mouth sending this hottie running.
Gunner Nix would have to be nuts to fall for a girl like me, but sometimes the craziest ideas are the best kind a girl can get.

ELIZABETH
"Everyone is *nuts* about this party."

Skye releases an impatient groan at my observation while I scan the room full of guests.

"You're not having fun?" My smile threatens over the rim of my champagne glass. "I'm having a *ball*."

"Enough, okay, Lizzie?" Her lips quirk despite her tone. "It is pretty, though. I'll give you that."

Our eyes skip around the ballroom, taking in the festive atmosphere and elaborate decorations adorning every possible surface. It's a giant holiday glitter explosion—all for the sake of balls everywhere. Or, more specifically, the Testicular Cancer Awareness Foundation.

"Oh, come on. I have like twenty more all stored up." Testicle puns are way too irresistible to waste.

Skye chokes on the mouthful of champagne she just sipped and shoots me a glare as she brings a napkin to her lips. "Tell me, why didn't I anticipate this?"

"I think that's a question we're all asking ourselves." I nod gravely in her direction before gulping down more champagne. Damn, this stuff is good. I'd ask what kind it is, but my bank account mostly favors alcoholic beverages in cans—or boxes.

Skye's head drops back, exposing the length of her neck and drawing my eyes to the ruby choker resting there. "I might have to fire you if you keep this up."

"Is that real?" Completely ignoring her comment, I extend my fingers to stroke—and possibly steal—the red stones. They'd match my dress perfectly, and I forgot to put on jewelry tonight. Skye smacks my arm away with surprising speed. "Ow." I snatch my hand back like wounded prey. "Watch the nails, Cardi B."

"Hands off the merchandise." Skye's crystal-embellished fingernail threatens to impale my chest. "Bronte gave it to me, and his hands are the only ones allowed near any of this." She circles her décolletage with a graceful hand, making it impossible for me to avoid looking her over and drawing comparisons between myself and the goddess that is Skye.

It's no surprise that she's managed to steal the heart of the owner of Asheville's own Arrows baseball team. Bronte adores how extra Skye is, and the two of them are a match made in diamond-encrusted heaven. Meanwhile, I linger down here in cubic zirconium land with my frizzy hair and closet full of paint-splattered overalls. Despite the number of times Skye has attempted to drag my ass to her "sorcerer of beauty" to spruce up my dirty blond locks and teach me how to wield an eyelash curler, I know a makeover won't do the trick.

"Well, pardon me, your royal highness." I fake a curtsey as well as one can without spilling bubbly everywhere. "And, by the way, you can't fire a volunteer."

"Watch me."

I gesture to the guests tipping back glasses and sampling goodies from the trays being passed around by uniformed waitstaff. "Who's going to clean this mess up at the end of the night if you kick me out?" Truthfully, I don't mind helping Skye and Bronte out at all. It's for a good cause, and there's enough Arrows-player eye candy to occupy me well into the night. My plan is to find a comfy corner and a bottle of champagne while I take in the view and wait for my instructions.

"Hmm. Good point. You may stay." She shoots me a sly grin. "But I might not introduce you to Gunner if you keep this up."

It's my turn to choke on my champagne. "He's here?"

The room threatens to spin as all the blood in my body rushes to my head, and the sudden need for more oxygen has me sucking air as if I've just surfaced from a ten-minute free dive.

"This is exactly why I didn't tell you sooner." I don't have to focus to know that Skye is shaking her head in exasperation. "He's just a man."

My responding laugh is just this side of hysterical. Gunner Nix isn't "just" anything. He's scruffily handsome, infinitely sexy in an unassuming kind of way, and one of the only people in this world who can tear me from my studio on a summer evening. Watching the man field balls with his tight pants and tall frame has become something of an addiction in recent months. But I never—not once in all the evenings I've watched him play from my couch or even from Bronte's owner's box at the Arrows' stadium—intended to actually meet the man in person! Uh, uh. No way. He belongs right where he lives in my lustful fantasies, not in reality.

"We've already been over this, Skye. Everybody knows fantasy is better than reality." I raise a quick finger in triumph as I continue, "It's like the time I walked into the unisex bathroom at One World Brewing right after Liam Hemsworth used it, and I found a turd floating in the toilet bowl. I haven't been able to look at him the same way since."

"That wasn't Liam Hemsworth." Skye blinks at me in disbelief. "It was Greg the bouncer."

"Says you. I know what I saw." We both know that all my arguing is just a front, but I still believe in what I'm saying—just like Skye believes if she keeps trying, I'll eventually get over my lying, cheating ex-boyfriend, Evan, and give dating a chance again. But choosing Gunner Nix to break the seal?

She's got to be smoking some strong stuff. The guy dates glamorous models and famous actresses, not local painters who hold Bugs Bunny in higher esteem than the pope and sometimes go grocery shopping in their pajamas.

"I can't believe we're having this conversation." Skye's head shakes in frustration. "Just meet the guy, for pity's sake. I promise he's just a normal person, and there will be no bodily functions involved."

"Except my vomit that'll probably land on his shoes when he speaks to me. You *know* I have a nervous stomach." I cover my belly with a protective hand.

Skye eyes me with impatience. "Again, tossing your cookies at your eighth-grade talent show had very little to do with a nervous stomach and very much to do with the four cheese dogs you ate before going on stage." Damn! I always forget how sharp Skye's memory is.

"Whatever. I know myself, and I know I don't need to meet Gunner Nix to live a perfectly happy life. End of discussion." I swipe a hand through the air and down some more champagne while Skye shakes her head again in what resembles pity.

I expect her to argue, but she narrows her eyes at something over my shoulder instead. "Speaking of fantasy, someone is living in a fantasy land of her own if she thinks this is happening." At her strangely intense tone, I glance behind me to see Bronte being chatted up by a tall, leggy brunette. "This will only take a moment." Skye sets down her glass and glides past me in her size eleven heels like she's preparing to take her turn on a runway.

"Hey!" I halt her with a hand to her elbow. "Before you go stick your flag in Bronte, you never told me what you think of the painting?"

She turns, giving me only half of her attention. "Honey, I haven't seen it yet. Which reminds me, you'd better set it out soon. The fundraising auction starts in an hour."

My head jerks back at that. "What do you mean? I set it up first thing when I got here."

This snaps her attention back to me. "That can't be. I came straight from the auction room before talking to you just now, and it wasn't there."

A prickling sensation starts beneath my scalp. "But..." This can't be happening. The painting is irreplaceable. Not only that, my students will be absolutely crushed if they find out our collaborative piece never made it to the auction. They worked so hard on it all month and were so damn proud. *I* was so damn proud. "There must be some mistake."

Without another word, I turn and weave my way between party guests and testicle-adorned holiday trees to the anteroom where all the auction items are on display. Row upon row of gift baskets, jewelry, sports memorabilia, artwork, and gift certificates lie before me on long, white-clothed tables. But I find myself grabbing the edge of the nearest one to catch my balance when I see the empty spot where our painting was sitting less than thirty minutes ago.

"Elizabeth!" A deep voice penetrates my stress haze, and I look over to see Bronte striding into the room, looking like a perfect half of a wedding cake topper come to life. "Skye said your painting is missing too." He stops in front of me and runs an uneasy hand over his silver-tipped hair.

I manage to nod. "Yes. I don't know where it could have gone. It was *just* here." I throw a hand out toward the table with the painting-sized gap, realizing too late that it's the same hand that still holds my champagne glass. Thankfully, it was mostly empty.

Like the dreamboat he is, Bronte doesn't even flinch before removing a crisp white handkerchief from his breast pocket and extending it to me. "This is very concerning. Who would steal from a charity auction?"

Skye's voice sounds from behind us. "Bronte!" We both turn to see her rushing into the room, hair and hips swinging like she's on a mission from Heidi Klum.

But she's not alone. Her arm is tucked into none other than Gunner Nix's suited one.

My gulp is audible, spurring Bronte to extract yet another clean handkerchief from his seemingly magic pocket and place it in my hand. "Just in case," he murmurs before moving to hold his hand out toward the new arrival.

Grab your copy of **Nuts About You** and read on for more fun! Available in ebook and paperback.

ALSO BY SYLVIE STEWART

Most titles available in Kindle Unlimited

Ale's Fair in Love and War (*Love on Tap*, Book 1)

Smooth Hoperator (*Love on Tap*, Book 2)

Deja Brew All Over Again (*Love on Tap*, Book 3)

Asheville Collection (Standalone Stories from the *Love on Tap* World)

* * *

Poppy & the Beast

Hot Flashes and Hockey Slashes, Hot Flash Hookups, Book 1

Mood Swings and Hockey Flings, Hot Flash Hookups, Book 2

* * *

Between a Rock and a Royal, Kings of Carolina, #1

Blue Bloods and Backroads, Kings of Carolina, #2

Stealing Kisses With a King, Kings of Carolina, #3

* * *

The Fix (Carolina Connections, Book 1)

The Spark (Carolina Connections, Book 2)

The Lucky One (Carolina Connections, Book 3)

The Game (Carolina Connections, Book 4)

The Way You Are (Carolina Connections, Book 5)

The Runaround (Carolina Connections, Book 6)

* * *

The Nerd Next Door (Carolina Kisses, Book 1)

New Jerk in Town (Carolina Kisses, Book 2)

The Last Good Liar (Carolina Kisses, Book 3)

* * *

Full-On Clinger (FREE ebook for a limited time)

Then Again

Happy New You

About That

Nuts About You

Booby Trapped

ABOUT THE AUTHOR

USA Today bestselling author Sylvie Stewart loves dad jokes, hot HEAs, country music, and baby skunks—preferably all at the same time. Most of her steamy contemporary romances and romantic comedies take place in North Carolina, a.k.a. the best state ever, and she's a sucker for hugs from her kids and a good laugh with her hot-nerd hubby. She also cusses like a sailor and can't bring herself to feel bad about it. If you love smart Southern gals, hot blue-collar guys, and snort-laughing with characters who feel like your best friends, Sylvie's your gal.

facebook.com/SylvieStewartAuthor
x.com/sylvie_stewart_
instagram.com/sylviestewartauthor
bookbub.com/authors/sylvie-stewart
tiktok.com/@authorsylviestewart
pinterest.com/sylviestewartauthor